THE PARADISE PROTOCOL

An Intergalaxia Novel

Anna Zogg

The Intergalaxia Series
By
Anna Zogg

The Paradise Protocol
Xerses Factor
The Terran Summit

The Paradise Protocol
An Intergalaxia Novel
© 2015 by Anna Zogg

Published by Mountain Brook Ink, White Salmon, WA 98672, creating fiction you can believe in.

In Chapter 3, Psalm 8:3-4 taken from The Voice™. Copyright © 2008 by Ecclesia Bible Society. Used by permission. All rights reserved.

In Chapter 6, the transliteration of the Lord's Prayer was written by Anna Zogg. The last line is the King James Version (Public Domain).

Edited by Sharon Hinck
Cover design by Nick Delliskave

Library of Congress Control Number: 2015942385

Print ISBN- 9781-943959-16-7

To Leo Zogg, my son,
a real-life Sean Reese

Acknowledgement

Hard to believe I originally wrote this story more than 20 years ago. During the time, I attended 2nd Writes (meeting weekly with Bill, Connie, Karla, Mar, Rich, Rick, Tina). I am grateful for their investment of patience, humor and expertise. Because of them, this book came into being. A huge thank you as well to Sharon Hinck, Virginia Smith and Marilynn Rockelman. You are all so very dear to me.

Chapter 1

Something...*someone* was out there. A slithering sensation flicked at the base of Aric's skull and snaked down her spine. This was the second time in an hour.

She gripped the bucket of fruit more tightly. Squinting, she peered into the thick foliage. The light of the twin suns barely penetrated the perpetual gloom of the jungle ecosystem.

"Julian?" Her voice sounded unnatural, scared. "That you?"

No answer. She heard nothing but the clacking kawyas. Forty feet above in the umbrella trees, the pterodactyl-like birds hung upside-down, yellow eyes bulging. They would alert her of anything out of the ordinary, and so far, they seemed unfazed.

"Okay, Julian, this joke's gone on long enough. Come out. *Now.*"

Still nothing. Merely her imagination. Again.

"He's dead," she reminded herself. "He's not coming back. Got it?"

She was the only living human on Empusa III.

Ever since he'd disappeared five months before, Aric had lectured herself, but the speech never banished the gnawing unease. Though she felt foolish talking aloud, hearing a voice—even her own—was better than nothing.

However, this creeping sensation was new.

She rubbed her neck. "I've wasted enough time. There's harvesting to do."

Her cramping stomach reminded her of the dwindling food reserve back at base camp. If she could hang on a few more weeks, the lean winter would be over.

An old regret played in her mind. If only the shipment hadn't been destroyed...

No use dwelling on that. Was she more upset about the missing supplies? Or the fact that SARC hadn't bothered to replace them?

A juvenile kawya flapped past, scoping out the fruit in her bucket. Aric waved it away. The honeypods were the first produce she'd found that season. A growing group of hungry creatures gathered above her. As though plotting how to steal the pods, the lazy kawyas clacked together like gossips at a corporate gathering.

She searched for more fruit, circumventing the exposed rhizomes of a huge spider tree. A mound of dirt under the roots gave evidence of a hibernating tereph. Deep underground, the predator's low rumble revealed it slept. She was about to move on when something caught her eye.

In the black soil was the partial imprint of a boot. Instinctively, she squatted. *Whose is this?* Heart hammering, she scanned the area.

She ran her finger along the moist edge. *Fresh.* The size denoted male. Fear pounded her. Then she shook it off. "This has to be Julian's."

No one would travel to edges of explored space. And SARC wasn't scheduled to send a replacement assistant for several months. So if it was Julian's, where had he been? How had he survived?

Aric sat back on her heels, pulse slowing. *I am no longer alone.*

Why relief? He made no pretense that he scorned her and her ideals.

Because bad company is preferable to no company?

Her solace was short-lived as she studied the print. It pointed toward base camp. Knowing Julian, he'd be hungry. He'd think nothing of tramping through her garden, demolishing weeks of work in search of a quick snack. She had to get back there. Now.

Aric set off in a jog. The heavy bucket, banging painfully against her thigh, forced her to slow. She couldn't run *and* carry the fruit. However, leaving the honeypods meant their loss. Above, the kawyas had left their perches and followed. The small party had grown into a squabbling mob.

She hastened on. When the bucket's edge cut her knee, she stopped. After wedging the pail between a spider tree's roots, she stacked branches around it. That should be enough to deter the kawyas. She hoped.

When she reached the clearing around the cabin and shed, she crouched in the brush to catch her breath. Camp appeared undisturbed. She sprinted toward the blindside of one building and flattened herself against the plasti-steel. With care, she peered around one corner.

Garden intact. Fence undisturbed. No movement. Where was Julian?

A moment later, a *whoop* came from the other side of the cabin.

She groaned. Sounded like he stepped into one of her jerry-rigged traps. She tilted her head back and banged it against the cabin. Didn't he remember she warned him about them?

Let him hang. Punishment for all the anguish he'd caused her. By disappearing without warning, he'd put their research in jeopardy. Right now, she had to take the offensive. If not, life would be more miserable than the months they'd spent together. How many times had he disrespected her as Team Leader? He seemed to take pleasure in provoking her, calling her "ma'am" as he pretended to salute her with an obscene gesture.

From a qualified scientist? Properly vetted and handpicked to work with her? Her two other assistants had not been as uncooperative and sullen as Julian.

I need to put him in his place. Remind him he's answerable to me. And SARC.

On the other side of the building, she could hear him swearing. She tried to harden her heart to his discomfort. Not possible.

SARC was right. She was too lenient to be a good leader. But that needed to change. Now. Squaring her jaw, Aric marched around the corner of the cabin.

The tangle rope trap had worked perfectly. Julian hung by one ankle, back to her. Repeatedly, he strained for a knapsack out of reach.

Knapsack? She stiffened. Right uniform. Wrong person.

The man hanging from the trap was not Julian.

Sean swore as he dangled upside down. What was this stuff around his ankle? He lifted himself, trying to loosen the knot until a cramping abdominal muscle forced him to release his hold. Swiveling, he assessed the distance to his knapsack and the knife inside. They lay a tantalizing eight feet away.

Fool! He should have kept the blade handy. His mind raced with unpleasant possibilities. Which would find him first? Aric Lindquist or an indigenous creature?

He might be able to reason with Lindquist. Not the bear-like creatures or those noisy birds that clattered incessantly. Lifting himself again, he reached for his boot. Maybe he could untie the laces and slip his foot out.

"You might as well give up," a cold voice warned.

Startled, Sean released his hold. He plummeted downward, swinging like a pendulum on an ancient Terran clock.

It was Lindquist, wearing what appeared to be a tailored animal skin. Where was her uniform?

"That's tangle rope." She pointed. "The more you fight, the tighter it becomes."

"So I'm finding."

His gaze traveled up her form, starting with feet encased in moccasins. She wore rough shorts and a tunic that didn't look very comfortable. She was part Lakota Indian. Was that why she dressed like one?

His head pounded from pooling blood. "You gonna release me? Or leave me hanging for some future meal?"

"Don't worry. I've been a vegetarian for quite some time."

"Then untie me."

"Not until you tell me who you are and why you're here."

Play nice. You can't afford to blow this. "Sean Reese, bio-technician. Replacement for your missing assistant, Julian Geoffreys."

"I didn't get radio confirmation. You shouldn't have arrived for another three months."

No radio—? SARC said they'd sent a message. No use arguing. "They broke protocol since you were alone."

"Is that so?"

He blew out a breath of frustration. "Look, the paperwork is in my knapsack. See for yourself."

Without another word, she spun on her heel. A huge sheathed knife rode at the small of her back.

She rifled through his belongings until he growled, "Front pocket."

Rising, she frowned as she read.

Had SARC done a convincing job? They crammed so much information into his bio they might have overdone it. How he was to pull off this charade was another story.

She indicated his pack. "This all you brought?"

"Yes, ma'am."

"Out here," her gaze flicked to the paperwork, "Mr. Reese, I'd prefer we use names."

"You sure you want to know what I'd call you right now?" He meant it as a joke, but no humor softened her face.

Without warning, she unsheathed her knife and stalked toward him. A chill gripped him at the grim slash of her lips.

Was she deranged? He'd been warned. Twisting around, Sean prepared to ward off the expected blow. The next moment, the ensnaring rope gave way and he fell heavily. Instinctively he rolled to his feet, then crouched, ready for her next move.

His stare met a bemused grin.

"You *did* want to get down, didn't you?" Lindquist sheathed her knife.

Still wary, he straightened. "Didn't think it'd be that abrupt."

She pursed her lips. "Expect me to catch you?"

As he unbound the remainder of the rope and slapped dirt from his pants, he shot several glances at her. Hanging upside down, he hadn't realized how petite she was. At six-two, Sean towered over her by at least ten inches. She must have barely met the height regulation for SARC, the Synecological and Astrobiological Research Center.

But what caught his attention were her green eyes. The hologram had not done them justice.

When her chin puckered, he realized he was staring.

Sean pointed to her clothing. "So what's with the outfit? You look like you'd fit right into the American west of 200 years ago."

A wry smile tugged at one corner of her mouth. "Like a squaw?"

"Maybe. Except you're too pale."

"It's this ecosystem." Her head tilted upward. "Umbrella trees block out most of the UV rays. You'll soon lose your tan too."

He had to ask. "No uniform?"

"Threadbare. All that's left are belts." She ran her

finger along the fabric, the only non-alien item she wore.

Lie number one—confirmed. Ten months ago her last assistant had brought her a supply, which she claimed had been destroyed. What had she done with the items? And why?

He shrugged. "You're the boss. Wear whatever you like."

Lindquist's eyes narrowed. "Here are your documents."

As she held them out, he noted her calloused palm and slim muscled arm. In three years, she'd lost the pampered look of a scientist working indoors breathing recycled air. The tidy cabin, thriving garden and clearing proved she was well organized, determined, skilled. He agreed with the inside reports. *Dangerous.*

With her foot, she nudged his knapsack. "Where are the rest of the supplies?"

Funny she should bring that up. He blinked in innocence. "Supplies?"

She opened her mouth to say something more, then apparently changed her mind.

"This is all I brought." The lie fell glibly from his lips.

"Anything nonstandard? I know SARC checks, but the forbidden still gets smuggled in."

"No ma'am." He smoothed his expression. "You looked through my stuff. See anything forbidden?"

Her face hardened. His "ma'am" irritated her. Way out of proportion.

"Let's get one thing straight, Mr. Reese. Unless you have orders to replace me, I'm Team Leader. We do things my way."

"Absolutely." He kept his tone cool. "I asked to work with you."

Her fingers plucked at the hem of her tunic. "Why'd SARC send you now?"

Nervous. She doesn't like that I showed up.

He spread his hands. "Who can understand the bureaucratic mind?"

Now that he was on his feet, confidence grew. The training locked in place. Observe. Assess. Prepare.

Her jaw flexed. "Find anything while you were snooping around?"

He managed a disarming smile. No use lying. She was not stupid. "Doesn't hurt to know who you're working for."

Good thing she had no idea who *he* actually worked for.

"Nothing piqued your curiosity?"

"Nope." He shrugged. That had to be the biggest lie so far. "But what's with the trap?" He sought the name of the planet's most dangerous predator. "Tereph?"

"They're for marauders."

"They? More than one trap?"

"Yes. There's another behind the shed."

Interesting that she would volunteer the information. "You expect pirates? Empusa III is so far off shipping routes that few know it exists."

She tilted her head. "Still pays to be cautious. We've all heard stories of murdered scientists."

Murder...intriguing choice of words. Hadn't she murdered her last assistant?

He indicated base camp in a sweeping gesture. "From what I've seen, you don't have much anyone would want."

"Let's hope *they* believe that." She motioned toward the cabin. "Thirsty?"

"Yes. It was quite a trek from the landing site."

"I didn't hear the drop-off ship."

"Newer technology. Much quieter."

She appeared to buy the lie. Good. His arrival two days prior had given him time to stash extra supplies and do some scouting. Though he hadn't located Geoffreys' body, Sean prided himself on his determination. He *would* find it.

"I have some juice you might like." She turned.

He followed. Her dark brown braid, bobbing against the knife's handle, drew his attention. Swaying with every step, the weapon reminded him why he was there.

Not for one second could he forget his secret orders to assassinate her.

Chapter 2

Sean stretched his legs under the table, frowning over the imitation wood-grain surface. Cheap plasti-steel? So were the walls and cabinets. The flimsy chairs and table wobbled. Why hadn't SARC replaced this with gallenium, a lighter and more durable material?

"This is a vegetable juice." Lindquist retrieved a container from the cooling unit. "Still a bit unripe, but the only thing available this time of year."

As she poured the thick liquid, Sean scrutinized every move of her hands.

She carried the cups to the table. "We call it

mathoke. Can't remember why now."

He smiled as though listening.

"We discovered thousands of bulbs shortly after our arrival. I found them to be the best match for human needs. If you process them a certain way." Her tone contained an element of pride as she slid into the opposite seat.

"Interesting name. And appearance." Leaning over, he studied the brown froth.

Watch your back. The warning from his colleague blared in his mind like a foghorn.

"Not only that, mathoke is prolific and stable. In a few weeks we can harvest countless bulbs." Resting her elbows on the table, she tilted her head.

He stalled, swirling the cup as though mixing the contents.

Without tasting hers, Lindquist merely watched. Her shoulders appeared relaxed, but he detected tension in the way she leaned forward. Was his drink laced with toxins?

A bemused look crossed her face. "You're acting like it's poison."

He sucked in a sharp breath. Oh, she was good. Very good.

Dark pink suddenly splotched her cheeks. Knuckles white, she raised her cup and tossed back her head. She rose. "If you prefer, there's always water."

Sean pretended to take a taste as she placed her cup in the sink.

"When you're ready, Mr. Reese, I'll show you

around." The chill in her tone could cause frostbite. Without waiting, she stalked through an interior door.

In seconds, Sean catapulted himself across the room and dumped the juice down the drain. "Not bad." He raised his voice as he noisily smacked his lips. Then he sauntered to where she'd disappeared.

"This is your room." She gestured. "Now that you're here, I'll move those crates."

When he stepped into the small space, she shrunk away.

Interesting. Lindquist didn't like him getting too close.

"I—I've been using this room as a storage area." Her body twitched in an awkward shrug. "To keep the common room tidy."

He studied her. Why was she nervous?

The bedroom contained a hammock, chair, dresser and a few crates. No windows. Illumination came through a skylight. "What's in the boxes?"

"Nothing now. Supplies. A long time ago."

Nothing? *Check them a.s.a.p.*

She cleared her throat. "I'll move them later."

"How about now?" He smiled.

"No, I can…"

Sean grabbed one by the handle. Despite the bulk, he lifted it easily. Maybe the crate *was* empty. But there were five others. Lindquist reached for one.

"No, let me." He hefted a second. "Show me where you want 'em."

She led the way out of the room and pointed.

"Over there. Until I make space elsewhere. Been meaning to clean out the shed."

Shed. Check. Investigate that next.

In no time, Sean moved the containers. All of them seemed empty. To make sure, he popped a lid. Nothing but a standard shipping crate with an air hole towards the bottom. And it *was* empty.

Lindquist stood a short distance away, puzzlement tightening her expression.

"I'm wondering what we can use them for." He snapped the lid back on. "Personal items, maybe."

"Go ahead. I have no use for them."

He approached the only other door off the common room and rested his hand on the knob. "This your room?"

"Yes."

"Mind if I look?"

Oh, yeah. She minds.

Her face clouded, but she shrugged. "Of course not."

Sean peered in, noting her room was identical to his. To be certain he missed nothing, he snapped on a light. "Ah, manual power switches?"

"No enviro-life systems allowed. We're phase two, remember?"

He took in the room's tidiness. Some personal items sat on a shelf—a book, child-sized locket, printed photograph. Later he'd come back and examine them at his leisure.

Behind him, Lindquist radiated discomfort.

He sought to mollify her. "How's the hammock?"

"Better than sleeping on the floor." She drew a deep breath, shifting from one foot to the other. "In the hotter months—just weeks away—you'll really appreciate it. Of course, in the wintere they're a bit cool. But with the cabin shut up tightly, nights aren't bad." She pressed her lips together, fingers twitching.

"Actually, I prefer sleeping outdoors."

"Not safe." She backed away, as though to entice him from her room. "This is the common area. Obviously. Kitchen, dining room, office."

Playing along, he followed. "What about restroom facilities?"

"Between the bedrooms."

"So, we share?"

"Yes." A blush rose to her cheeks. "No shower booth, unfortunately. But there's a stream not far from here." She spread her hands. "That's it as far as living quarters."

"What else do I need to know?"

"Be tidy. I loathe sloppiness, both personally and professionally." Her chin lifted. "We're here to research. I expect you to comply with established standards."

So that's how it's gonna be?

Sean resisted the urge to salute. "Yes, ma'am."

Sucking in a breath, she took her time answering. "Please. I'd prefer Aric."

Aric? Using her first name would take some getting used to. He gave one nod. "Do you rely completely on solar power?"

"Yes. Again, typical for our phase."

What restrictions did that entail again? Glancing around the common room, he picked up enough hints. Rows of bound journals lined two shelves while the small desk boasted a box of pencils. An archaic radio sat on a built-in corner shelf. No electronic equipment, no computer. That meant his neuro-gun, bio-scanner, and other equipment were strictly taboo.

Good thing they were hidden in a cave.

He pretended to be a student reciting his lessons. "In phase two, we're allowed only basic survival equipment."

"Exactly." Her posture relaxed. "Solar pumps for water and waste removal, biodegradable paper for notes and so forth."

"And you've taken the next logical step in getting most of your food from the land?"

"Not most. *All.*" Her voice rang with pride. "My garden provides the greatest percentage. I forage for other items, but I have no outside source. Since SARC's shipments have been spotty," she spoke more slowly, "I've learned to be self-sufficient."

The blatant lie again jarred. He'd personally seen the manifest of what they'd sent—over a year's worth of food packets, medical supplies, gardening tools, personal care items. Had she destroyed those along with her uniforms?

He shouldn't goad her, but he couldn't help asking, "No food packets? None at all?"

"The last shipment was accidentally destroyed."

Guess she was going to stick to that story.

Lindquist tilted her head to one side. "You apparently didn't bring replacements?"

Again, he admired her ability to deflect. "No, I didn't." He smoothed his expression. "A week's worth of packets, if that."

She rested a hand on her hip.

What? She's pretending indignation? Like I'm hoarding food?

In truth he was, but she didn't need to know that. Or why.

Her eyes narrowed. Then making a sound of impatience, she brushed by him.

He joined her in the clearing, her stiff back declaring she chose to maintain her duplicity about the shipment.

"I relocated some fruit and vegetable plants from the plains. Because they are UV dependent, I have to preserve the clearing and the opening through the umbrella trees."

He came up beside her. "And too great an opening will jeopardize the ecosystem?"

"Very good. It's about time you showed you had some training."

The sarcasm bit. "It was a long trip here. I've not quite recovered from sleep suspension."

She crossed her arms. "Better get over it soon. I'm not letting you shirk your duties."

"I'm not adverse to hard work."

Did she roll her eyes? Sean squelched his amusement. *Amateur.*

A wave of impishness came over him, especially as the silence grew. "Do you mind a question? I'd rather not get my head bit off."

Lindquist cast a sidelong glance. "Go ahead. Your risk."

He placed a hand on his heart. "Your humble student was wondering about the relationship between the umbrella trees and the ground cover."

Visibly struggling to keep a straight face, she lowered her gaze. "The trees rely on the jungle succulents to sustain them. When one dies, the others fill in the gap to protect the ecosystem."

"So this clearing has upset the balance a little?"

"Yes. But because the opening isn't immense, we determined the damage was minimal."

He assessed the gap. "Looks like the growth is endangering your solar collectors."

"Yes." Trepidation flitted over her features as she looked skyward.

"How often must the trees be trimmed?"

"About once a month—a Terran month, that is."

"And how do you accomplish that?"

She took a shaky breath. "I climb up and hack off branches with a machete."

Really? Her bio stated she had a phobia of heights.

"Looks like the job's about due." He watched her reaction.

"Mm-hmm." She rubbed her neck. "I'll have to do

it in the next few days."

"Can't wait to help."

She shot him a surprised look. Or was that skepticism?

Again she rubbed her neck. "Other than food gathering and prep, I catalog animals and plants. Although, lately, I've been too busy with survival." A cloud passed over her face.

Survival? Was she trying to lure him into sympathizing? "I thought synecology was your area of expertise."

"It is. I'm most interested in the Edenoi."

"The creatures on this planet?"

She bristled. "The *humanoids*. SARC classified them as such."

"That's what I meant." He'd merely skimmed her quarterly reports. Her passion for preserving their way of life had influenced first contact protocols, from SARC to the more recently formed Intergalaxia organization. "Why'd you call them Edenoi? Instead of..." He paused over a name. "Empusites?"

"I think you just answered your own question." She grinned. "Empusite sounds like a skin disease."

He couldn't help his laugh.

"And Empusae sounded too..." She paused. "Diabolical."

Was she going to say "mythical?" Some at SARC speculated that she'd named the humanoids after the fabled Garden of Eden. Like this planet was some sort of paradise?

"So you had no say in naming this planet?" He waited for her reaction.

"My choice was shot down."

He tilted his head in sympathy. "Too bad."

"Edenoi are male and female, producing offspring. Their culture is simple, even—even childlike." She stumbled over the word. "They're *not* on the same level as artificially enhanced animals."

So, that was her hot button. A perfect in.

Sean softened his tone. "I'm eager to study them. Since you value them so highly."

Distrust still colored her expression.

He stated the obvious. "Are you looking forward to Empusa being upgraded to phase three?"

"No." She shook her head. "Everyone on the original team agreed that interfering with the Edenoi would alter their natural development. We'd end up destroying them."

"I read some of the initial reports. And the input of your other assistants over the years."

"Then you know we can't go to phase three." Her voice rippled with distress. "SARC would be violating their own standards of ethics."

"Doesn't matter to some."

She raised her chin. "I'll fight them if they try to reclassify Empusa III."

"Even if it means having to return to Earth?"

With pupils dilating, her reaction seemed out of proportion to his questions. What was she afraid of? Or who?

Finally, she answered. "If I had to." Perhaps realizing she'd said too much, Aric pressed her lips together.

Maybe she was as possessive of this planet as he'd been told. This was *her* world. After all, didn't the Greek demigoddess Empusa lure men and then murder them, like she lured Julian Geoffreys to his death? Because he somehow threatened her and her world?

He reviewed SARC's directive—get evidence of Geoffreys' demise and any other breaches of protocol. When the next info-beacon went out in three months, Sean was to signal them he was prepared to place her in custody until a ship arrived.

Then the secret orders to eliminate her. The only imperative was to make it look like an accident.

But why rush? No ship would come until after he sent the info beacon. Everything had to appear on the up and up with SARC. Because Sean would cool his heels for several months, he could afford to play along. For now.

Aric cleared her throat. "I need to make a trip into the jungle. Mind being left alone for a few?"

"Not at all. I'd like to settle in." He strolled toward the fenced garden, listening as the succulent growth squished under her retreating footsteps. Search the shed or follow her?

Definitely follow her.

"No. *No!*" Aric ran toward the scattered branches. Her bucket lay tipped on its side.

"You greedy..." She shook her fist at the kawyas above her while they clacked, oblivious to her outburst. "All that hard work. Gone." Fighting tears, she sank onto the soft black soil.

Honeypods were difficult to find, even more arduous to harvest. A kawya fluttered past her, scouting out more food.

"Go away." She waved a hand.

With a squawk, the creature swooped to the cluster above her and hung with the rest of its family group.

"Don't try to charm me with your beady lil' eyes. No more handouts today."

When she grabbed the bucket's handle, she noticed a small honeypod within the roots of the spider tree. Eagerly, she crawled into the space, but the faded red peel proved it was inedible.

She flung it into the cluster of kawyas. "Here. You missed one."

Chatter abruptly ceasing, they flapped to avoid the fruit missile. They resettled above her, silent while their heads swiveled to keep her in sight. Aric couldn't help her chuckle. They were quite comical. To a point.

She assessed the bucket, glad to see no damage. The kawyas had probably fought over the meal. Given a reason, they could be aggressive.

Again she crawled under the roots, looking for any fruit. Nothing. No honeypods for her dinner. Correction, *their* dinner. She now gathered food for two. No longer would she be eating alone, working alone, living alone. That would take getting used to again.

For weeks after Julian's disappearance, she'd hated the solitude. Hated jumping at every unusual sound or any unexplained event. Like some of her possessions disappearing. Had he taken them before he'd wandered into the jungle? And where had he gone? He must have been ill.

Again she berated herself for not seeing the warning signs. But Julian had displayed none of the symptoms that were precursors to Empusa III's one known illness. She remembered too well her own bout less than a year before. The migraine, the nausea, the extreme fever.

Rising, she stared at the impressions of her hands in the soft black soil. The remembrance of the tereph den slammed into her mind. Of course! That boot print she'd seen was Sean's. Had he been spying on her while she picked honeypods?

Aric tried to recall exactly what he'd said about his arrival. Had he lied?

"What's he up to?" She spoke into the growing dusk.

Nothing about him fit SARC's profile. He didn't belong here. If she didn't know better, she'd have pegged him for one of those telecomm body builders, complete with an aerobi-suit. His sandy blond hair seemed to curl perfectly. That cleft in his chin would make some women's knees buckle, no doubt. Innocent brown eyes...

He reminded her of a sleek cat, all muscle and grace. Quiet. Deadly.

She dismissed the image. According to his paperwork, he was a bio-technician, heavy on a broad range of topics, but light on field experience. And she was still Team Leader. Though she blew it with her last assistant, she determined this time would be different.

I can handle Sean Reese.

Chapter 3

Sean reached base camp ahead of Aric with seconds to spare. Before she entered the cabin, he opened his knapsack and dumped personal items on the floor of his quarters. From the common area, he heard the clatter of pans and the thumping of cabinet doors. After a few minutes, he sauntered out, yawning noisily.

An array of foodstuffs lay on the small kitchen counter. She scooped some into a pan and turned on the stove. "All settled?"

He rubbed one eye sleepily. "No. I sorta snoozed while you were away."

"Enjoy it while you can."

He strode to the open cabin door. An urge to pop on the news swept over him. Not possible. Comm-panels were forbidden on Empusa III. Already, Sean missed the babble of a dozen voices vying for attention, his evening habit. The infernal quiet—except for the never-ending cacophony of those birds—grated on him. He could understand how someone could go nuts living there.

"So, Sean, tell me about yourself."

"Not much to tell. Career is everything. Studies." He shrugged. "Who has time for hobbies?"

Her lips pursed. "Looks like you've taken time to work out."

Obviously too much if she's noticed. "Eh, that's not really a hobby." What was perfect for his SARC security job was wrong for a planetside scientist. No use worrying about it now, though.

"Any siblings?"

"Just me."

"Parents still alive?"

"Unfortunately, no." The lies were beginning to add up. "How about you?"

"I had a sister who passed away about the same time as my dad. Only my mother is alive now."

No lies there. "Where does she live?"

"North America. Western sector."

"Ever live there?" Sean already knew the answer, but wanted to keep her talking.

"For a time."

"So your outdoor skills come naturally."

She made a face. "No. I hated camping and anything to do with the outdoors."

"Then how'd you end up as a synecologist on a backwater planet, light-years from Earth?"

"Just blessed, I suppose."

Blessed? Interesting phrase.

He cocked a brow. "Need help?"

The gelatinous mass on the cooktop began to pop like boiling tar.

"I got it." Aric stirred vigorously as she adjusted the heat. "Tonight is your last night to relax."

Was that what she'd said to Geoffreys before luring him into the jungle and murdering him? How could Sean trick her into revealing where she'd stashed the body?

Maybe she hid the corpse by an Edenoi village. If their biological makeup was similar to humans, that could be why he hadn't picked up a reading on his bioscanner. In that case, he would have to convince her to take him out to the plains.

"Dinner's ready." She ladled what might be considered stew into his bowl as he slid onto a chair.

"That was quick."

"Leftovers. I threw in a few more organics."

The contents of his bowl looked like something from a bad Asian restaurant. All the colors were wrong. The broccoli-looking things were rusty orange while the pea types were sickly yellow. Those and other "vegetables" swam in a semitransparent gray gelatin. Sean wrinkled his nose.

"Sure this is edible?" To buy time, he tilted the bowl as though assessing the stew. He'd wait until she took her first bite.

"Of course. I've been living off Empusa III's bounty for quite some time."

"Huh." He drummed his fingers on the table. "Maybe I should eat my rations."

"And how long will they last?"

He watched her expression while she put out other dishes. No contrivance that he could see. Still…

"Not long, I guess."

"If I were you, I'd keep the food packets for a rainy day."

"I thought Empusa III had no precipitation." He hoped his quick answer proved he knew something. Already he'd erred a number of times.

Cheeks flushed, Aric sat across from him. She lost the small furrow of worry that etched a miniature line between her brows.

The glow suits her. She doesn't look as pale or harried.

"You know what I mean." She pushed back a stray strand of hair. "For emergencies. Or save them for when you can't stand my cooking."

"You're welcome to them."

Her face tightened. "No thanks."

Why refuse? Because she had her own more-than-adequate supply?

Sean jabbed the mass with his spoon. "Guess I'd better learn to cook this stuff then."

"If you took over, I'd have more time for studies."

"Be glad to."

When she frowned, Sean made certain he didn't alter his smile.

Clearing her throat, she drew her spoon and bowl closer. "Mind a moment of silence?"

"Not at all."

She folded her hands and closed her eyes while Sean watched under hooded lids. Was she praying? *No way.* His mind raced as he attempted to recall what her bio said about religious preference. He'd seen no fetishes in the cabin.

Another mystery.

He waited for her to begin eating. Knowing he'd blown it earlier with the juice, he dipped his spoon into the stew before she did. But he made certain she took the first bites.

"Not bad." He scooped out a third spoonful.

She inclined her head modestly.

"Although the textures are kind of strange. This looks like it should be more crisp." He held up the broccoli-type vegetable. Then he fished out what appeared to be a legume. "And this should be softer."

"Appearances can be deceiving."

That they can.

Had his expression given his skepticism away? Her eyes narrowed. "You'll learn in no time."

"I'll have to. Or we'll both starve."

She chuckled. "I'm not letting you back out. You already said you'd cook."

"Warning—I'm not that great." He mirrored her relaxed grin. "I'd appreciate lessons. Since you're going to teach me everything else."

"Very well." She seemed to ponder his request. "But it's going to cost you."

Sean schooled his expression to remain unchanged, but her words brought him up short. Cost him? Like it cost Julian Geoffreys?

Don't let down your guard. Even for a second.

The warning that his long-time friend, Jayden, gave him flashed through his thinking. *"If she's as brilliant as they say, she's equally as cunning. Watch your back, buddy."*

Given time, Sean would track down what happened to her last assistant. When he did, he would take two bodies back to Earth.

Standing at the clearing's edge, Aric watched the sky. Blazing yellow faded as the Alpha sun dipped below the horizon. Its shy twin began to flaunt marvelous colors. Dusky pink morphed into scintillating red, then violet. Shimmering stars burst into view, playing hide-and-seek behind swaying fronds.

"When I gaze to the skies and meditate on Your creation," she recited from Psalms, "on the moon, stars, and all You have made…"

Though Empusa III had no moon, the evening

lightshow always filled her with awe. The stark, black silhouettes of the umbrella trees only intensified the celestial hues.

"I can't help but wonder why You care about mortals." She closed her eyes as a cool breeze blew against her. Yielding to impulse, she lifted her hands and stretched upward. Slowly, she loosened her braid, untangling the mass. The strands billowed, easing the day's stress.

"Looks like it's going to be a gorgeous night."

Gasping, she wheeled. Sean stood behind her.

"I didn't hear you." She pressed a palm to her chest to slow her heart's frantic pace.

"Sorry." He casually put his hands behind his back as he nodded toward the opening. "I've never seen a sky that color before."

"It's common here." She fought for nonchalance. The cat image again prowled through her mind.

Though he stood at a respectful distance, he wasn't observing the sky.

Why is he looking at me that way? His expression fluctuated between admiration and distain. Because of her appearance? More than once, she'd caught his raking assessment.

She shifted from one foot to the other under the intensity of his brown eyes. The breeze stirred, teasing her hair into a dance. Aric twisted the strands together.

"I didn't mean to impose." However, he didn't walk away.

Hands dropping, her hair spread across her shoulders. "You aren't."

This is stupid. She was the leader, he was the assistant. It didn't matter that they were alone on an alien planet. She had shared a cabin with Julian for months.

Then why do I feel like I can't catch my breath?

Nerves. Back on Earth, she would have been dressed professionally with nothing out of place. Not hair streaming across her shoulders or her wearing something out of a caveman museum exhibition.

He frowned. "Are those creatures always that loud?"

She hardly noticed the kaways' clacking anymore. "During the day, yes. After both suns go down, they'll settle. We'll get a well-deserved break."

"What about nocturnal animals?"

"Only the tereph. And their prey."

"Tereph—they resemble bears?"

"Complete with claws and fangs. However, they're hairless, white—almost albino." Aric couldn't help shuddering as she recalled her first days on Empusa III. The original team of which she'd been part had observed a tereph kill a banwok. Up close. Nightmares had plagued her for weeks.

"Now that warmer weather's here, their hibernation period is almost over. Night travel won't be safe. In fact, standing in the clearing won't be wise either."

Did admiration flit across his features? Had to be her imagination in the growing dusk.

"What other dangers are there?"

"The kawyas aren't normally aggressive. But if

you're down for any reason, watch out."

"Then I'd better not let myself get 'down.'"

She grinned at his word play. "I'm sure you'll get homesick."

"Did you?"

"Certainly." She kept her tone light. "I miss my family."

"Family? I thought you said only your mother was living."

"Right. I meant just her."

She turned. Very few knew about Ella. Her daughter was now seven, living with Aric's mother. Her throat tightened as she counted up the years they'd been apart. Too many. But the only way to protect Ella was to keep her existence secret.

"I suppose you have a male interest waiting for you back home?"

"Are you kidding?" Despite his intrusive question, she managed a small laugh. "No one would wait that long."

"Not even a husband?"

"I tried marriage once. Didn't work." She pressed her lips together.

Sean was very good at prying information from her without giving any away. Though his paperwork didn't indicate it, she wouldn't be surprised if he had psychological training. Perhaps SARC had sent him because they were concerned about her mental health? That would explain his premature arrival. They rarely deviated from routine.

Then why hadn't they sent him five months ago? Right after she'd sent the emergency beacon about Julian's disappearance?

"Wow." Sean's exclamation drew her attention to the heavens.

The second sun slid below the horizon, violet darkening to aubergine. The kawyas abruptly stopped their racket as though their power source disconnected. The night stilled except for the whispered breeze through the spider trees.

"I never tire of the sight." She sighed, again contented. "Next year, the orbit shifts and both suns go down almost simultaneously. One minute it's light, and the next, space black."

"I hope I'm around to see it." His voice fell low on her ear.

She swiveled. "You should be. Or is SARC replacing you at the end of this year?"

"No. I'm contracted for a total of...fifteen months."

Why did he hesitate over the number?

"That means we'll be spending two Christmases together." She bit her lip. Why had she brought that up?

"I like Christmas." He grinned. "Although I'm sorry I didn't bring any presents."

Realizing he'd moved closer, Aric backed away. "We'd better get inside."

Without waiting, she headed indoors. Despite her warning, he didn't immediately return to the cabin. As she straightened the common room, she heard him in the shed. What was he doing out there?

The similarity between his behavior and Julian's struck her. *Don't be so jumpy.* Sean was merely getting settled. Scoping out the lay of the land. He wasn't Julian.

She couldn't blame Sean for snooping. This planet—and she—must appear strange after the cosmopolitan life he'd left a month before. No doubt, he needed time to acclimate to his now-rustic situation.

Sean soon returned. Before heading to bed, she showed him how to secure the cabin.

Later, as Aric lay in her hammock, she listened to him move about his room. Dresser drawers opened and closed. The sound of fabric rustled through the walls. Footsteps. His throat clearing. All foreign sounds, yet welcome.

SARC didn't abandon me.

She could finally lay aside that fear, one that had haunted her for five long months.

Then again, the timing of Sean's arrival struck her as odd, considering SARC's notorious frugality. Shipping him there, at the fringes of deep space outside their normal schedule, nagged her. He should have arrived within a month of her emergency communication or not until January, still three months away. Why now?

SARC was up to something. Something big for them to invest that amount of resources.

A chill gripped Aric at the obvious reason—they planned to go from phase two to three. In the years she'd lived on Empusa III, she had been vocal about maintaining the status quo. If she were right, then Sean's untimely arrival heralded something more ominous than a mere replacement for her missing assistant.

Had SARC sent him to spy on her? Ferret out weaknesses so they could disqualify her as Team Leader? If so, all her work would be in jeopardy.

Every quarter when she sent an info-beacon, she had requested replacement supplies, more gardening tools and even a female assistant. All unheeded. If they planned to replace her, their aloofness now made sense. And if she were right about Sean, then she should answer his questions with as much frankness as possible. Go about her routine. Give SARC no reason to replace her.

For how long, though? Her tenure as Team Leader would be up in fifteen months when she rotated offworld. The nearer her end date, the more she ached to be with Ella. After a mandatory sabbatical, SARC would give Aric the option of returning to Empusa III, but would she? Nearly four years of her career contract remained until SARC would release her.

How could she stay away if what she suspected was true? Like little children, the Edenoi were defenseless.

She turned in her hammock and gripped the taut ropes. Ella had her grandmother. These humanoids had no one.

What if I'm the only one who will protect the Edenoi?

Chapter 4

Pale light filtered into Aric's bedroom. Yawning, she luxuriated in stretching. Wakefulness seemed to elude her. Then realization struck. A man slept one room over, but that didn't mean she could indulge in indolence. She had work to do.

Mindful of being quiet, she dressed and gulped down a small glass of mathoke juice. Since this was Sean's first morning, she would cut him a little slack. As she slipped on her moccasins, the day's needs rushed at her. Water, weed, clear brush, harvest produce, wash, repair...

She prioritized and headed out. The garden was always the first and most vital task. No garden meant no food.

As Aric strode through the clearing, she yanked her hair into a braid. The first thing she spotted was the damaged fence. Something had shredded the tangle rope strung between posts of spider roots. She surveyed the three-inch rodent-like prints—*banwok*. Probably blundered into the rope, then thrashed to escape. She studied the sky. Fix the fence or water the plants? The Alpha sun was already sending out heat waves, a reminder she was behind schedule. Watering first.

She filled the bucket under the solar pump, then hauled it to the ever-thirsty plants. The breeze at her back helped push her along, but after ten trips, the bucket grew intolerably heavy. She slowed.

Why didn't SARC send her a hose?

Though grateful for the bucket, Aric couldn't help her daily grumble. A hose wasn't illegal for a phase two planet, even for her strict standards. She paused to flex her arm and shoulder. Then she again moved from the shadows under the umbrella trees to the spotlighted garden.

A spicy scent assailed her, vying with the ever-pervasive fungal odor. As she whirled, water sloshed down her leg. Sean headed across the clearing.

His aftershave. Inhaling deeply, she savored the pleasurable scent.

"Good morning."

She nodded a greeting. As her arm went limp, the

plasti-steel container banged her thigh. The weight jarred her less though than his disarming smile.

"Let me." Warm fingers enclosed hers as he grabbed the handle.

Where was her tongue?

"What do you want watered?"

"Garden. Plants." She waved in the general direction.

The weight seemed insignificant to Sean who carried the bucket with a bent elbow. "These?"

"Yes." She hurried to catch up. "I'll take it from here."

"I got this. Show me where and how much."

She pointed to the nearest plant. With care, he poured a stream of water next to the vegetation.

"Enough?"

"A little more." She pulled herself up. "Without the deep root systems like the jungle trees have, these plants wither without adequate water. Out on the plains, they get soaked by the morning dew. But here, they don't get enough moisture. Without my help." Why was she babbling? She clamped her mouth shut.

They made their way down the row, Sean quickly grasping how much water each plant needed. When the pail was empty, he went back for more.

After a while, she insisted on taking a turn. Bad idea. As she worked, she felt his scrutiny. Chatting about the insect life in relation to the garden didn't ease her discomfort. After a few minutes, she relinquished the bucket and retired to repair the fence.

When he was done, he called to her. "Now what?"

"Only weeding. I can take care of that." She didn't relish the idea of him staring at her while she demonstrated which plants needed to be pulled.

"Oh?" He struck a stern pose. "Seems we could get a lot more done if we both worked."

"All right." Truth to tell, help would be a great change.

She quickly finished the fence repair, then again joined him. With a gentleness that belied his size, he carefully removed the invaders without disturbing the other plants.

Late into the morning they labored, Aric growing hotter with the rising temperature. When the suns peered over the rim of the opening, her skin tingled. Though the labor wasn't that difficult, Sean repeatedly swiped an arm across his face. His damp shirt clung to him. However, the warmth only intensified his cologne. When he rose and stretched, she stared in fascination as a bead of sweat rested at the base of his throat before trickling out of sight.

She tore her gaze away. "I think we're due for a break."

"You're the boss." He brushed off his hands. "See you inside."

Managing a nod, she pretended something caught her attention. With the racket of the kawyas, she didn't even hear him stride away. For a long moment, she stared at the plants. Then she glanced back at the cabin. Was he watching? Rubbing her neck, she wondered at that nagging tickle.

You've got more important things to think about than his spying.

Truth be told, she probably was something of an oddity. A social misfit.

In minutes, the growing heat forced her to retire to the cabin. Sean sat at the table, sipping mathoke juice.

He set down his cup. "Anything else on the agenda for today?"

"Work on the clearing."

"Why? Your garden seems to be getting plenty of light."

"To keep tereph away. They don't like open spaces. You wouldn't care for one tapping at the window."

He grinned. "Agreed."

"I sometimes journal in the afternoon. With the clearing taking so much time, I'm a little behind."

He turned to glance at the shelves. "You've got two sets of books?"

"One scientific, one personal. Feel free to read or add anything you want. Got any questions I can answer?"

"How about if you refresh my memory about Empusa III?"

"All right." Aric retrieved a container of mathoke bulbs from the cooling unit.

As they chatted, she peeled the organics. At first she worked alone, then Sean found another paring knife. For about an hour, they discussed the twenty-hour cycles and the fourteen-month years, which happily coincided with Earth's time frame. His questions revealed an impressive grasp of subjects. They discussed the mostly harmless animal life. Compared to Earth, Empusa III had few dangers.

"Anything else?" She scooped the peels into a pile for the compost bin.

"No, except you've done a remarkable job here."

"Thanks." Her cheeks grew warm.

"I mean it. I'm honored to work with you."

Aric shrugged. Something about the way his eyes flicked when he spoke. Were his compliments contrived? Or a test?

"I'm sure I haven't done any more than the average scientist."

He didn't answer. Why not? Because he'd worked with others who were extraordinary?

She brushed her hands together. "Hungry?"

"Sure. I'll put the mathoke back in the cooler."

This time she showed him how to prepare the vegetables. Sean stood attentively beside her, his devastating aftershave filling her senses. No matter how she tried to maintain a distance between them, the gap kept getting smaller.

He seems relaxed. Why aren't I?

Because he was there to evaluate her. She reviewed the protocols of handling waste, agonizing about every area that she'd let slip over the last several months.

"These are okay raw." She placed her hand on one pile of vegetables. "These, however, are semi-poisonous until cooked."

"Oh?" He chopped khatseer stalks into bite-sized pieces.

"Let's just say the stomach cramps would make you wish you could die."

Instead of the expected smile, he frowned over his task as though he were having difficulty taking the bark off. "Do you only eat organics?"

"For now. I'm vegetarian as I told you. Not by choice, though." Aric dropped the vegetables into a pot. "The original team tried a variety of animal proteins. All horrid."

"So much for my hunting skills."

He spoke so forlornly that she laughed.

As the stew cooked, she showed him where she stowed the compost bucket. She frowned over its grubbiness when she realized it could use some cleaning. Next time she emptied the bucket, she would scour it.

After they finished eating, she went outside to survey the clearing. The jungle had reclaimed a sizable portion.

Sean came up beside her. "What's the scowl for?"

"I can't believe I've gotten so far behind." But this was merely another task in an avalanche of needs. She sighed.

"Then let's get busy."

He labored hard, hacking away vegetation with a second machete. Then with a long-handled shovel, he dug up some of the more stubborn plants while she pulled at the roots. The exertion made her drip with perspiration, even in the shade. After an hour she stopped to get them some water.

He took a deep drink and wiped his forehead. "I feel like a nineteenth-century farmer. Without the benefit of horses or oxen."

"Don't push yourself. You're not used to the low oxygen. Or heat." She didn't want him to think she was a slave driver.

Face flushed and shirt molding his back, he nodded. "You usually do all this by yourself?"

She shrugged. "I'm used to it."

"I doubt that."

What did that mean? Aric glanced at him, but he had already turned to remove a spider-tree root. She joined him, tugging on the fibrous strand.

"It's got to give." He clenched his teeth. "Soon."

The root suddenly snapped, the momentum flinging them backwards. Sean let go while she landed on the ground with an undignified *oof*.

She couldn't help but laugh at the way he'd staggered. "Was that some new dance?"

"I was going to ask you the same thing." With a sigh, he sank beside her.

"If it is, I definitely need more practice." She gingerly touched her sore elbow.

He lay back, chest heaving. Watching out of the corner of her eye, she longed to stretch out as well. Instead, she rubbed a sore spot on her thigh.

"We needed a break anyway." He rolled to his side and propped his head on one hand.

She held up the tuber trophy. "I didn't let go."

A slow grin spread across his lips. "Good for you. Although if you had, it might have saved you a few bruises."

"They're nothing. I get injuries all the time." She touched the newest cut on her knee.

Sean didn't respond. Something flickered in his eyes.

Slowly, she sucked in a breath. *How do you do that? How do you make me forget everything but you?*

Or was this another test? Aric jumped up. While she brushed herself off, he rose.

Words stuck as she pointed to a different section. "I think I'll work over there for now."

"Suit yourself." He rose and began filling the hole they'd created.

Drawing a deep breath, she grabbed the machete and hacked at the vegetation. For the rest of the afternoon, he never met her gaze. When the murkiness of the jungle deepened, she called it quits.

"We still have a lot to do." Sean wiped his brow.

"No use killing ourselves for a few more feet."

Something closed in his expression at her choice of words.

What did I say?

"I'll come in after a bit." She swiped her hair off her forehead with the back of a dirty hand. "You go on ahead."

After a brief nod, he strode toward the cabin.

Staying to survey their work, she sighed in satisfaction over the pile of uprooted vegetation. After several more sessions, she'd have time for what she really wanted to do—study the Edenoi. Had it really been over seven months since her last excursion to the plains?

Then she noticed the way the umbrella trees closed around the solar collectors. No, they needed to be done first. Soon.

She stretched to relieve her soreness. Despite the heavy labor, the day had turned out better than she'd expected.

Her pleasure vaporized the minute she entered the cabin. Several food packets lay on the table. This was his idea of cooking? Or another test?

"Help yourself." Sean motioned to them.

She stared at them, then him. "No thanks." She stalked past him and rummaged in the cooling unit. As she feared, the equipment didn't seem to be keeping the food as cold as needed. And the cabin lights were definitely dimmer.

She grabbed cold fruit and sponge bread out of the cooler. Since Sean had already torn into a food packet, Aric didn't offer him anything. They consumed their dinner in silence. When she finished, she washed her dishes and put them away. Apparently, he found his food bars particularly delicious because he was eating a third with relish. The wrappers lay scattered on the table.

She remained by the sink, indecisive about what to do next. Work on journaling? Weariness hounded her.

He held up a bar. "Last one. Last chance."

What part of "no" didn't he understand? Julian had once tried to make a gift of his food. Though he'd never said anything directly, Aric got the feeling he was trying to barter.

What was Sean after?

"I'm tired. Good night." She marched past him to her room. Soon she lay in her hammock, staring into the darkness. Despite her exhaustion, she couldn't sleep.

Some unnamed fear nagged at her. Or was it Sean that unsettled her? When he complimented her, she got the distinct feeling his praise was a calculated lie. Like he hid some truth behind flattery. It reminded her of…

A shudder quaked through her at a memory she refused to name. She'd once fallen for a man's flattery and attentions. Never again. He still worked at SARC, in a greater position of power. As much as she wanted to return to Earth, she feared being under his control again.

Empusa III was safer.

As she listened to Sean moving about the common room, she turned and pulled the blanket over her shoulders.

Chapter 5

After rising early, Sean stood at the window to watch Aric. Since his arrival her schedule had not wavered from gardening, food prep and working on the clearing. He'd given her ample opportunities to sneak away. She hadn't. For three days, she'd not broken protocol.

Neither his search of the shed nor perusal of her room yielded any suspicious evidence. Not only were things not adding up, the multiplying mysteries were beginning to irritate him. The simple task of finding Geoffreys' body and gathering incriminating evidence grew more elusive with each passing hour. He needed proof...if for no other reason than to write a convincing report to SARC.

And for him, to justify her execution.

Her movements outside the window distracted Sean as he slipped on his shirt. She was up earlier than normal, hauling water. Her predawn rising might suggest she didn't want his help. She was a tough lady to have survived alone on an alien world for five months. Not many science teams, let alone a single woman, could pull it off without modern equipment.

After the gruesome demise of two teams on Laotis 12, that planet reverted from phase three back to one because of the outcry on Earth. SARC capitulated to the public's demand, not wanting Intergalaxia to take advantage of the situation. They'd been vying for control for years, planning to absorb SARC and other organizations.

Aric turned on the solar pump. Water trickled into the bucket. Fingers resting on the handle, she shook her head. Her hair, loosely bound, caressed delicate shoulders. She raked fingers through the stands, then braided them. Her tunic rode up, drawing his attention to her slender legs.

Castigating himself for getting distracted, Sean gulped. What was it with her outfit? She'd explained the material came from a buffalo-hide tree, whatever that was. The fabric appeared rough.

Why wear something so uncomfortable, especially if she had an alternative? One insurmountable truth— no sane person would willingly forego supplies that would make life easier. He recalled the report from Aric's last assistant.

"I'm not sure what she did with her uniforms, but they're gone," Julian Geoffreys had relayed. *"Aric blames me for their destruction. Not only does she dress like the humanoids, she believes she is one."*

Then the odd last lines.

"I'm worried about her mental health. And my life."

Outside, Aric set down her bucket and looked up. To assess the trees? She spun on her heel. Her expression and body broadcasted tension, from the frown on her face to the rigid muscles in her neck.

As Sean finished buttoning his cuffs, she disappeared into the shed. *She's gonna trim branches without me?* Even though he'd offered to help, she apparently didn't want to wait. He smoothed back his hair. In moments, she reappeared with tangle rope and a machete.

After setting her knife aside, she wound a length of tangle rope about her torso. Taking care, she slipped the machete through the cords across her back and headed for the nearest tree.

She wasn't kidding about the task. Grabbing hold of the trunk, she inched her way up. He went outside for a better view. Only when cool dirt squished between his toes did he realize he was barefoot.

"Getting started without me?"

Face pinched and knuckles white, she looked down from fifteen feet.

He tried again. "Want some help?"

"If you like climbing, then yes." She continued upward, progress slow. Torturous.

After stepping back to appraise the situation, he decided at least two other trees needed to be trimmed.

When he reached the shed, he lashed rope about his waist. If this stuff could hold him by the ankle, it would have no trouble keeping him secure. He located the other machete and slipped it through the strands as Aric had. Bare feet would be perfect for the job.

Leaping onto the tree opposite her, he gripped the trunk. Miniature ridges made the ascent fairly effortless. His youthful tree conquests and rock climbing now came in handy. This was easy by comparison. As Sean worked his way up, the ridges became more pronounced, providing better finger holds.

He attained his treetop long before Aric reached hers. After locking his legs about the trunk, he put the machete between his teeth. Then he unwound the rope from his waist and lashed himself to the bole. Arms free, he hacked at the branches.

They sliced off with ease, yellow sap spraying him. Compared to the day before, this task was cake. He reveled in the dizzying height and the magnificent view of the morning sky. The expanse shimmered with a pale pinkness, tinged with crystalline blue. No clouds blotted the skies of Empusa III, allowing the unrelenting suns to beat down on the planet.

As he moved higher, he viewed the aptly named umbrella, spider and tangle rope trees. The branches of the immature umbrellas drooped as though half-opened. Sean supposed that when they reached maturity, their limbs would spread like their giant siblings. From his perch, the brown spider trees looked like squatting arachnids prepared to pounce. The abundant tangle rope trees elbowed other foliage. Their long, stringy strands reached down to the black soil or tangled in the succulent bushes. They reminded him of something in Gigi's kitchen. A mop? His great-grandmother stubbornly clung to that outdated tool.

Across the distance, Aric worked slowly, her mouth a grim slash.

He couldn't resist. "Having fun?"

Without breaking her rhythm, she glared. Like a drowning victim with a rescuer, her arm strangled the trunk. She had reason to be afraid. A plunge from this height could be fatal.

Fatal.

What if she fell? The idea worked in his mind. With orders discharged, albeit passively, he could leave with a clean conscience. In a few months, he'd be back on Earth with all the luxuries of the late twenty-first century. His employer would be happy, SARC somewhat satisfied, and life would progress to the next sweet step. His triumph would vault him onto a new path, one that would guarantee success in his ultimate mission.

If that could be done without touching Aric, so much the better.

"This good enough?" Sean called to her.

She stopped to survey the job. "Clear a few more

on the side facing me."

Looking up, he shielded his eyes from the blinding yellow sun, the first to rise above the horizon. He grunted as he climbed higher.

"Be careful." Her voice got lost in the noise of spongy leaves rubbing together. They squeaked like inflated balloons. Before he could lash himself to the trunk, Aric screamed.

Did she fall?

A gray blur sped past, leaping over his arm. As Sean slipped several feet, guilt battered him. Had his idle thought come true? Pulse racing, he grappled for finger holds. His gaze raked the damp black soil, looking for her broken body.

Where was she?

"By the stars." He slipped further, frantically searching.

"I forgot to tell you," Aric's comment floated to him, "watch out for zeheeks."

His heart thrummed so loudly in his ears, he couldn't determine where her voice was coming from. Sean finally saw her clinging to her tree. Several seconds passed before he understood he hadn't heard Aric scream, but the creature he'd disturbed.

She wasn't wounded. Or dead.

"They're harmless, but they do squeal when upset."

"*Now* you tell me." He fought for an even tone. "What'd you call them?"

A brief smile flashed. "Zeheeks."

Why am I relieved she's still alive? Swearing quietly, he pushed the question away.

He peered up. How many more animals were hidden in the mottled green and brown? He inched his way up, then prodded the tree's heart with his machete. Several striped zeheeks squealed their displeasure before scampering down the trunk. They reminded him of lemurs. Most ran over him in their haste to escape.

You big wimpwoid. They're more afraid of you. He chuckled to himself. "Probably having a nice nap when a big ol' ape scared 'em."

"What'd you say?" she called.

"Nothing." This was one for the books. Jayden would get a kick outta this tale.

When no more were evident, Sean secured himself and resumed cutting. The last branches came off quickly and he shimmied down.

Since Aric still worked in the first tree, he scrambled up the next. In a short time he finished, despite the number of zeheeks that ran over his shoulder. As he clambered down, he noticed her absence from the treetop. Looking below, he spotted her.

From his height, she appeared so small, vulnerable. Why did she have to die?

That isn't my concern.

He had an assignment. Without fulfilling it, Sean jeopardized the bigger mission. He didn't need to have proof of her guilt before carrying out orders. Wrestling with his conscience was a luxury he couldn't afford.

When he was still several feet up, he pushed away from the trunk and leaped down. Her expression changed to horror. As she cried out, she rushed forward. Her palm, under his elbow, cushioned his landing. Together, they straightened.

She drew a shaky breath. Hand lingering, her lips puckered in a circle of worry.

For the first time, Sean noticed her eyes were more teal than green. A strand of hair escaped her braid to caress her cheek. He gulped. Despite her primitive clothing and disheveled appearance, she was beautiful. Why hadn't he noticed that before?

She backed away. "You startled me. I thought— thought you were falling."

"Not me. I'm like a feline. Always land on my feet."

Her eyes were huge and her face paler than usual. Was she really afraid?

He gestured. "Should we gather these branches and dispose of them?"

"Yes." She seemed to mentally shake herself. "Of course."

They hauled the limbs to the edge of the clearing. In a short time, they finished removing the mess. She stood beside the pile of branches, fingering the spongy leaves as though uncertain of what to do next.

Say something. Anything. "How about some breakfast?"

"Probably lunch time by now."

He assessed the position of the suns. "Yep, morning's about gone."

But Aric didn't lead the way into the cabin. She tapped on the branch, that little furrow again between her brows.

Hands on hips, he waited.

"Thanks for your help." She spoke slowly.

"No big deal." He worked to sound flippant.

Still, she didn't move, eyes narrowed as though she were dissatisfied with his response. "I really mean it. You did most of the work. And I appreciate it."

Sean shrugged off her thanks. He didn't want her to gaze at him with her huge, gorgeous eyes and melt with appreciation because he did a job she hated. He didn't want to notice the scrapes on her legs or the smudge of yellow sap on her cheek. Most of all, he didn't want to think of her genuine fear of his getting hurt.

Before she said anything else, he turned and stalked toward the cabin.

Soon. She had to die soon. Tonight or tomorrow. Before his resolve weakened.

Chapter 6

Aric crouched at the stream's edge, splashing water on her face, arms and neck. After settling on her favorite flat rock, she sighed. How long since she'd allowed herself the luxury of a good soaking? Too long. She was always in a hurry—to eat, bathe, sleep. Hurry, hurry, hurry. Everyday tasks hounded her every moment.

Not now, though.

She dipped her feet into the cool water, not minding the sting of the scratches she'd gotten from tree climbing. Nothing would mar her delight at the prospect of a decent bath, even if the water wasn't warm and the homemade soap not the best smelling.

"Thank you. Thank you, God." She leaned back. The branch cutting was done. Done for one glorious month. Her multiple sighs drove away any lingering tension as she closed her eyes.

The suns' lightshow danced across her eyelids. A deep contentment rose within her—rare in harried days and restless nights.

"And God…" She stopped, unsure of what to say. Words seemed so inadequate. "God of the heavens…"

How could she express her overwhelming thankfulness?

The kawyas, involved in their usual clattering and croaking, seemed to turn down their volume. A quiver ran through Aric. Did they quiet in anticipation of the Creator's worship?

Head bowed, she pulled her feet from the water and sat cross-legged. Still her posture didn't seem right. Lifting hands with fingers spread, face upwards, her spirit seemed to soar.

"Father, in heaven, may Your name be praised. May Your kingdom come and will be done, as it is throughout the universe—on Earth, on Empusa III, everywhere. Thank You for every day providing enough to eat. Forgive me for all my wrongs, as I forgive those who have wronged me. Lead me from temptation. Deliver me from evil."

She took a deep breath, finishing the prayer in the time-honored tradition. "For Thine is the kingdom, the power and the glory forever. Amen."

Bowing her head, Aric allowed her fingers to slowly sink to the cool stone.

A long interlude passed before the world came back into focus. The rippling water bubbled up into her hearing, then the clattering kawyas. The smell of decaying brush filled her nostrils and the air's damp earthiness caressed her skin. She basked in lingering contentment one more moment.

Bath, right. She rose. The afternoon warned it would soon disappear.

She rechecked the location of her moccasins, knife and towel, all hanging on the knobby roots of a spider tree. Grabbing the bowl of cleanser, she spied out the best place to step into the stream.

She tiptoed into the rushing water, testing her footing. Moving until she was thigh-deep, she stripped off her clothing and tossed them onto the dry stone. Quickly now, for the water chilled her to the bone, she scooped a handful of the creamy cleanser as she lowered herself into the stream.

Wrinkling her nose, she smeared the pale olive goop over herself. The cleanser wasn't Terran soap, but it did the job.

The snap of a branch shattered her preoccupation. Covering herself with a bare arm, Aric sank into the water. She held up the bowl of cleanser, ready to hurl it as a weapon.

Not Sean, surely. *And Lord, please, not a tereph.* The predator should not yet be hunting. Still a chill ran through her, caused by more than the water's temperature.

Peering into the dim jungle, she looked for what caused the sound. Her teeth began to chatter. She couldn't stay in the stream much longer. A banwok plodded from under gnarly tree roots and drew nearer. The eighteen-inch omnivore snuffled her tunic. Did it think her clothing a zeheek?

She fumbled for a small stone in the streambed. "Go away!"

The huge rodent gurgled.

"Scram!" She tossed the missile but it bounced harmlessly.

Ignoring her, the animal nudged her clothing with a bristly snout. A horrible mental picture of returning to camp wearing only a threadbare towel flashed through her mind. Now she wished she'd taken the time to hang the garment beside her moccasins in the tree.

"Get away." She splashed water. The banwok's olfactory glands twitched while its pale color changed into a rainbow of hues.

Moving closer, she continued to yell and splash. The omnivore suddenly jumped as water touched its nearly hairless hide. With an indignant grunt, it shuffled off. Aric waited until the animal was safely away before emerging to retrieve her tunic and shorts. Without toweling off first, she slipped on her clothing.

All thoughts of a leisurely bath fled. Sitting on the bank, she quickly cleaned her legs and feet. Because the sky grew dusky, hair washing would have to wait.

She dried off, then headed to camp.

When she entered the cabin, a pleasant surprise awaited.

"You made dinner!" Aric couldn't help her smile.

"No problem." Sean had his back to her.

She passed through the brightly lit common room. "I'll put my things away and be right out."

By the time she returned, he was ladling stew into bowls. As she leaned forward to enjoy the aroma, her stomach growled in anticipation. "I had no idea I was so famished. This smells wonderful."

"Don't get too excited. These are only leftovers."

"I don't care." She waited till he sat then bowed her head. Biting her lip, she caught herself before praying aloud. Some team members hadn't appreciated her "moment of silence," let alone the occasional "amen" that sometimes slipped out.

This time she thanked God not only for the meal, but Sean's preparation of it. Then she added her gratefulness about the branch cutting. Finally, she prayed for her mother and Ella.

Fifteen months. In just over a year, she would see them again. *Please keep them safe, Lord.* But no prayer would ease the longing in Aric's heart.

She'd swallowed a couple bites before realizing Sean hadn't taken one. "Aren't you hungry?"

"Yeah." He stirred the food, then took a halfhearted taste.

"You keep dawdling, I'll eat yours too." When he didn't respond, she added, "I'm hungry enough to...to eat a tereph."

A small grin tugged at one corner of his mouth. Was something wrong? He probably didn't know how to respond to her unusual exuberance. Could she blame him? After all, she'd been strictly business since his arrival. He'd never seen her playful side.

Did she even have one?

Bowl empty, she rose. "Did you heat enough for seconds?"

"If not, you can have some of mine."

"How can you *not* be starving?" She ladled the remainder of the stew into her bowl. "Especially after you did most of the work today."

He made a small sound as he shrugged.

Pressing her lips together, she resisted making a comment. Maybe he was tired. Other team members had complained of fatigue in the first weeks after their arrival. Julian had been downright ill for almost a month. Too much exertion could have an adverse affect, especially for those not used to the gravity and lower oxygen.

She should be more considerate. A little kindness and appreciativeness on her part wouldn't kill her. Before Sean was done, she finished her meal and began cleaning up. When he rose as well, she said, "Nope. Sit and enjoy your dinner."

"I'm really not hungry."

"Fine. But I insist you relax."

With obvious reluctance, he lowered himself to his chair while she bustled about. In no time, everything was done.

Sean was still sitting at the table, a faraway look creasing his face as he stared toward the radio equipment. Was he homesick? Maybe he had a girlfriend waiting.

She hated to break into his thoughts. "I know it's early, but I think I'll head to my room. Read a little. But I'm sure I'll conk out soon. Do you mind?"

His gaze finally met hers. "No."

"Tomorrow, if you're up for it, why don't we take a hike? There's a ridge not far from here. Great view."

"If you want."

She hesitated before heading to her room. *Be kind, remember?* But how? The minutes ticked by.

Say something. But words stuck in her throat. Why was this so hard?

She walked toward him while he still sat. As she approached, he swiveled, expression guarded.

"About this morning." She chewed her lip when his brown eyes regarded her. She let out a breath, then took another. "I know I already thanked you, but I wanted to let you know how much I appreciate all you've done since your arrival. You've made life..." She struggled for the right words. "You've made *my* life much easier."

She stuck out her hand. Isn't this what people did? To show appreciation?

Slowly he rose, taking her hand. His strong fingers could easily crush hers, yet his hold was gentle.

Swallowing, she shook his hand, once. Then she

backed away. "Have a good night."

Not until she lay in bed, covers drawn up to her neck, did she realize Sean was the first man she allowed to touch her. In years.

Sean paced across the dark common room and back, unable to wear himself out. What was wrong with him? Pressing a fist to his forehead, he wished for the millionth time he had some weights or a punching bag. Something to work off what was eating him.

And this infernal silence! He was going nuts.

Leaning his hands on the window frame, he looked out into the black night. What he wouldn't do for a CU right now. A dozen voices on his comm-unit would drown out that one voice in his head that would not shut up. His own.

Why didn't you kill her this afternoon? You had the perfect chance.

He squeezed his eyes shut, but the image of Aric by the stream continued to haunt him.

He had followed her, confident she would finally lead him to Julian Geoffreys' body. If not that, her stashed supplies.

But she hadn't.

As he stared through the window, the scene replayed before him.

He tracks Aric to the stream. With her back to him, it

will be the perfect assassination. When he creeps forward, she does something disturbing. Inexplicable.

She raises hands, tilting her face to the heavens in some pagan ritual. No, not pagan. She utters the word "God."

When he peers around the tree trunk, her expression stuns him. Immeasurable ecstasy. Amazing peace. One word bursts into his mind: worship.

She begins saying a prayer that he recognizes. It's different, yet the same.

What was it? Where had he heard that before? A memory tugged at his mind, one he couldn't place. Didn't want to. He slammed the door to his thoughts as he thumped the window frame with a fist.

I shouldn't have witnessed that. No one should.

He'd trespassed in the throne room. Of God.

How Sean got away without her hearing was a mystery. He'd tripped on a root as he wheeled and ran, not stopping until he'd stumbled into camp.

When Aric returned, she acted as if nothing unusual had happened.

Had she really been oblivious to his presence? He shook his head, reevaluating. No, not oblivious. She had been wholly consumed by something else. *Someone* else.

The accusation flared. She should be dead. She should be face down in the water.

Flopping to the floor, he did pushups until his biceps screamed. Then he flipped over. No matter how many sit-ups he did, the pain in his body could not override the agony of his mind.

Which burned more—the failure to assassinate her or the transgression against God?

Muscles cramping, he lay panting on the floor for several minutes. An idea struck him. What if he didn't *cause* Aric's death?

Unless he found Geoffreys' corpse. That would be the deciding factor.

The notion grew.

Find excuses to be alone. Access your equipment in that cave. If you find the body, confront her and...

And finish the job as originally planned.

In a few months, he'd be back on Earth. He'd settle in the good graces of the powerful man who owed him. No longer would Sean need to pose as a security guard at SARC. No more mind-numbing rounds, inane gossip. The completed favor would open more critical doors.

Despite his strategy, training warred with logic. By not assassinating Aric, he disobeyed *them*—those he feared more than the man who'd ordered the hit. *"Your mission is to do the job, then get back to Earth."*

With all the money and manpower already invested, they'd have his head if he blew this.

He rose. Ignoring his open door, he slammed his body into the hammock. The bolts creaked ominously.

Do the job. *Do the job.*

"I will," he growled into the darkness. "I *will* finish this."

Chapter 7

Humming a tune, Aric tended the garden. Sean's open door gave her an opportunity to confirm he still slept. Let him. She could get everything done in plenty of time before their hike. Besides, he'd earned the extra rest. Warmth stole over her as she imagined their next fifteen months together.

An unusual aroma arrested her. Could it be...? Her nose twitched. Coffee?

She jogged to the cabin and flung open the door so forcefully it banged the wall. The delicious bouquet hit her full force.

Sean stiffened as he stood by the stove.

"I'm sorry," she said with a little laugh. "I didn't mean to startle you."

"Good morning." Dressed in a taupe, knee-length robe, he took two cups from the shelf. Sandy hair tousled, a pale shadow graced his chin and cheeks. "It's not quite done yet."

"Is it coffee?" She wasn't sure she could trust her senses. "Earth-grown java?"

"Want some?" He set the cups on the table.

"Absolutely." She plopped down on a chair in front of the nearest cup. Fingering the handle, she realized her hands were filthy. She rose to wash them but was quickly back in her seat.

"This might come out a little weird since it's boiled." He poured steaming brown liquid. "You'll probably get a few grounds."

"I don't care." She couldn't tear her eyes from the stream. Leaning forward, she inhaled the aroma.

"I didn't bring creamer or sugar."

"No matter." Grasping the cup, she reverently lifted it. The first careful sip delighted her as did the next. Finally, she grew aware that Sean wasn't drinking his own, but merely studying her. His expression contained almost regretful wonder.

"I hope *you* don't mind there's no cream or sugar."

"No worries. I'm enjoying watching you."

Her cheeks grew warm.

"Sorry I didn't share sooner." He scratched his cheek. "Forgot I had some."

"I'm amazed you brought the one item I crave

most."

He tilted his head, a half-smile playing on his lips. "You don't know what else I've got in my knapsack."

"Can't be better than this." She trailed one finger over the cup's handle. "Make coffee every morning and you can sleep in all you want."

"Yes, ma'am."

She grinned, then took another sip. "Aren't you going to have any?"

He started as though suddenly aware of his own coffee. "Of course."

"You'd better guard it. I won't pass up leftovers like last night."

He moved his cup protectively closer. "You'd have to arm wrestle me for it."

"You got a deal."

His brown eyes rose to hers, something hidden in their depths.

She was the first to look away. Before she could finish her first cup, Sean rose and poured a second.

"Thank you."

"I didn't bring a lot. From here on out, we'll have to ration."

"No problem." Without thinking, she added, "You're so different from my last assistant."

He set the pot back on the stove. "What ever happened to him, by the way?" Sean spoke with studied indifference.

The room suddenly lost its coziness. Why'd she open her big mouth?

Her report contained everything SARC needed to know. He had to have read it. But somehow she knew he wanted more than mere facts.

Aric loosened her hold on the cup. "Truthfully, I don't know. Julian was an insomniac. Roamed at night, preferred to solo scout." She took a deep breath. "I got up one morning and he was gone." Again, she paused. "I searched the jungle for a week."

"Only a week?"

"I couldn't travel farther. The garden needs constant care, since it's my only food source. Besides harvesting."

His face wore a speculative look.

"I did find something, though." She spoke slowly, aware that her confession might make her sound deranged. "I saw what I thought was a body, but didn't get a good look."

"Why not?"

"The remains were across a ravine. It was late and the tereph had not yet fully cycled into hibernation." She ran her fingers along the table's rough edge, rethinking the event. "When I returned, I couldn't find anything. My speculations were in the report I sent to SARC."

"Yeah, I read it." Sean shrugged. "I thought there might be more to the story."

She fought with herself about saying more. "I...I didn't include that Julian and I never got along. And over time, things seemed to deteriorate."

"Oh?"

"I started to compile a list of ethics breaches. After he disappeared, I destroyed it. No point besmirching a dead man's reputation."

His eyebrows rose. "You're convinced he's dead."

"He has to be. All he had was a standard-issued knife. He'd never survive without food, shelter or protection. Not for five days much less five months. Even with my knowledge and experience, I doubt I could."

"What happened to his clothing? Personal belongings?"

"Some of those disappeared too." She shrugged.

He was scrutinizing her with that piercing gaze she remembered from his first day.

If she was going to tell, she should tell all. Still, the words came slowly. "I understand as Team Leader, I'm responsible. But Julian gave no indication he was mentally unbalanced. SARC vetted him, right? I still can't figure it out."

He passed a hand over his chin. "How soon after his disappearance did you send the emergency beacon?"

"Six days."

Sean's eyebrows rose. "Why'd you wait so long?"

"Julian was a loner. It wasn't unusual for him to take off for an entire day."

"And leave you to do all the work?"

She shrugged. "I figured he'd eventually show up."

Sean seemed to take his time absorbing the information.

"I searched as far from base camp as I could,

but..." She sighed.

Confessing to him felt right. At least she no longer carried the full burden.

She finished her coffee. "Anything else you want to know?"

Though he seemed to have more questions, he shook his head. "No. That's plenty."

"You still want to hike? We have to head out soon if we want to go today."

"I'm always up for adventure."

She smiled. "Okay. While you get ready, I'll pack a lunch."

Chapter 8

As they climbed a steep path, Sean puffed and cursed his weakness. Where was the oxygen? He'd given up on conversation long ago.

When they reached a wall with an overhanging rock, Aric paused. The ledge widened, allowing a comfortable space to escape the burning suns. Opposite, a sheer cliff dropped a hundred and fifty feet. The calls of the kawyas, rising on the moist updraft from the jungle, sounded tinny in the distance. Besides them, nothing could be heard but the soft whisper of wind and his labored breathing.

"Let's stop here a bit." She peered about the area

before sitting.

Without the fine sheen of perspiration on her forehead, he wouldn't have guessed she'd hiked nearly two miles. She didn't even look winded.

A furrow of concern settled between her brows. "You okay?"

"You're shaming me." He consumed a deep breath as he bent and rested hands on knees.

"I'm accustomed to this planet. You'll adjust."

"I hope so." An ocean of sweat gushed from his temples. He wiped it away with his sleeve. Slowly, he lowered himself beside her.

After slinging her canteen off her shoulder, she offered him a drink.

He declined with a shake of his head. "I got water."

"This is mathoke. A better refresher."

She's genuinely concerned. Sean detected no contrivance in her expression.

"Thanks." He unscrewed the cap and drank.

"Not too much." She stayed his hand. "In large amounts, the juice can sedate you. Since you're not acclimated."

Nodding, he handed back the canteen.

"How long…" He gulped air. "How long before that happens?"

"Hard to say. When we first landed, the medics diagnosed us as having something similar to hypoxia. Every team member exhibited some symptoms."

"How'd you react?"

"I had a headache for about a week."

"That's it?"

"People respond differently." She spread her hands. "Be grateful you're not like Julian. He vomited almost every day for a month."

"I *am* grateful."

He leaned his head back. Her story was plausible. In his report seven months prior, Geoffreys hinted his life was in danger. Was paranoia the first step? He'd gone off his rocker, packed his clothes and wandered into the jungle. If that were the case, Sean would find bones instead of a shallow grave. He thought through SARC's mandate to get proof of Geoffreys' death. Not so simple anymore. As far as ascertaining Aric's mental state...again, not so simple. Sean vacillated between believing her to be a pathological liar and a victim.

However, those were moot points when he considered his secret orders to assassinate her. The man who'd sent him didn't tolerate disobedience.

She touched his arm. "Sure you're okay?"

"Yeah." He opened his eyes. "I was only resting."

"It's not far now. Can you make it?"

"Give me one more sec." Again he closed his eyes, sensing every atom of the woman beside him.

Though petite, she possessed a core of strength that he was only beginning to realize. Her slim arms, shapely legs and lean body all spoke of hard work. Yet he detected her vulnerability, inexplicable with her hard-shelled exterior.

She couldn't be a pathological liar.

Yes, she could. He'd interrogated people like her

before.

I need evidence. He abruptly rose. "Let's go."

He determined to squelch any weakness, physical or otherwise. For some reason, his military training came back to him. The sergeant yelling in his face. No thinking needed. No reasoning allowed. "Do your job, soldier. Just do your job."

I will not fail. I can't.

As before, Aric led the way while he trailed behind. When they reached the top, he remained standing to keep his muscles from cramping while she unpacked their lunch.

Unlike the black soil of the jungle floor, the stony surface of the ridge gleamed white. The olive and brown branches of umbrella trees spread out below, creating an illusion of a solid canopy. Aric pointed out the open plains where the Edenoi settled. Fields for planting and groves of whippet trees were out of sight.

"Tell me about the buffalo hide trees," he said.

"The hide is actually the pelt of an animal that lives on the host. They have a symbiotic relationship. The Edenoi harvest it, much like we would strip cork trees or shear wool. Doesn't seem to hurt the creature, which grows more covering." Eyes shining, she grew animated. A true teacher.

"What do the Edenoi use it for?" He sat beside her as they snacked.

"Mainly for clothing and tents. Sometimes they dye strips for ornamental use."

He enjoyed listening as she shared her knowledge.

"What first piqued your curiosity?"

"I saw the tree groves by an Edenoi village. They are unique looking." Her cheeks darkened. "The knowledge came in handy when my uniforms wore out."

He nodded, refraining from commenting because of the taboo topic.

"I discovered the more I tanned the hides, the softer the cloth became."

"But it's not as comfortable as woven textiles or syntha-fabric?" He met her gaze.

"No. Unfortunately. But it's served me well."

Served her well? Sean had already observed the chafe marks on her delicate skin.

"What's on the other side of this ridge?" He pointed in the opposite direction.

"I've never explored too far beyond a couple of short trips during the winter months." She began putting fruit away. "That sector is like the one we live in."

"And there's always plenty of work to do at the base."

"Yes." She seemed relieved he didn't insist they go on a longer excursion. "I've found the tereph population greater there. Possibly more aggressive."

"And knives aren't much of a defense."

"One theory I don't plan to test."

He chuckled. "What you wouldn't do for a neurogun."

"I've never needed one." She rose and brushed off her hands. "Besides, I couldn't kill a tereph."

Interesting. "Not even for self defense?"

"In three years, one's never threatened me. I just stay out of their way."

She pointed out landmarks and explained the Edenoi's occasional skirmishes. With only primitive clubs and farming tools, the various tribes didn't do too much damage.

The suns rose higher in the sky. Sean touched his tingling skin. "I'm beginning to bake."

"Then let's get to base. Why don't you lead?"

The trek back was almost as tiring as the climb. Though his core temperature hadn't risen significantly, his brain began to feel cooked. However, he did experience the effects of the juice Aric had shared. If his mind felt foggy, at least his body had regained energy.

She lingered as though reluctant to leave. Or was she allowing him to set the pace? He slowed when he came to the overhanging rock where they'd rested earlier. Against the wall, an object glittered on the ground. A gemstone? He leaned over to pick it up.

"Sean, no!" she shrieked. Darting forward, she jerked his arm.

He swiveled. *What...?* One moment, she stood beside him, the next teetered at the cliff's edge. Clawing air, she slipped over the side.

His hand shot out. Fingers clamped her tunic. Instinctively, he braced for impact. When she hit the sheer rock, his shoulder jarred. The force yanked him to his knees.

Seconds crawled. He braced against the ground

with his free hand. Her weight pulled him downward. The image of her ashen face struck him as she scrabbled to right herself. Her mouth screamed with silent terror. Beyond, the vast abyss yawned.

Let go.

The thought came out of nowhere.

The perfect, accidental death.

Sweat burned his vision. His grip twisted.

Loosen your fingers. Let go. Mission fulfilled.

"Sean!" Green eyes shimmered. "I'm slipping."

Lip bloody, her face constricted with terror. Raw knuckles strangled his wrist. Her hair billowed on a draft of air.

I can't. His vision cleared. *I can't let her go.*

"Hang on." He pulled steadily. The muscles in his shoulder convulsed. Pedaling feet propelled her upwards. With Sean's final grunt and jerk, she shot up and slammed into his arms. Together they staggered backwards. His spine hit the wall, knocking the wind from him.

For uncountable moments, she crumpled against him, fingers clutching his shirt. Pain ebbed into awareness. Her softness pressed against him. She felt so fragile in his arms, vulnerable. In need of comfort.

When she raised unfocused eyes, he stared down at the pinched whiteness underneath her sunburned nose and cheeks. He couldn't help himself. With his thumb, he smoothed the blood from her lip.

"You okay?" His voice sounded husky, even to himself.

Her mouth moved, but she made no sound.

"If you said we were going base jumping, I would've brought my chute." He forced a grin. When she began trembling, he tightened his grip about her waist. "Anything else besides your lip hurt?"

"No." The word burst from her. "All over."

For her sake, he chuckled. "Nothing hurts, just everything?"

Her grip tightened as she arched to look behind. She shuddered violently.

Worried her knees would buckle, Sean held on.

Color slowly crept into her face. "You save...saved my life."

"Yes." He couldn't trust himself to say more.

Whatever the glittering object was that he'd nearly touched was now gone. He considered asking her about it, but Aric still appeared in shock. Under the sunburn, her expression grew more pinched. Her fingers spasmodically clenched his shirt.

Time to get her back to the cabin.

Sean tugged her arm. "Let's get out of here."

Not until they were at camp did Aric lose her pasty look. As he followed her into the cabin, he noted her limp had become more pronounced. She repeatedly rubbed one wrist. When she opened the cupboard to get cups, he reached for them.

"Let me." He tugged them out of her hands.

"I can—"

"No. Sit."

Slowly she obeyed.

He poured some juice. "What was that shiny thing you didn't want me to touch?"

A blank look skipped across her face. "Oh, that." Aric drew a breath as she flexed her hand. "An insect that emits acid."

"It would've burned me?" He handed her a cup.

"Yes." She stared into her drink. "If you picked it up, you'd have been in agony for a week."

He absorbed her explanation in silence. "Seems pretty insignificant in exchange for your life."

Her grip tightened around the cup.

"However, thank you." Sean drew closer and rested his fingers on her shoulder.

Aric glanced at his hand, then rose abruptly. "I think I'll go lie down for a bit." The words seemed as strained as her expression.

Why was she so eager to get away from him? For a long time, he nursed his juice as thoughts ricocheted in his head.

I couldn't kill her.

He downed the drink. No. Aric Lindquist wouldn't die by his hand.

Borrowing the words of his great-grandmother, he spoke aloud. "Well, Sean, you grabbed a rattler by the tail. Now what're you gonna do?"

Gigi had a plethora of phrases that came in handy

now and again.

The obvious answer was to take the offensive. If he were to unravel the mysteries, he needed to be proactive. The clock was ticking. In a little over two months, Aric would radio her scheduled report. As her assistant, Sean was required to make an entry. SARC would be waiting for news.

That part isn't a problem.

He fully expected to have enough information to satisfy them as far as her mental state and what had happened to Julian Geoffreys.

But as far as the other…

The man who'd ordered the assassination wouldn't be as forgiving. Once she sent her report, he'd know that Sean had failed. Another assassin would be sent. One who wouldn't hesitate.

Two months. His gaze landed on her personal journals. They would be a good place to start getting answers.

Settling in a chair, he flipped to the most recent entry and began working backwards. Although Aric was frank about some things, she obviously kept secrets. If he were to save her life—both their lives—he needed answers.

He would use whatever means at his disposal.

Chapter 9

"What a great idea." Aric pulled the plug on the storage container. Water gushed from the bottom to fill the irrigation ditch.

Sean grinned. "It'll save hours of work."

"Absolutely." She studied the supply crates, set up at both ends of each garden row. All they had to do was fill the bins with water, then remove the plug at the bottom. Though they still had to haul buckets, time would be saved by not having to water each individual plant. "Don't know why I didn't think of this earlier."

"You were busy with other things."

Like survival. Aric smiled, warmed by a rush of

gratitude. Finally, someone understood her harried life. That is, before his arrival. Her days had considerably slowed, giving her time to catch up on little things, even journaling.

Stepping back, she waved toward the rows. "Looks like the plants are getting plenty of water."

"As long as we maintain the ditches."

"That should be easy." She cleared her throat. "Mind doing the weeding? I have a task that needs to be taken care of." Her moccasins had grown thin in the soles.

"Not at all."

She headed toward the shed. Inside the building, buffalo-hide pelts were curing. She fingered the pliable material. Perfect.

After setting a plastic tub outside by the pump, she filled it half-full. Kneeling, she submersed the buoyant hide.

As she held the material underwater, she watched Sean work. Had it been a week already since the episode on the ridge? Since then, something had changed between them. And in him. He no longer dawdled in the morning, but was up as early as she, gardening or working on the clearing. They'd removed so much vegetation that she could again see the original boundary markers.

He looked so incongruous as he made his way down the rows of plants. How did he manage to always have a near-impeccable uniform? And perfect hair? He was definitely the city type, not the backwater planet variety. Next to him, she felt grubby. Shabby. Even though he had generously shared his soap and shampoo. Incredible luxuries.

Because of his help, she could finally catch her breath. If all went well, they could soon plan a trip to the plains.

When she released the hide, it no longer leaped out of the tub, proving it was sufficiently waterlogged. She hauled the material out and began to beat it with the handle of the spade.

"What are you doing?" Sean approached, eyes on the creamy hide.

"Breaking down the fibrous tissues. Easier to work with." She grunted from the effort.

He continued to observe while her cheeks heated.

"Want me to take a turn?"

"In a minute." While she worked, he leaned against the shed, arms folded. The longer he scrutinized her, the more self-conscious she became.

Couldn't he return to the garden? She held her tongue to keep from voicing the thought. When he refused to leave, she gave in.

"All right." She handed Sean the tool. "Don't strike too hard. The hide needs to be a little firm."

After several inept attempts, she laughed at him. So he was incompetent at *something*.

"Here. Like this." Aric grasped the handle. Guiding his hands, she demonstrated how the hide should be struck. But their combined effort didn't work either. He was too stiff, unable to bend enough to give the pelt a good enough whack. Or their timing was off. He muttered a profanity, but quickly apologized.

Finally, she was laughing so much, she had to stop. Sean, too, had a bemused grin on his face.

"I'm sorry." She didn't want to tell him he was a klutz. "You must be too tall."

"That. Or something." He straightened. "I think I'll return to the garden where I *know* I'm useful." He went back to weeding while she rhythmically beat the hide. However, she was aware that he looked in her direction several times.

Finally, the pelt was pliable enough. Using her templates, she cut the pieces for her moccasins. She hung the leftover portion to dry. A large needle and some stripped tangle rope thread were the only other things required.

Into the cabin she headed. She needed to act quickly while the fabric was still moist. Gathering her things, she sat cross-legged on the floor.

Sean came in. He stopped by the door before heading to the cooling unit. "Want anything to eat?"

"Not now." She continued to sew. "Thanks."

Consumed in her labor, she was vaguely aware of him moving about the room. She paused though, when he set a cup of coffee beside her.

"Thank you." When she glanced up, he was staring out the door.

"Doesn't the quiet get to you?"

Aric grinned. "Are you kidding? With the noise of the kawyas?"

"I meant in the evenings. Don't you miss the news? Movies? Music?"

"I used to turn on SARC's info-station. They broadcast once a week. Even though Empusa III is so far out, I still could pick up their signal."

"Why'd you stop?"

She punched the needle through the hide before answering. "The solar collectors, for one. The radio takes a lot of power."

"But we solved that with the tree trimming."

"True." She shot him a grateful smile. "However, something's wrong with the radio. Julian checked, but couldn't fix it."

"Ah." Sean's mouth puckered. "Mind if I look?"

"Not at all."

Was he so versatile he knew about electronics? When he switched on the radio, the room filled with ear-piercing static.

He hastily turned down the volume. "Sorry."

While he fiddled with dials, Aric went back to her project. The material grew stiffer, making the task more difficult. As she labored, she was aware of him taking the radio down from the shelf and setting it on the table. When he asked about tools, she told him where to find some.

Peace settled on the room. She'd nearly completed one moccasin. In the years she'd lived on Empusa III, she'd sewn more pairs than she cared to recall. What would her mother say about them? Aric had never made an issue about her Lakota Sioux blood, but it was important to her mother. *And my ex.* He'd used her ethnicity to gain the trust of partisan groups. He'd also used her father's renown as a scientist to ride the wave of publicity.

She pushed the unwanted thoughts away. Regardless of what her ex-husband had swindled from her, she retained a far more valuable treasure—their daughter, Ella. He didn't even know about her. Before Aric had a chance to tell him she was pregnant, he'd abandoned her.

Will Ella even remember me? After all these years?

Back stiff, she shifted. Her gaze met Sean's over the top of the radio. For some reason, heat flooded her face. Then she chided herself. He couldn't read her mind.

"What's the prognosis?" She tilted her head toward the radio.

He grinned. "I think we can save it."

"Good. I don't want to miss sending my quarterly report."

His face tightened. "No, you wouldn't want that."

She rose and stretched. "Do you need new parts?"

"Some wiring should be replaced. Since we apparently don't have any, I improvised."

"Wonderful."

"Don't get your hopes up." He put the radio back on the shelf. "When's the next broadcast?"

She studied her homemade calendar, pinned to the wall. Then she stared at her journals, which were out of chronological order. Had he been reading them?

Sean was still waiting for her reply.

"Looks like tomorrow night."

"We can try the radio then."

Aric sat back on the floor. As she resumed sewing, she shot another glance at the journals. Apparently he looked at only her personal ones. Not the scientific accounts still lined up perfectly. Why would he be interested in those? Of course, they weren't off-limits, but she found it odd that he would choose the personal ones first.

"Something else to drink? Lunch?" He put away the tools.

"Later for me." She concentrated on threading her needle.

Didn't he have something to do? She clamped her mouth shut, determined not to recommend he work on the clearing. Or tree trimming. He would know it was a ploy to get him out of the room. However, the longer the quiet stretched, the more she grew aware of him sitting a few feet away.

His chair creaked as he crossed his legs. "Do you believe in God?"

She sucked in a quick breath. "What a question."

"You pray before meals."

"Then obviously, I do." She ducked her head.

He was quiet for a few seconds. "How can you—as a scientist—believe in God?"

"How can you, as a scientist, *not* believe in God?" she shot back.

"I've never thought much about Him."

"So, you *do* believe." When he frowned, she added, "Since you referred to God as 'Him.'"

"Merely a traditional reference." He shifted in his chair.

Good. She'd finally made him uncomfortable. Before he returned to that topic, she asked, "How long have you worked for SARC?"

"About thirteen months."

"And before that?"

"I did some consulting work with the science department at the United International University in—"

"I know where it's located." As glibly as possible, she constructed a trap. "Then you must have known my father."

Sean shook his head. "Dr. Lindquist was before my time. I only worked at UIU for four years."

"You just missed him, then."

"No." His lips pursed. "Didn't your father die nine years ago?"

"Yes." She bent her head to hide the fact that she'd tried to catch him in a lie.

Guess I should stick with sewing.

"So, after all your work, how long do your moccasins last?" Sean asked.

"Six months. Give or take."

"And you like them?"

Shrugging, she stabbed the needle through the still-porous fabric. "They're better than nothing."

He made a sound of agreement. Or was it skepticism?

She regarded him. "Hinting you want a pair?"

"You offering to make some?" One eyebrow rose.

"Yes. If you'll wear them. I'm not going to work this hard only to have you turn them into a decoration."

"Never."

"Then I'll make you some." She added a caveat. "Only if you *don't* help."

He laughed. "Gladly. Should I get the other piece from the shed?"

"Yes, I mean, no. The hide needs to be soaked first."

"I can do that."

After he left, she rose. Her fingers were sore but strangely, the prospect of doing another pair didn't bother her. The footwear would be a great thank you to him for saving her life.

She drank her now-cold coffee. When she caught sight of Sean outside, she smiled as she watched him immerse the hide in water. Rolled-up sleeves revealed corded arms. The frown of concentration on his brow somehow gave him the appearance of a small boy intent on completing a project for his teacher.

When the hide suddenly bubbled up and sloshed water into his face, she laughed. Apparently he hadn't heard her because he didn't look toward the cabin. Instead, he shoved the hide back under the water's surface, jaw tight with determination.

For some reason, she couldn't tear her gaze away. *Why do I feel so...so...?*

She couldn't identify what that was.

Resting her back against the wall, she rubbed her upper arms. She spoke sternly. "The moccasins are merely a gift, a thank you. Nothing more."

But even as she spoke, Aric knew she didn't tell the whole truth.

Later that evening, Sean noticed Aric by the window, peering out. When he entered the common room, she didn't even turn. "What's going on?"

Engrossed, she started when he spoke.

She threw him a glance. "Tereph. First one I've seen this season." Her voice grew strained. "Please cut the interior lights."

After the room plunged into darkness, he joined her at the window. "Where is it?"

"Give your eyes a sec to adjust. You can't miss it."

He didn't have long to wait. A massive and pale form moved cautiously along the edge of the clearing, zeroing in on something. How big was that thing? Sean guessed it was easily 550 pounds. From the distance, he couldn't make out more details. "What's it after?"

"Probably banwok."

The tereph suddenly lunged. Aric gasped when the shrill squeal of its victim pierced the night. As the predator backed toward the cover of the jungle, its prey continued to screech. The sound grated on Sean's nerves while he stared in horrified fascination. Though he could see nothing, the shrieking indicated the tereph was still nearby.

"Is it playing with its food?"

She turned a tight face toward him. "No. Tereph always devour their prey alive."

"Seriously?" In spite of himself, he shuddered.

"I've never seen one venture that far into the clearing. Must be extra hungry to take that risk."

Sean absorbed her words. "One thing's for certain. When you say it's time to head inside, I won't dawdle."

A ghost of a smile crossed her lips. "Now that they've emerged from hibernation, we definitely will be taking more precautions."

Starting now. Before they retired, Sean rechecked the door to make certain the cabin was secured. As far as he was concerned, Empusa III had lost some of its charm.

Chapter 10

Sean padded across his bedroom in new moccasins. Several times over the last few days, he'd caught Aric's pleased smile after she'd checked his footwear. They were great for everything except shoveling dirt or uprooting shrubs. Cool and soft, the moccasins were perfect for traversing the damp jungle floor.

As he shaved, he contemplated his strange new life. *Like using this razor.* The soothing ritual, more than the primitive tool, enamored him. On Earth, his comm-panel would be blaring the latest news. Back there he'd even had one installed in his bathroom so he wouldn't miss one item of importance. With his electronic gadgets plus the comm-panel, he could drown out ten clusters of kawyas.

Outside, they were happily chattering. As the razor scraped over his foam-laden face, Sean could even hear himself think. In the next room, he could hear Aric preparing for her day.

He'd given her plenty of opportunities to slip away, but she disappointed him by picking berries or studying plants. The items in her room didn't help either. The photo was of her as a child, with her sister and parents. The locket was a mystery. The book, *Life's Uncertain Highway,* was unimportant, a gift from her father.

Sean bent to rinse his face as water streamed into the basin. He patted his skin with a towel, not even missing a drying booth. Was the convenience and speed of the electronic wizardry worth all the noise?

After dressing, he found Aric working on her journal. As with most things, writing consumed her. Never had he met such a task-oriented person, proven recently with her moccasin making. She hadn't stopped to do more than snatch a bite to eat before finishing in the evening.

What could he give her in thanks? An idea hit him. Returning to his bedroom, he retrieved something she might appreciate. He carried the item behind his back, feeling like a schoolboy with a gift for his teacher. He'd once seen an old lithograph at Gigi's that reminded him of how he must look.

Gigi...a distant memory tugged at his mind. He'd

been at her house. Was he four or five?

He'd asked about a book of paintings in her parlor. One he remembered in particular was a man hanging from a large T-shaped pole. Huge spikes pierced his hands. Spectators surrounded the victim, wearing expressions of sorrow or scorn.

Sean had asked Gigi what the men were doing. What had she said? Buried under years of suppression, the memory eluded him. But now, without the hustle and bustle, the recollection began to crystallize.

"Yes?" Aric turned in her chair, interrupting his thoughts.

Later, he would have to revisit that. "I've got something for you."

"What is it?" Her smile encouraged him.

"This." He presented the pale green material.

As she rose, she shook it out. "One of your shirts?"

"Never worn." He shifted from one foot to the other. "I thought you might like some fabric."

"For what?" Puzzlement wrinkled her brow as her fingers caressed the item.

Why was she making this so difficult? He ran one hand through his hair. "For—for making yourself some clothing. Or whatever."

Her cheeks flamed.

Sean hurried to explain. "It's a thank you for the moccasins."

"Oh, that." She glanced up, catching the grin he'd allowed himself. Both of them shuffled their feet. Sean couldn't help his chuckle as he thought of how they must look. Like two teenagers on their first date.

By the stars, you're over thirty, not a kid anymore.

"Well." She smiled brightly. "I'm done journaling. Interested in a swim?"

"Cold, shallow water doesn't sound that inviting."

"Not in the stream. Somewhere *much* better. It's a bit of a hike…"

He could tell that she wanted to surprise him. "What about swimming clothes?"

"Wear what you like. I'm going in this." She smoothed the hem of her tunic.

"All right." Sean headed to his room and quickly changed into shorts. Nothing else he owned would be appropriate. He'd not come to Empusa III to go swimming.

Carrying two towels, he returned to the common room. Where was Aric? Glancing around, he discovered her door ajar. Through the three-inch opening, he caught sight of her profile. Lost in thought, a soft smile tugged at her mouth. His gift lay on the hammock, her hand resting on it. Was she pondering how to use the material?

Her fingers moved across the shirt. Then she startled him by raising it to rub it against her cheek. Heart thumping against his ribcage, he gulped. Was she more enthralled by the fabric or him?

Undetected, he backed away, then reopened his bedroom door. Noisily, he closed it as though he'd just come out. Good thing Aric tarried. He needed the extra minute.

Cheeks flushed and eyes sparkling, she joined him. Could she see his pounding pulse?

"Ready? Let's go."

Water geysered from a cliff into a pool forty feet below. On the perimeter, Aric stood waiting for his reaction. Face beaming, Sean grinned as he took in the surrounding hedge of white rock and eddying water. Only the chartreuse and sepia lichen clinging to the sheer walls marred the perfection. The water too, was the wrong color, somehow both violet and pink.

"Is it safe?" He dipped his toe to the water.

"Absolutely. The kawyas don't like this much water."

"I'm betting they don't like the noise competition."

Aric laughed as she slipped off her moccasins and dropped the towel. "Last one in is a putrefied garbage scow."

She dove. As she swam toward the other side of the huge pool, he didn't follow. Sean seemed content to examine a handful of sand that he dug up at the shallow end. The temperature of the water wasn't as warm as the last time she'd been there, but she refused to let anything detract from enjoyment. The pool was an oasis in a desert of work that always pressed against her.

Squinting into the sky, she noted how the umbrella trees had still not closed the gap. Branches strained across the expanse from both sides.

After half an hour, she headed back towards Sean. "What do you think?"

Oblivious, he floated like flotsam.

As she swam closer to get his attention, she accidently splashed him.

"Hey!" Sputtering, he thrashed upright.

"I said, what do you think about our private pool?"

"Fine," he growled, "until you half-drowned me."

"Half...?" She made a sound of derision.

"Yeah, with a gallon of water."

"I only splashed a little—"

"You call this a little?" He scooped a tidal wave toward her.

As water hit her face, Aric reflexively inhaled, then coughed. The next minute she was sloshing him as fast as she could while he retaliated. In moments, they were both laughing uncontrollably. Realizing she'd never win, she plunged underwater.

She hoped Sean would be so surprised by her sudden disappearance that he wouldn't follow her behind the falls. Behind the veil of water, she'd hide.

Lungs nearly bursting, she swam deeply below the surface. Ahead, she could see massive air bubbles where the falls crashed into the pool. *A few more yards.* Arms aching, she skirted the roaring cauldron.

She shot up and sucked in a huge breath. Pausing only a second, she pulled herself up to crouch on the small ledge. Peering through the undulating liquid curtain, she looked for Sean. Where was he?

Confounded, she rose and stared.

She was still gaping when something cool snaked across her foot. Sean's grinning face bobbed below. Before she could react, he yanked. She teetered, over compensated, and fell forward. Flailing, she fought as the falls pummeled her, thrusting her deeper into the pool.

She lost all sense of direction, then panicked. Water pinned her below the surface. Out of air, she swam deeper, then back toward the inside of the falls. As she battled her way up, Sean joined her, pressing his hand against the small of her back. Side by side, they rose.

Clutching the rock's edge, Aric fought for breath. She wrestled the mop of hair that plastered her face.

"Thanks." She hoped her tone carried all the asperity she intended.

"You're welcome."

Obviously he'd missed the sarcasm.

"I mean thanks..." she paused to cough, "for nearly drowning me. Guess you got your revenge."

"I didn't intend to."

She wished she could dunk the lout. However, not only was he stronger, but an expert swimmer. Better than she.

Sean merely grinned, expression devilish. His sandy hair had gone curly. Golden sparks of light danced in his eyes.

As the moments ticked by, his smile faded. He drew closer.

Paralyzed, Aric couldn't make herself swim away.

He held onto the ledge behind her, arms moving to cage her in. His biceps bulged as though he strained against some incredible force. The light disappeared from his eyes as he leaned toward her. The water grew colder in contrast to his radiating warmth. She shivered.

Run away!

Buffeted by the churning pool, she clung harder to the rock, every atom coiling with tension until she felt she would explode. Any second, he was going to kiss her.

Go. Go now.

Aware that he could outswim her, she submerged. Deeper and deeper she swam. Her eardrums screamed in pain as she reached the rocky bottom, swiveled, then planted her feet. She shoved with all her might and eventually ended up beside her towel on the dry rock. With shaking arms, she pulled herself out of the pool. Grabbing her moccasins, she ran into the jungle.

Chapter 11

The mile return took Sean twice as long because he lost his way on the poorly marked trail. When he finally reached camp, he was hot and tired. So much for a relaxing afternoon.

He expected to find Aric in the garden. Nope. She stood at the kitchen sink, peeling vegetables. Her spine remained ramrod stiff when he passed her to put away his things and change. Neither of them spoke. By the time he left his room, she was outside checking the garden.

He rested his hand on the makeshift fencepost. "Anything worth picking for dinner?"

"No."

"Need some help?"

"Not really." She continued to lift leaves and pluck stray weeds.

For several moments, he watched. Not once did she meet his gaze. As soon as he entered the enclosed space, she rose and brushed off her hands. Without a word, she headed toward the shed.

So, is that how it's gonna be?

After puttering a few minutes, he gave up. The well-tended garden didn't need any work...not until Empusa III mysteriously sprinkled weeds in the soil during the night. Instead, Sean popped the crate lids and assessed the water levels. Might as well take care of this now.

He surprised Aric, standing on tiptoes, peering out the shed's window. Looking for him? As soon as she saw him in the doorway, her face reddened. She swiveled on her heel and pretended to check the curing buffalo hide. Because she wrongly concluded he'd returned to the cabin?

This would have been comical if he wasn't still irate about finding his own way back from the pool.

"Aric, we need to—"

"I'll go make dinner." Flattening herself, she edged by him.

He turned to watch her literally scamper into the cabin.

Fine. If that's the way she wanted it.

Sean grabbed the bucket and filled the reservoirs. Water sloshed his leg when he carelessly dumped it into the bin. Shaking his head at his sodden pants, the real reason he was irritated struck him.

I shouldn't have tried to kiss her.

But she wanted him to. If not, she should have run off. Immediately.

She hadn't. For one who was so concerned about rules, she made it apparent that the "no relationships" directive meant little to her. At least, that's what he'd assumed. She'd sent him all the "come hither" signals with which he was well acquainted — coy smiles, glancing at him under her eyelashes, open body language. He was merely answering her invitation.

Stupid mistake. He shouldn't have given into temptation. If not for professional reasons, for personal ones. His stay on Empusa III would be so much more complicated if he became involved with her.

Sean finished filling the crates and put the bucket away. When he entered the cabin, Aric was hunkered over a bowl of stew, engrossed in one of her scientific journals.

At the desk. Not at the table.

The message was unmistakable — *leave me alone.*

Very well. If she could pretend nothing happened, so could he.

After he changed his pants, he grabbed his own dinner. He deliberately reached past her to pull the earliest journal from the shelf. Her startled look nearly made him laugh. Because of his proximity? Or the fact that he chose her personal writings?

She'd said to feel free to read whatever she'd written.

With a *thwump*, he let the journal drop open on the table. He dove into his meal, unable to concentrate on her finely written account of her first days planetside. Repeatedly, his gaze returned to her as she sat mere feet away. Her back to him, she doggedly ignored him.

What had happened to Aric? Her ex must have really done a number on her—proven by the fact that their divorce had been so disagreeable, she'd changed her name back to Lindquist. Sean had heard Mitchell Harker had a big mouth and an even bigger ego.

But what about all the rumors about Aric? Her Center profile called her a maverick who rebelled against authority and standard procedures. She finagled her way into the exploration field, some say by bargaining with sex. What a laugh. Despite skimpy outfits, she was exceedingly modest. How did she get to be Team Leader if she was only qualified to be a biotechnician?

The answer magically appeared under Sean's fingers. *"After the engineers finished constructing the base, I was stunned when I was named Team Leader. Sara fussed, declaring she was better qualified, but the order came directly from headquarters. Ram might claim it was his idea, but I wonder if my friend influenced him."*

Ram? Sean's pulse quickened at his first tangible clue. Did she mean J. Bertram Barkley, director of

SARC? Sean pondered the use of his nickname. Ram. Maybe the gossip about Aric wasn't groundless.

Wait. Barkley wouldn't have sent his sweetheart to the fringes of space. Four years ago, he was the Division Supervisor of planetary contacts. His position gave him the power to send her anywhere. Why Empusa III?

Perhaps Barkley and Aric had split up after a brief affair.

Sean reread the account. Apparently she didn't know who was responsible for naming her Team Leader. Inside reports hinted Barkley had been coerced. Her account now confirmed it.

Aric's chair scraped as she stood with her empty bowl. As she washed her dishes and put them away, he couldn't tear his gaze away. She moved with unearthly grace. Her outfit couldn't hide the curves of her body. Luxuriant hair loosely framed her face—soft, inviting, a temptation for any man. She was a beautiful, desirable woman.

Then he knew.

Barkley had wanted a relationship but *she* had turned him down. Had he doctored her files as a result?

Sean felt like the universe split open to reveal his stupidity. Not for almost kissing her, but for missing the obvious. He had to test his theory, though.

"You're aware Dr. Barkley is now SARC's director?" He kept his voice casual.

Her face tightened. "Yes. Appointed a year ago?"

"We needed a forward-thinker like him. Don't you agree?"

She slowly put the journal she'd been reading back on the shelf. Her fingers smoothed the books back into place. "I've no doubt he's qualified for the position."

"You know he's also chairman of the board?"

Shock rippled across her face as she met his gaze. Her fingers still rested on the journal.

Sean leaned forward. "Surely you must have known him before you came here."

"Yes." She drew out the word. "I knew him."

He tilted back his chair and balanced it on two legs. "A real ladies' man. Distinguished. I hear women find him irresistible." He withheld the information about Barkley's remarriage and child.

Her averted eyes didn't denounce her, but her clenched jaw did. Without saying another word, she continued to straighten the books on the shelf. Yeah, Aric gave him her answer.

So why did Barkley want her dead?

In the heat of the morning, Aric tugged at a root in her garden. She muttered curses not only on the fibrous strand, but on every male that spanned the galaxy. Especially Ram Barkley.

"A ladies' man?" She panted. "Distinguished?" The fury at Sean's comments surprised her. She always knew Ram would rise to power. He would do, say and become anything to get what he wanted.

Slumping, she dabbed at the perspiration on her forehead. Was she upset by the news about Ram? Or because of what happened at the pool yesterday? She inhaled deeply.

I should never have allowed Sean to get so close.

His actions had provoked nightmares—ones she thought permanently gone. She squeezed her eyes shut to ward off the memories, but they came nevertheless. Ram grabbing her, flinging her to the floor of his office, pinning her while she fought him.

Once, she thought him a friend. What an idiot she'd been. After her divorce, loneliness became unbearable. Ram zeroed in on her vulnerability. Not until that one night—that dreadful, revealing night—did she find out the truth about him. He hadn't listened when she begged him to stop. If a division manager hadn't banged on the door of Ram's office and demanded he answer...

Aric shuddered. The near-rape robbed her of serenity. Fear stalked her every moment as Ram hounded her at SARC's headquarters with his veiled threats. Not until she left Earth did she experience any peace.

She rose and retrieved the shovel from the shed before heading back to the garden.

For three years, Ram had left her alone. Was she a fool, thinking she was safe by staying under the radar? His complete control of SARC might explain the numerous oddities of late—her ignored requests, missing supplies, Sean's untimely arrival, his incongruity.

Jabbing the shovel into the ground, she grunted from the effort of trying to dislodge the root.

Ram planned to upgrade Empusa III to phase three. With his position and power, no one would oppose him.

No one but me.

Ram's modus operandi was sickeningly familiar. He wouldn't hesitate to harass, coerce or ruin her credibility to get his way. He'd done it before.

How did Sean fit in? She recalled the admiration with which he had spoken of Ram. What had he said? Ram was the kind of leader SARC needed?

What was once a question was now confirmed— Sean was there to discredit her.

The next logical questions quickly followed. Was the incident in the pool a test? To see if she would break the no-relationships directive?

Heedless of dirty hands, she pressed her fingers to her temple. If only she could ask him. If only she could *trust* him. As she leaned on the shovel, the aroma of coffee alerted her that Sean was up.

I can't face him. Not now. But where to escape?

Abandoning the shovel, she hurried to the shed, grabbed a bag and struck off into the jungle. Not until she was well over a mile from base camp did she slow. And scold herself. The kawyas began their morning clatter, reminding her she'd left the safety of camp too early. Foolish to trot into the habitat of the tereph. Though nocturnal, some had been known to linger in the morning after a night's hunt.

Aric found a whippet patch next to the ridge. Maturing mathoke bulbs littered the ground. After clearing a space, she sat. Harvesting was easy. She plucked them off their delicate stems and shoved them into the buffalo-hide bag. In no time, she had plenty. Instead of returning to camp, she ran her hands over the knobby whippet tree roots that nestled below the surface.

"Please give me wisdom, God." She raised her chin toward the sky.

She had to keep Sean at arm's length. Maintain the objective relationship required by the Center between team members. Disregard any personal feelings she might have.

And how do *I feel about him?*

She studied the white bark of the whippet trees, the delicate fronds of the branches that stirred in the morning breeze, the crystalline blue sky beyond, the white rock of the ridge. Again, she ran her fingers over the roots, struggling to answer.

It doesn't matter how I feel. Abruptly she rose and slung the heavy bag over her shoulder.

Sean would be worried about where she was.

"He's fine. He doesn't have to know everything." Then Aric growled at the annoying habit she'd developed of arguing with herself.

As she trudged toward camp, she knew she needed to prove herself. Not only to SARC, but to Sean. "Exactly how?" As the strap cut into her shoulder, she shifted the load.

Throw herself into getting camp into shape. Now that she was no longer worried about survival, she could concentrate on the little things that had slipped over time—journaling, the clearing, cataloguing.

Not only that, she would resist Sean's charm. No matter what, she would stick to the directive. She resolved not to notice his sweet lopsided grin. Or the look in his brown eyes as he watched her when she prepared meals. Or his softened expression after she prayed. Or the way he...

"Enough!"

Many moments passed until she became aware she was leaning against an umbrella tree and was staring off into space. She might as well admit it.

I've fallen in love with him.

"Where have you been?" Sean fought to control his voice the second she entered the cabin.

She lifted her chin. "I needed to collect some mathoke. We're almost out so I—"

"Without telling me first." He gritted his teeth. "I look out the window and you're in the garden one minute, the next you're gone."

"I admit I should've—"

"You got that right." He clenched his fists to resist shaking her. "I thought that you..." He paused, realizing what he almost said. *That you were checking on your supplies.* Instead, he said, "That you'd lost your mind like Geoffreys."

She instantly melted into contrition. "I'm so sorry. I didn't ..." She pressed her lips together. "It'll never happen again. I promise."

His shoulders relaxed. Truth be told, he wasn't sure what irked him more—her disappearance or that he'd relaxed his vigilance. By the time he discovered she was gone, he couldn't find her.

Or was he upset because she was avoiding him?

Then he realized she hadn't moved away. Lips parted, her eyes were huge pools of teal. Inviting. All he had to do was lean forward mere inches...

Whoa. He straightened. What was he doing?

He'd almost blown it yesterday. He was not going to do that today. No matter how soft and tempting she appeared.

Stepping back, Sean cast about for a reply. "Apology accepted."

She glanced away. Finally.

"Where did you say you went?" He rubbed his forehead.

"There's a mathoke patch a mile or so from here. Along the ridge."

He knew the place. Not far from the cave with his equipment. Good thing he hadn't rushed to get his scanner to track her. He would have blundered into her. And blown his cover.

"You leave the bulbs outside?"

"In the shed. We can lay them out in the clearing

tomorrow morning early. The ultraviolet light cures them. After one full day, they'll be ready to process."

"Okay." He stalked toward the window. "I finished pulling the root out of the garden. The one you started. Did the watering. The usual."

"Thank you."

He studied her out of the corner of his eye. Her hand was resting on the back of the chair, fingers caressing the plasti-steel. What had come over her?

He should take advantage of her vulnerability while her guard was down. He'd been trained to ferret out the truth. If she were still reluctant, the obvious course of action would be to become physically involved with her. In a short time, he would get to the bottom of why Barkley wanted her dead. And after three years. The answers lay within her, and it was his job to get them. By any means.

"I'll refill the water bins." Without another word, he stalked away.

As he hauled buckets of water, he castigated himself. Never in his career had he struggled with the ethics of his orders. But ever since he'd landed on Empusa III, every decision was fraught with implications.

If you don't steel your resolve, you'll both end up dead.

But how far could he push Aric? How far and still be able to live with himself?

Chapter 12

"Is this good?" Sean found a cleared space at the edge of the jungle where they could spy on the Edenoi. At long last, Aric had given the go-ahead for a trip to the plains.

She made a face, but he caught sight of her expression before she smoothed it out of existence. "Sure."

The area—small for both of them—obviously bugged her. Before she changed her mind, he slung off his knapsack. He straightened their things while she crouched and squinted through the trees.

Around them thousands of whippets, like giant white asparagus, reached skyward. They had little competition from the immature umbrella trees that bordered this patch. The whippets thrived in the transitioning ecotone.

Sean fingered a delicate fern-like leaf. "These the ones that give us mathoke?"

"Mm-hmm." She was already peering through an opti-scope to the plains below.

"I thought you said the bulbs were prolific."

"They are."

"Then someone's harvested here. Or these trees aren't producing much."

That got her attention. Aric frowned as she stared at the ground. "I've never seen the Edenoi collect mathoke."

"Another page for your journals." He smiled, inviting her to chat. The last couple days she'd been reticent. Since he'd finished reading her personal journals, he'd moved on to the other ones.

Scope pressed to her eyes, she again looked to the valley. "Oh! I see a group of Edenoi working their fields. You don't want to miss this."

Tilting his head, he studied her shapely legs. *I'm not. Believe me.* He was pleased she'd lost some of the gauntness from his first weeks on Empusa III. Was she healthier because of him? Her curves only added to her feminine allure.

He settled beside her with his own scope. After fiddling with the gadget, he studied it. How was he supposed to see anything with this archaic instrument? With no electronics, the thing was all lenses and plastic.

However, it gave him an excuse to watch Aric some more.

A smile played on her lips. Did the Edenoi really captivate her that much? Or did she secretly like having him so close? When his elbow brushed hers, she didn't jerk away.

"Look." For some reason she was whispering. "They're preparing the soil for sowing."

"Okay." He too whispered. "But I don't think we're in any danger of being overheard from this distance."

She chuckled, then spoke in a normal voice. "Aren't they fascinating? They're working like the ancient farmers of Earth."

Truthfully, he was more interested in her than them. After he adjusted his opti-scope, Sean finally got a good look at the Edenoi.

They're quite beautiful.

No doubt anatomically humanoid. They appeared elf-like with large eyes and silky golden hair. Their taupe skin indicated resistance to the ultraviolet light of the twin suns.

"What's their average height?" Sean couldn't remember.

"Under five feet for males. Shorter for females."

Again, their beauty struck him. "So why have I never seen holos of them?"

She stared, alerting him that he'd blundered. "SARC's directive. In covert procedures, we allow alien races some privacy."

"You mean clandestine, not covert."

She frowned. "What's the difference?"

"Clandestine means 'hidden' as opposed to..." He paused, realizing he again erred. "Well, SARC's presence on Empusa III is known. 'Covert' implies deniability."

Making a sound of skepticism, she gazed across the plains. "How would you know that?"

Sean didn't answer. *Fool.* He needed to guard his tongue. A novice's lapse. He turned his attention back to the fields, more intrigued by the humanoids than their actions. How had Aric once described them? Childlike? Petite and perfectly proportioned, they wore the same buffalo-hide clothing she did. Some were dyed with a shimmering silver.

"What do you find so fascinating about them?"

She hemmed. "Everything. I've written extensively about them."

"Give me a for instance."

"Okay." She paused, like a kid trying to pick one present out of a stack of gifts. "Their society on the whole is peaceful. They have minor squabbles, but from what I've observed, they settle differences quickly. Of course, because we allow them an element of privacy, we can only speculate."

"And you prefer it that way."

"Absolutely. I can't imagine how we could damage their culture." She studied him. "I've done some detailed cataloguing in the science journals. If you're inclined to read them."

"I plan to. Especially since I've seen the Edenoi for myself."

She smiled. With them being so close—mere inches—he could feel the warmth of her body. Could smell the sweet floral scent of her skin. Her pupils dilated as her gaze flickered to his lips.

She wants me to kiss her. Doesn't even realize she's asking.

He clenched his jaw. Rotating his head ninety degrees took more effort than bench-pressing two hundred pounds.

Idiot. Next time, he needed to find a bigger area to spy on the Edenoi.

Finally Aric turned away and he could breathe again.

"Looks like they're about done working." Disappointment rippled through her voice.

The group left the field and disappeared behind a hill. Shoulders tight from his cramped position, he set aside his scope and turned over.

Perfect time for a nap. But if he suggested it, Aric would scamper off like a shy doe. The fronds above him swayed, their movement mesmerizing. He closed his eyes.

After a while, he could tell she grew restless. Her sigh, soft grunt, and tendon popping told him she was stretching before she resettled.

"Hungry, Sean?"

"Not yet."

Though she blew out her breath, she didn't move

away.

He carefully crafted his question. "Your contract with SARC ends next year, right?"

"My offworld tenure does. However, my career contract doesn't for another four years."

He cracked an eye. "Think you might extend? The tenure part, I mean, and return here?"

One shoulder rose. "It's crossed my mind."

Again, he shut his eyes. "Doesn't SARC require team leaders to undergo some physical and psychological testing between assignments?"

"Yes, and a mandatory sabbatical."

He kept his lids closed, but could hear a change in her tone. What made her nervous? The time off or the testing? Or being on the same planet as Barkley?

"You know we'll ship off Empusa III at the same time." She spoke slowly.

Interesting that she would bring that up. He kept his tone casual. "Yeah. I guess." Again, he waited before adding, "Maybe we'll run into each other in Seattle." Holding his breath, he waited for her response.

She took her time. "I doubt SARC will let you sit around headquarters too long. They'll ship you off to another planet as soon as they can."

He opened his eyes and tucked a hand behind his neck. "Why would you say that?"

"You're too good of a bio-tech to waste your talents on Earth." Then perhaps realizing what she said, she blushed.

Sean inclined his head. "Thanks for the compliment."

Chewing the inside of her lip, she abruptly rose. "Well, I'm hungry."

As she grabbed the knapsack, he slowly sat up. "I can always turn down my next assignment."

"If you wanted to commit career suicide."

"Eh." Then he mentally drew himself up short. *What am I thinking?* His stint at SARC would be terminated and he'd be back in New Washington, waiting for his next mission.

She brought out some food. "Change your mind about lunch?"

"Sure." He grabbed sponge bread and ate in silence. What if Aric shipped out to another world? She could be incommunicado for years.

"What happens during phase three?" He was supposed to know, but conversation was preferable to his gloomy thoughts.

Her expression grew pinched. "More science teams. Electronic equipment. More camps."

"But SARC's presence would still be invisible to the Edenoi, right?"

"Yes." She inhaled, then shut her mouth. Finally, she said, "But phase three always leads to phase four."

"Always?"

"The whole point is to prepare for integration."

He absorbed the information in silence. Was that why Barkley wanted Aric out of the way? But what benefit would phase four be to the director personally? How could Empusa III, with its sticks and stones, add to his burgeoning dominion? Sean blew out a breath of frustration.

As she stared at him, a furrow etched between her brows. "Are you planning to recommend phase three in your report?"

He brought himself back to the present. "Report?"

"Yes, the quarterly info-beacon. You're responsible for writing one as well."

"Oh, that." He nearly blurted *no*, but perceived this was another way to keep the doors of communication open. "I reserve judgment at this time."

Aric opened her lips to protest, then pressed them together.

How can you worry her like that? Jerk.

He looked down at the fruit he held. "After I read the journals, I'd really like to hear more about why we should maintain phase two."

There. He could live with that.

Her face relaxed. "It's a deal."

As they ate, the heat built, the trees confining the escalating temperature. With the vegetation about them, Sean felt as though they were in a large cooking pot.

As she finished her meal, he invited, "Tell me more about Empusa III."

"After we built base camp and were done with the preliminary studies, we learned the Edenoi had no natural enemies."

"Except the tereph."

"Actually, they pose little danger. The carnivores

stay out of the plains, away from the settlements. And the Edenoi rarely venture into the jungle except to harvest one medicinal plant."

"Mathoke?"

"No, I was referring to tahor. I'll have to show it to you sometime." She grinned with some secret knowledge.

"And this medicinal plant is used for...?"

"Scrapes and cuts. As far as diseases, we've seen no evidence to support the Edenoi have any bacterial or viral enemies. Animals aren't really a danger either. They tend to stay in their habitat." She studied the sky. "It's getting late. Let's see if they're back."

He put away the rest of his food while she again took up her position and panned the area with her opti-scope.

"They move to another field?"

"Or they may be done for the night."

"How far is their settlement?"

"A couple miles that way." She pointed as she sighed in disappointment. "I was hoping they'd work longer."

He too wished that. Was there something about the Edenoi that had caught Barkley's interest? "You open to a suggestion?"

She peeled her eyes away from the instrument.

"How about if we move closer to their settlement? We've got enough supplies to last the night."

"It wouldn't be safe."

"You said the tereph don't go out onto the plains.

Are there other dangers?"

She sucked on her lower lip. "Not really."

"We'll head back to base camp early tomorrow. What do you say?" He could tell she was weakening. "Just tell me what to do."

"All right. But remember. We've got to stay out of sight."

Aric couldn't help her sigh. For an hour, she'd been staring out across the plains and had seen nothing but birds. She fidgeted, wishing the Edenoi would come back and give her a reason to back out of their planned trip.

But what if the humanoids didn't return to this field? A wasted day for the small glimpse of their farming techniques. She and Sean had only two options, return to base camp soon or spend the night on the plains. They couldn't remain on the fringes of the jungle and be safe from the tereph.

Everything in her said moving closer to the settlement would be a big mistake. What if they were seen? Yet at the same time, the idea excited her. This could be the opportunity to finally convince Sean about the planet remaining in phase two. Once he viewed the Edenoi up close, he would fall in love with them like she had. Having him on her side would be a tremendous benefit once they returned to Earth.

"We should probably rest, Sean. Before we head out."

"Sounds good to me." He settled and seemed to instantly fall asleep.

Typical. Committed to a plan, he appeared to shut off his mind and give himself wholeheartedly to oblivion. She fidgeted. First a mathoke bulb seemed to grow from the size of a marble to a baseball underneath her. She squirmed and then yanked it out. Next, a whippet root jabbed her. Then the Alpha sun blinded. Aric growled, ready to give up.

When her gaze lit on Sean, she quieted.

While slumbering, he lacked the element of keen watchfulness. With his eyes closed, the feral intensity slept as well.

A three-inch scar ran under his jaw. How had he gotten such a peculiar injury? He rarely volunteered information about himself. So much she didn't know.

So much she wanted to.

His bio sheet said he was thirty-four. Really? How had he retained his youthful visage? Perhaps it had to do with a guiltless conscience, unspoiled by regrets or tragedies.

Not like me. Oh, Ella. She sighed, remembering every detail of the last time she'd seen her. Ella's purple shirt and matching pants. Her pigtails. The scrape on her elbow. Before Aric entered the space-training program, her mother and daughter had flown to Seattle. After meeting them at a hotel, she and Ella had played, drawn pictures and giggled together.

And later, she sobbed her heart out. But what choice did she have? In the middle of her master's program, Mitt had pressured her to sign a ten-year contract with SARC. Little did she know he already planned to abandon her. SARC finished paying for her master's degree, but it was small compensation for the fact that they owned her—body and soul—for ten years. If only she'd read the small print, which said they could send her to any assignment. Even to the fringes of explored space.

For the hundredth time, Aric was glad she'd told no one at SARC about her daughter, especially Ram. That was one thing, at least, she didn't regret.

Protecting her daughter—keeping her existence secret—had been the smartest thing Aric had ever done. She longed to be part of her life. But with Ram as director and chairman of the board, how could she remain in Seattle? Unless...

Her gaze again rested on Sean.

Perhaps she could transfer to a different division. Her good friend, B.J. Matheson, could find her a position in his department. She would persuade her mother to move to Seattle with Ella, somewhere on the fringes of town. Somewhere Aric could watch over them both. *I know I could make it work.*

Content with her plans, she finally settled to nap. As her mind drifted, she became aware of Sean's breath tickling her cheek with his every exhale. With him close, she felt safe.

Chapter 13

Sean blinked and yawned. Beside him, Aric slept. He gauged the time of day. They had perhaps an hour before they could move down onto the plains. The Edenoi retired early, which would make evening travel less risky.

The kawyas were clacking, telling him by their calls that they were happy. Despite the reassuring sound, his mind skipped ahead to the possibility of tereph coming out of their dens. However, Aric insisted they only emerged at night. By then, they would be close to the Edenoi settlement, concerned with remaining un-detected.

The heat continued to build. Aric's lips were parted, emitting a soft hiss of air. Cheeks flushed, girlish innocence replaced her usually guarded expression. Was this the real Aric Lindquist? Someone who slept without fear or regret?

Not like me.

He noiselessly rose and grabbed her journal to fan her. In repose, she sighed then settled more deeply into dreamland. When his arm grew tired, he stopped. Each time she stirred from the heat, he cooled her.

The suns slid toward the horizon, one ahead of the other. Streaks of blue and violet splashed the panorama, deepening as the light faded. In the late afternoon, the air cooled, giving Sean a chance to put away the journal before she awoke.

Squatting beside her, he debated how best to rouse her. "Aric, time to go."

She sleepily opened one eye, then yawned.

"Rise and shine, Sleeping Beauty." The name from an ancient fairy tale seemed apt. Then he remembered the maiden was supposed to be awakened with a kiss.

She stretched, moaning in the process. Riveted by the sight, Sean swallowed hard. Even in the innocence of awakening, she was incredibly alluring.

Drawing in a quick breath, he walked away. While waiting on the fringe of the jungle, he listened to her gather their things. When ready, they left the whippet patch. With the pack on his back, Sean stepped into the glowing sunshine.

Aric pointed. "Let's head that way." As they

crossed the plains, she shot looks about them.

"Expecting problems?"

"No. Just nervous about open spaces."

"You've been in the jungle too long."

She grinned.

Sean studied the grass-like growths under his feet. As soon as he moved on, the plants sprang upright, leaving no evidence of their passage. "Well, that's weird."

"What is?"

"The grass."

This time she chuckled. "Not grass, but miniature trees."

He stopped. "You're kidding." He squatted to get a better look. The short green growths did kind of look like a miniature version of the whippets. Between them grew chartreuse-colored lichen. Together the brilliant green gave the plains a lush appearance.

"I hate to interrupt," she said, "but we have a date at the Edenoi settlement."

Peering up at her, he grinned. "We have a date?"

She reddened. "You know what I mean."

Enjoying her consternation, Sean straightened slowly. "Okay, boss."

They traveled to a lower elevation, then up a hill. When they reached the cultivated fields, they paused to take note of the farming techniques. The humanoids had left their tools, confident their things would remain undisturbed during the night.

Skirting the field in order to leave no footprints, he

followed Aric who seemed to know where she was going. A half hour passed before they spotted the settlement. More wary now, they stopped often to survey the region with opti-scopes.

"What I wouldn't do sometimes for a bio-scanner." She studied the area.

Thinking of the one he'd hidden, he clamped his mouth shut. But an impish curiosity swept over him. "Perhaps I can get you one. My buddy could smuggle one in the next shipment."

She thrust the opti-scope away. "Don't you dare."

"If one would help maintain our anonymity—"

"Absolutely not. Even if we don't agree, we obey the rules."

He shrugged. "Merely a suggestion."

A maverick, the words of her bio read, *unwilling to follow orders.*

What a crock. Aric was a stickler about regulations. Barkley had really messed with her reputation. From all the inside reports Sean had read, he should have known that everything the director touched he corrupted.

"Let's move closer." She put away the scope. "The Alpha sun will go down in about fifteen minutes. We'll have less than an hour to observe the Edenoi before they retire."

"Remind me not to invite them to all-nighters."

She chuckled. "They're definitely early-to-bed, early-to-rise types. We'll have to look sharp in the morning."

They lay side by side on a hill overlooking the tents. Clustered in a natural hollow, the settlement was organized and clean. On the outskirts sat a crude well. Beyond the village, hides stretched across tall poles. A grove of peculiar, tall stumps captured Sean's attention. A fringe of orange flowers grew on the tops, appearing like bizarre flattened hats.

"What's up with those?" He pointed.

"They're buffalo hide trees. Too bad we're not closer. I can't wait to see your first encounter with them."

"Why?"

"You'll know when you touch them," was her mysterious reply.

"And those?" He pointed to pelts stretched across poles. The humanoids stood on crude ladders, gathering something from the surface.

"Ovens where they both dry and cook food. The hides serve as a storage area as well."

"Fascinating." And he meant it.

"They don't usually use fire but rely on the slow processes of the suns. Everything about them is slow, orderly, methodical."

Like her? He wanted to ask, but didn't. Aric might be offended by the implication. The more time he spent with her, the more he admired her. She was no slacker in a hurry to tout her discoveries to the world, but a true scientist who loved learning for knowledge's sake.

He touched her arm. "I hear your reports have started a new movement of empathy on Earth. Many are clamoring for contact with alien races."

"But the Edenoi wouldn't be ready for that yet."

"True. But in the time you've been here, SARC and Intergalaxia have made contact with more than a dozen humanoid species who are far beyond the Edenoi developmentally."

"Really?" Aric's eyes widened. "Intergalaxia too? They used to be a piddly organization."

"They've grown."

She pursed her lips. "When I left, SARC and Inter-G together contacted merely a handful of other civilizations. The rest of the twenty-odd planets were either phase one or two."

"They've made tremendous strides in communication. I've lost count of the phase one planets. There must be thirty-odd phase two and three. I can't recall how many phase four planets there are now."

"I guess they don't take five years to do a stage one sweep anymore."

"Some restrictions haven't changed." Sean rifled through his training, but couldn't remember exactly what a stage one sweep was. "The science teams are still in charge with enough influence to restrict what type of information is released to the public. SARC fully complies. And Intergalaxia ensures that—if for no other reason, competition."

"I'm glad." Aric's tone was grim as she again peered through her opti-scope. "I can't imagine what kind of damage marauders would do to a planet that was rumored to be wealthy. Humankind is still greedy."

For power and wealth. Some things never changed.

"How about we spend the night in that grove of whippets?"

"Where?" He looked through his opti-scope.

"To the right of the encampment. In the morning, we can make a quick getaway to the jungle."

He nodded. "Out of curiosity, how many settlements are there on Empusa III?"

"Probably thirty or so. That estimation is based on long-range scans from space."

They both turned their attention back to the Edenoi who gathered in the center of their settlement to eat. Intrigued, Sean watched both females and males serve their companions. The children and elderly were given special consideration as they sat together on hides in the center of the adults.

Aric gripped his arm. "There's the chief. He's the one with the plumes."

The leader's headdress was decorated with tall orange and blue feathers. His body shimmered with pigment.

"What's with all the silver dye?" Sean wondered aloud.

"I think it's a sign of honor. Remember my mentioning tahor? They harvest the plant for its dye too."

"It's rather unusual." At first, the chieftain glimmered with silver, but as the suns set, the color appeared more iridescent.

"Tahor also has an unusual odor. I once dug one up out of curiosity. Big mistake, though the medicinal attributes are beneficial."

"What does it smell like?"

"Worse than rotting eggs." She wrinkled her nose. "Why they dye themselves with that is beyond me."

"Probably smells like roses to them."

She laughed.

The Alpha sun slid to the horizon, splashing everything in gold.

"Any others wear the dye?"

"The chief's family members. Perhaps minor officials. Oh, and the workers who dig up the orbs. I guess they're honored for doing the potentially dangerous work."

Sean continued to watch them. "What's going on now?"

"Not sure."

A female, covered in silver, rose and stood by the chief. He pointed at her and gesticulated excitedly. Then the chief moved in front of her and waved about her with his hands. The movements, slow and graceful, followed the curves of her head and body. Was this some worship ritual? He stepped aside and another Edenoi, a female, came forward and did the same thing to the immobile young woman.

"I believe," Aric said slowly, "they are honoring her for some reason."

Sean agreed. Even the children took turns, their silent praise strangely moving. At that distance, he could see no sign of verbal communication.

"Aren't they beautiful?" Aric breathed beside him.

A tent flap opened and a magnificent male stepped out. To Sean's unpracticed eye, he appeared younger than the chieftain. His body was dyed and the head-dress he wore boasted of huge blue and white plumes.

The younger male approached the female. He did none of the adoration movements. Instead he raised both arms, elbows bent, palms facing her. Attention fixed on them, the villagers waited.

"I wonder..." Sean broke off as the female slowly raised her hands, mirroring the male's stance.

A high-pitched shrill pierced the air. Aric drew an excited breath. "I think this is a wedding!"

The chieftain moved between the couple, separating them before they touched. He gestured to one then the other. Then he pointed toward the second sun that perched above the plain like a glowing blue ball. With his arm, he swung in a circular motion four times.

The young male and female moved apart without looking back. No one hindered them, rather most of the crowd followed the young woman to her tent. Their raised hands undulated in a slow swaying motion.

"I don't understand." Aric's voice held a note of frustration.

Sean burst out laughing as the scene became clear to him.

"What's so funny?" She lowered the opti-scope.

He couldn't answer for a moment, freshly amused by her indignation.

"Well?"

He squelched his laughter. "Though I know little of the Edenoi, I *do* know something of the male species. If this was a wedding, I doubt the groom would have trotted off without his new wife."

She flushed. "But everything we saw—"

"Think about it," he interrupted. "If this isn't a wedding, what could it be?"

The glow from the sinking sun emphasized the blush on Aric's cheeks while her teal eyes glittered. *She's beautiful.*

"This must be a wedding announcement."

He nodded. "Perhaps the ceremony will take place four days from now?"

Her expression lit up. "I believe you're right."

"Should I assume we'll be the uninvited guests?"

"I wouldn't miss it for the world."

They turned back to the group, which had resettled in the center of the village.

"Now what're they doing?" Sean asked.

"The best part."

"What does that mean?"

Aric's eyes twinkled. "You'll see. Or rather, you'll *hear.*"

Saying nothing more, he watched the group. They sat in a circle, unmoving, waiting. As soon as the second sun blinked out, a siren song rose into the air. The sound built and built as dozens of voices joined in melody.

Shivers of pleasure ran up and down Sean's spine at the alien—but transfixing—sound. To his untrained ear, the music reminded him of a combination of human vocalization, cellos, and organ. The Edenoi rose as a body and slowly walked to their tents, still singing. When the last flaps of the tents closed, the music ended.

Beside him, Aric breathed deeply. Neither of them spoke or moved. In the fading light, her face and hooded eyes reflected utter contentment. No, more than contentment. He'd seen that look before.

By the stream. When she had been praying. Worship?

No doubt the singing had been beautiful, but for some reason the sounds affected her more profoundly. Why? Obviously she heard something he was deaf to. Again, he was struck by an odd emptiness. And an unnamed longing.

What does she have that I don't?

He vowed to find out.

Chapter 14

"This reminds me of when I used to jump on the bed." Cross-legged, Sean bounced up and down. The pliable whippet trees underneath him bent and sprang back, like natural coils.

Aric chuckled. "I wouldn't recommend standing on them. Doesn't work as well."

"Ah, so you've tried."

She pressed her lips together to hide her smile. "If SARC asks, I'm pleading the fifth."

"Okay then. It'll be our secret."

Still grinning, she settled. The whippet patch where they planned to spend the night was almost as small as the one he'd picked earlier, except in this case they had no choice. Aric had bypassed the more mature whippet trees which ranged from stiff branches to stout poles, the support beams the Edenoi used for their ovens.

Sean followed her example and lay down. With his back to her, he kept sliding her direction. The third time he repositioned himself, he growled.

"Something wrong?" she asked.

He considered joking that the whippets conspired to push them together. "Nope. Not a thing." He anchored his foot under a small, bent tree.

Gonna be a long night.

"So how come I've never heard about the Edenoi singing?"

Aric took her time answering. "I mentioned it in one of my reports. As vocalization."

"You deliberately downplayed it?"

Clearing her throat, she shifted. "I suppose."

He carefully chose his words. "I would have called it...melodic praying."

From the sudden movement of the whippets, he could tell she jerked upright. "Now why would you say that?"

"Seems a more appropriate description." He looked over his shoulder. "They look like you when you pray."

For a long time, she said nothing. *Open up, Aric. Let me in.*

Tension radiated from her, but she remained silent.

Turning away, he shifted an arm to pillow his

head. "I'm not going to write a report about it if that's what's worrying you."

"Who said I'm worried?"

He chuckled. "You're very protective of your Edenoi. Like a mother hen."

Again, he heard a catch in her breathing. Why were they so important to her? Barkley would obviously know from her first reports, but was that motivation for murder? Something must have changed in the time she'd been on this planet. The key had to be here.

"You know," he said quietly, "your early essays on the Edenoi were very provocative. I wouldn't be surprised if they'll be used as guidelines for noninterference in humanoid cultures."

She took her time answering. "I'm flattered."

Rolling on his back, he stared at the stars. Like a spray of diamonds, they glittered and twinkled, all the more dazzling without the umbrella trees to block them. After the shrouding darkness of the jungle, this cool brightness was hard to adjust to. "Give praise where praise is due."

"That's kind of you to say."

"Since your radio is a little wacked, you haven't heard all the hubbub about the coalition of planets under Intergalaxia." Sean withheld the information that her equipment appeared sabotaged. Or was it because of Geoffreys' ineptness in trying to fix it?

Facing him, she propped her head on one hand. "Like I've said, Intergalaxia used to be a fairly inconsequential organization."

"They've reorganized. And now have a very charismatic and powerful leader. SARC makes most of the initial contacts, but Inter-G sets up liaisons between them and Earth."

"And who monitors their activities? The Universal Security Forces?"

Something in her tone caught his attention.

"They do some. I'm sure." He scratched his chin. "You got something against USF?"

Her whole body tensed, from her tightening neck muscles to her curling knees. "My family had a little run in with them."

Run in? Her words didn't match her reaction. "Care to elaborate?"

She took her time answering. "A security breach at the university where Daddy worked. Everyone was investigated. Let's just say USF was more than thorough."

"That doesn't sound particularly unpleasant."

Aric drew a sharp breath. "They were like Nazi Germany's Gestapo. They turned all our lives upside-down, interrogated Daddy until he couldn't sleep from worry, poked their noses into every aspect of our lives..." She bit her lip. "Sorry. The whole episode was very upsetting. To all of us. Daddy was never the same."

"Sounds like an overzealous agent in charge." He'd have to ask Jayden to check it out. Regardless, since the passing of the New Privacy Act Bill, USF couldn't get away with such practices any longer. Still, Sean was curious about the details. "They catch whoever was responsible?"

The tightness in her shoulders relaxed. "Yes. So, I guess USF redeemed themselves."

"That's good to know." He spoke casually. "Since SARC is answerable to them as well."

And Barkley. The file on him was a mile long.

She nodded slowly. Her mouth had again pursed. Because she was reliving the incident with USF?

Glancing up, Aric caught his stare. He relaxed his expression.

"I meant to ask," she said. "How many planets are part of Intergalaxia's coalition now?"

"Eleven, I think."

Her eyes widened. "Eleven? Wow."

"They're getting to be a formidable organization."

"I'd say." She turned on her back, hands resting on her stomach as she looked toward the heavens.

He watched her out of the corner of his eye. A faraway look settled on her face.

Shut out. Again. What was she thinking? He wanted to know for more than professional reasons.

"Maybe," he said slowly, "when you get tired of working for SARC, you could find a position with Inter-G."

Her gaze darted in his direction. "Aren't they headquartered in New Washington?"

"Yeah."

She studied him a moment. "That's a long way from Seattle."

His pulse sped. *Why'd she bring that up?*

With her master's in synecology, Intergalaxia would be a better fit. Their abundant contacts would more than satisfy her love of alien cultures. Perhaps she could break her contract with SARC?

The next thought hit him in quick succession. If she lived in New Washington, he could see her more often. But would she want to see him once she knew who and what he really was?

Sean turned away from her. "Good night." He again anchored his foot, then slowed his breathing so that she would think he fell asleep.

Assuming he made it back to Earth alive, Barkley would manufacture some reason to bounce him out of SARC. Sean had no proof of Barkley's orders to kill Aric. Those had come through the head of security. With the two men loosely connected, the flimsy evidence would fall apart in court. No, Sean needed something concrete.

He'd have to access his hidden equipment and send a message to Jayden, his handler. And tell him what?

I didn't follow SARC's or Barkley's orders. I think Barkley ordered the hit on Aric because he wants revenge, only I can't prove it. I have no evidence, only speculations. Great news, though, I'm attracted to the woman I was supposed to assassinate. How's that for remaining objective and on track with our mission?

Sean squelched a sound of derision. No, he was on his own.

Behind him, Aric yawned. The answers, he told himself yet again, lay with her. He had to somehow prove he wasn't her enemy. Had to get her to talk about everything in her past so he could sort through her history and find out why Barkley wanted her dead.

But in return, she would expect veracity from him. He'd dodged details about his position at SARC. How much could he open up? How much truth could he share? He couldn't even talk to his own family about his real career. They thought he was a nutrition and fitness instructor at a corporation based in New Washington, on temporary assignment in Seattle. *What a joke.*

Had it really been three years since he'd spent a holiday with them? Sean pushed that regret away to concentrate on Aric. Her even breathing, deep and restful, confirmed she finally slept.

He was beginning to doze when a howling in the distance made him start. It sounded like a wild dog. Make that two—no, three. Big ones. Without moving too much, he lifted his head.

"Aric!" He kept his voice low.

"Hmm?" She mumbled sleepily, then shifted her weight.

"What's that noise?"

Again, a sharp barking sounded, this time closer. The call was answered by another.

"Nothing. It's…" Her voice drifted off.

Nothing? He continued to listen, but the dogs—or whatever they were—scampered off. He began to relax. Suddenly he became aware that Aric turned over in her sleep. True to their nature, the springy whippets happily pushed them together. In her state of unconsciousness, she pressed against his back. He didn't dare move, afraid she'd awaken and blame him for the lack of space between them.

She sighed softly in her sleep, the sound coming to his ear on a whisper of a breeze. His throat tightened.

Gonna be a really, really *long night.*

Gradually, he succumbed to fitful sleep. In the predawn, as he drifted out of semi-consciousness, he discovered he had turned toward her sometime during the night. She was curled up against him while his arm lay possessively over her.

Aric awakened to a soft call. Stretching, she forced her eyes open. First she saw the gray-pink sky, then Sean's expressionless face.

"G'morning." He crouched nearby.

"Morning." Her back felt chilled, as though missing a warm presence. She blinked away her grogginess.

"Sleep well?"

"Yes. Thanks." Self-conscious, she leapt up. The rising dew dampened her skin.

She shook out her hair, untangling it while he watched. Like the day before, she felt hurried. As though aware of her consternation, he turned away and stared at the whippet trees. After re-braiding the tresses, she was ready to depart.

"Let me carry that." He reached for the knapsack.

"You hauled it around yesterday."

"I insist." Ever thoughtful, he gently, but firmly, pulled it from her hands.

She bent to straighten the whippets, removing all evidence of their presence.

"I don't think the Edenoi will suspect we've been here." She sought to fill the silence. "Animals sometimes sleep in the grove."

"Like the ones we heard barking last night?"

"What about last night?" She straightened.

Sean made a face. "I knew you were talking in your sleep."

Alarm flooded her. "What did I say?"

"Nothing embarrassing." He chuckled. "You started to name the animal, then fell back asleep."

"Oh." She bit her lip at her foolishness. "Probably a plains bird. Harmless."

Brow cocked, he stepped closer. "What deep, dark secrets do you have, Aric Lindquist?"

"Nothing." Her tone squeaked in an unconvincing manner.

"Really?" Playful charm settled on his face. "I'll tell you mine if you tell me yours."

An ugly memory sprang into her mind. *"Just play along, Aric. I'll make it worth your while,"* Ram had crooned. *"We've got compatible body parts. Show me yours and I'll show you mine."*

Sean's grin faded. She flinched when he suddenly

reached up and touched her arm.

"Forget I asked." Without saying anything more, he turned and walked away.

Trembling from the recollection, she followed him. What had he seen in that ten-second interval between his question and abrupt departure? Aric didn't need to tell him the shameful secret about her and Ram. To some degree, Sean guessed. But what was he going to do with the information?

Chapter 15

As Sean stood at the window, he watched her pull weeds. Many time, Aric stopped to note the sky, the plants, the soil. Gardening seemed to be a tonic. She always appeared happier afterwards.

More than once, he'd caught her kneeling in the dirt, eyes closed, head bowed. Was she praying? He would silently retreat, again aware he intruded. More and more he found himself wishing for whatever she had. Something Gigi had too. As he looked back, he realized his great-grandmother clung to some archaic religion. The Christian sect? But life and time blurred the details of what exactly she believed. Aric, too, seemed to have the same faith. He longed to question her about her beliefs but sensed she wasn't ready to share.

When she suddenly jumped up and ran across the clearing, he snapped to attention. By the time he headed outside, she was talking to something in her hand. As he approached, she glanced up, a silly grin on her face.

"Look, a baby." Aric held up a small puff of fur, not much bigger than a four-inch grav-game ball. "I saw her fall and had to rescue her."

Sean stared at the creature that was a tangle of gray-stripped fur. The thing had arms and legs, or perhaps it was all legs. Sharp toes clung to her hand while round, lime-green orbs unblinkingly studied its captors.

We're the captives, not captors. He fought a ridiculous urge to baby talk. Perhaps its charm came from what it did to Aric because she smiled so softly at Sean that his throat tightened.

He gulped at the wistful look on her face. "Is it one of those 'zacky' things?" He purposefully stumbled over the name.

"Zeheek." She caressed the fuzz with a delicate finger. "Isn't she precious?"

Huge ears unfolded. Was that purring he heard?

"It's...interesting." The thing startled him as it sprang and landed on his chest. Sean kept from swiping the creature off, as if it were a large, angry bee.

Aric giggled. "Don't be frightened. She won't bite."

From the adrenalin rush, he felt hyped up enough to go into mortal combat.

She stepped closer. "I'll get her off you."

"No. I can manage." He didn't want her to think he was afraid. With more gentleness than warranted, he grasped the tiny creature. The zeheek wouldn't let go. Spiky nails dug through his shirt and into the skin of his chest. When more than a dozen tiny needles impaled him, he hissed.

As he tugged, flesh ripped. "Ow!"

"Here. Let me." She didn't bother suppressing her giggles.

"No. I got this."

Their hands locked over the zeheek. Ears flattened against its head. Its whimpering cry sounded like a newborn human's.

"Don't scare her."

"I'm not," he said. "You're the one threatening its comfortable perch."

Her giggles burst into full-fledged laughter as a brown stream erupted from the zeheek. Doubling over, Aric fell away. If he hadn't been wearing the excrement, Sean might have laughed too. He held his soiled shirt away from his chest, trying to preserve a semblance of dignity.

At least the smell wasn't horrendous. While the creature mewled, he maintained his hold on the zeheek and shirt.

"I—I'm sorry." She wiped her eyes. "It's just that you…" She couldn't finish the sentence as she pressed her hand over her mouth.

Sean decided he'd have to stand there forever before he understood what she wanted to say. For some reason, she found the whole situation unbearably funny.

She tried again. "You shouldn't have...oh, I wish you wouldn't look at me that way."

"What way?" He used his driest tone.

"Like you want to strangle me and your—your furry friend."

"Not my friend. *Yours.*"

She nodded, eyes still gleaming.

Actually, he didn't hate this as much as he pretended. Who was he to complain if this made Aric happy? Ears fanning out again, the zeheek settled. However it still wouldn't release his shirt.

"Tell you what," he said. "Give me your knife and I'll get this off in a flash."

She recoiled, her face instantly changing to horror. "No. Don't hurt it."

"I was only kidding."

Brows drawn, she cocked her head to one side, studying him as if she wasn't certain she should believe him. But the humor was over.

"So how do we get this little gal back to her Momma?" It was the only thing he could think of that would reassure Aric.

She chewed her lip, looking upwards.

"I'd be glad to shimmy up the tree and return her to the nest." Sean nodded in the direction of the nearest umbrella tree. "Or whatever they have up there."

"She's able to climb. Take off your shirt and we'll put her next to the tree."

"All right." He made a face. "How do I get it off without getting this on me?" With his chin, he pointed to the wet spot.

"I'll help." Aric stepped forward.

He didn't move, enjoying the way her fingers fumbled with the buttons. Big mistake. She glanced up and caught his grin.

"Never mind. You can take off your *own* shirt." Cheeks red, she backed away.

"Be glad to. Could you hold our baby?"

She cast a narrowed glance at him.

"Please?" Tilting his head, he smoothed his expression.

She moved closer and cradled the zeheek. With one hand, he held his shirt away from his skin and the other, worked the buttons. A teasing comment poised, but his mischievousness faded.

A deep blush marked her cheeks. Under the delicate skin of her throat, her pulse quickened. This wasn't a game to her. How could he so blatantly flirt with her, like she was soulless?

Someday I'll disappear from her life and move on to my next assignment.

Was that all she was? An assignment?

For the first time in his life, he grew ashamed of himself.

"Mind helping with the cuffs?" He spoke softly.

Perhaps sensing his change of attitude, she complied without hesitation. In no time, his shirt was off. She held it and the zeheek next to the tree. The creature sprang nimbly to the ridged surface and zipped to the top.

"There." He brushed his hands. "All's well that ends well."

Aric surprised him by wadding up his shirt and flinging it at him. He deftly caught it. "What's that all about?"

"Making me worry you were going to harm her."

"Never." He held up three fingers and saluted. "SARC's honor."

"We don't have a pledge."

"We do now. I just made it up."

Still pretending indignation, she suppressed her grin.

He couldn't help his sigh of relief at their restored camaraderie. And, he vowed to himself, he wouldn't treat her so callously in the future. Aric deserved only his best.

She deserved...

"Back to the garden for me." She turned on her heel.

He stood staring after her, shirt crushed in his fists. Time to be honest...with himself, for once. He took a deep, mental breath.

Aric deserved a man who would cherish and love her. One worthy of her love. A man who would sacrifice everything for her—career, friends, reputation.

Anna Zogg

Life.
> *I'm not that man.*
> The bitter truth pierced his soul.

Chapter 16

They skirted the edge of the jungle, searching for the best spot to spy on the Edenoi. A number of humanoids gathered, exactly four days after the wedding announcement.

"This good?" Sean had already asked that question a half dozen times.

"Should be."

As soon as she settled, she'd grow discontent. Again.

This time, he remained standing. Any second she'd start to fidget.

She threw a glance at him. "What's up?"

"I'm waiting for you to grow unhappy with the

limited vision. Or something else."

She made a sound of indignation. "I will not."

Tonelessly whistling, he tapped his foot.

She tsk-tsked, rolling her eyes.

This time Sean took the offensive. "I'm going over there." From where he stood, he could see a curve in the whippets that would give the right amount of cover *and* an unimpeded view.

"Suit yourself."

He strode away. Finding a comfortable spot, he dropped the knapsack. This *was* better. From his vantage point, he could see most of the wedding party, which apparently was comprised of two villages. He counted at least seventy adult Edenoi.

Through his opti-scope, he located the groom, dressed even more regally. His tall plumes, as well as the buffalo hide he wore, were of the deepest silver. Elaborately braided tangle rope fringed his tunic.

Another male, with equally impressive feathers, stood nearby. The groom's father?

"Is that...?" He stopped when he remembered Aric was still in their previous "perfect spot."

He turned his scope in her direction, then laughed when he caught her watching him. Her head jerked back toward the humanoids. He again watched the distant crowd, then sighed. This would be a lot more interesting if Aric were there. For another fifteen minutes, he remained where he was, then got up. Might as well eat humble pie.

As he picked up the backpack, snapping branches

betrayed she moved in his direction. Hastily, he dropped it and plopped on the ground.

"Oh, hi." He made his expression reflect surprise.

"How's it going?"

"Good, good." He scooted over, but had trouble suppressing a chuckle. "Plenty of room. Great view."

Her eyes narrowed. Oh, yeah. She knew he had been about to leave.

She settled beside him. "What do you think so far?"

"Looks like the kids are going to get hitched."

"I agree." Her expression glowed with excitement.

He turned back to the scene below. The group parted as one chief brought his daughter forward. They walked slowly, their movements as precise as ballroom dancers. All the important players in this drama were covered in various amounts of silver.

He stared at their headdresses. "Where do they get those feathers?"

"From a plains bird that you might have heard." She pulled the opti-scope away.

"The one that sounded like a jackal?"

"Yes. I had quite a time tracking it. Couldn't catch even one."

After some elaborate bowing and hand signals, the two chiefs faced each other. The rest of the Edenoi surrounded them.

"Think they'll sing again?" Sean wondered aloud.

"Possibly, in celebration. Only at this distance, we won't be able to hear."

"That's too bad." He truly was disappointed.

The group settled for a feast. Since nothing appeared to be happening, Aric made small sounds of impatience.

"Why don't we have lunch while we wait?" Sean reached for their bag.

Several times she glanced at the sky while they ate. "We don't have much time before we have to head back."

Sean nodded, his mouth full of fruit. "Did you want to spend another night near the settlement?"

"I would love to, but with all the extra visitors, I don't want to take a chance."

"Good point."

"You look disappointed."

"I am." He smiled sheepishly. "Their singing…" What could he say about how the music affected him?

"Gets to you, doesn't it?" She smiled softly.

Strangely, he felt vulnerable. An odd emotion. "I've had enough. To eat." He rose and put away the remainder of his meal. Squatting, he again looked below. "Something's happening."

Aric hastily set aside her food to see.

The bride had risen from the feast and approached her affianced in a slow, rhythmic march. Covered in silver, her tangle rope skirt swept the ground. Holding up her hands, she moved directly before her young husband-to-be. Then she backed away in a teasing fashion.

Sean chuckled at the look on the groom's face.

"What's so funny?" Aric asked.

"Sure you wanna know?"

Her eyebrows rose. "As a bio-tech, your opinion is important."

"Okay." He drew the word out in a teasing warning. "I was thinking that regardless of the culture, women are the same. The Edenoi female is provoking the male to follow." He added, "Like a human."

Aric made a sound of indignation. "That was a great observation about the *Edenoi*. Thank you very much, but your conclusion about *humans* was unnecessary."

"Isn't synecology the study of *all* cultures and peoples?"

"Your pronouncements are appreciated. However, not the addendum." Though she spoke sternly, he detected the gleam in her eyes.

He laughed as he peered through his opti-scope. "Does this mean I get a 'D' in...?"

Something in the Edenoi's clothing captured his attention. Adjusting the focus, he blinked as sweat stung his eyes. Aric replied, but he missed what she said.

Continuing to dance, the bride undulated with slow movements. With the suns directly above, a different light was cast on the group below. She and the groom were the only ones who were standing.

Sean fine-tuned the instrument. Again, something flashed in her tangle rope skirt. Then the couple sat. The mysterious item was no longer visible. He continued to stare.

"What's so fascinating?" Aric asked.

Pulling the opti-scope away, he smiled. "I was hoping you could copy that dance later."

With a sound of irritation, Aric smacked his arm.

"For purely scientific reasons." He spoke with mock seriousness. "Someday SARC might ask you to demonstrate."

She growled.

Relieved she'd dropped the interrogation, Sean returned to his perusal. If he had been more caught up in their teasing, he would have missed the flash in the bride's clothing. For the rest of the ceremony, the group remained seated. But enough of the female was visible to Sean for him to continue examining her.

Fine-tuning the instrument to filter out color, he scrutinized her. That helped. The odd glimmer flashed again, no longer camouflaged by silver. Dull, crystalline stones embedded the bride's skirt. He looked at the other tribal leaders and detected smaller crystals. His pulse quickened.

Can't be!

He framed a question, forcing his tone to sound casual. "When do you think we can do another overnight survey?"

She looked at him, brows raised. "Maybe a couple weeks?"

"Great." In an instant, he decided he couldn't wait that long.

"I'm pleased the Edenoi interest you."

You have no idea...

"Does this mean you changed your mind about

recommending phase three?" She spoke slowly, working hard to sound nonchalant.

"I'm definitely going to endorse phase three." As her face clouded, he added, "In about eight hundred years."

Her surprised smile, bursting through her growing worry, was worth the teasing. However, he reconsidered when her eyes glistened.

"I agree with you, Aric. The Edenoi need to be protected. SARC *must* maintain phase two."

She ducked her head. Finally, she said, "Thank you."

First honest thing I've said since I landed.

However, truth had to stop there. For a little while at least.

What had he seen in the Edenoi's clothing? He needed to find an opportunity to slip away and access some of the specialized equipment he'd hidden. Until then, he would have to be content with speculation.

"What surveys did the original team do on Empusa III? Eleven years ago?" Sean sat across from her as they cataloged their Edenoi excursion.

"Just the usual."

"Any mineral sweeps?"

"Those as well." She looked up from writing. "Why do you ask?"

"I was reviewing my studies, but I don't recall those details."

She made a sound of mild interest. "They did the standard scans from space, but didn't take samples from Empusa III. No harvesting was allowed. Not then, not now."

Not wanting her to think he was too interested, he didn't press for more information. He couldn't chance that she'd say anything to SARC. "Before you send off your report, do I get to read it?"

"If you like."

"I would." He had another reason for asking. He had to ensure she didn't send the info-beacon early. "When does it go out?"

"In about a month." She rose and checked her calendar. "Twenty-nine days."

"Once we finish our report, think you'll send it sooner?"

"We can't. SARC is a stickler about schedules, especially for their offworld teams. Besides, we have to wait for the relays to line up to get the signal back to Earth." She indicated the radio. "Since we're using older technology."

"Okay." Relieved, he calculated the minimum time before another assassin could show up. Twenty-nine days plus travel time. More than ever, he was aware of the proverbial ticking clock.

"You look worried." Her head tilted, lips pursed.

"I was trying to decide what I'd like to include in my report."

"Don't forget you can send personal letters, too."

"That'd be great. I'll send my family Christmas greetings."

She frowned. "I thought you said your parents were gone."

"I have a couple cousins I keep in contact with." Sean scratched his chin. Looking away, he berated himself for slipping. How much longer did he have to keep lying?

As long as he was on Empusa III. And well beyond that.

I can never share the whole truth with her.

Rationality warred with training. Every day he spent with Aric increased the chances of blowing his cover. He felt torn between his oath of secrecy and desire to be honest with her.

"You're lost in thought again."

He straightened. "Sorry. A lot on my mind."

"Care to share?" Her green eyes were wide, inviting.

How I wish...

"Just thinking of my cousins."

"Okay." Though she smiled, he could tell she was disappointed. Aric was learning to read him. Either that, or he was giving away too much.

He passed a hand over his forehead. "I think I'll hit the sack." He stopped at the threshold to his bedroom. "Thank you."

"For...?"

"Sticking with your convictions about the Edenoi."

A blush crept up her cheeks. "You're welcome."

Before he said something stupid, Sean shut his door.

Later, arm tucked behind his head, he lay thinking. Eleven years ago, Barkley controlled mineral sweeps done on pre-phase one planets. Had he gone back through the initial reports and altered Empusa III's? Until Sean verified his suspicions, he would have to be content with speculation.

Once he got proof, how much could he share with Aric?

His arm muscles tightened.

I have to tell her…

No, he didn't. Not unless he wanted to end up in prison. He knew what *they* would do if he opened his big mouth. Regardless of the reason.

But how much longer could he continue the multi-faceted charade before he royally messed up?

Chapter 17

J. Bertram Barkley tilted back his office chair. Running his fingers over the fine Lapsia leather armrests, he took an expansive breath. The executive suite he'd been anticipating for months was now finished. With SARC's dedication festivities over, work could resume. However, his new office granted him boundless power.

As Ram touched the rim of the desk's surface, the station flickered to life. The command screen demanded voice and numerical entry codes. The final verifications involved palm and retinal scans. Lights illuminated under the black cerami-coat top, indicating all systems functioned. He grinned with smug satisfaction at the design he'd helped create.

Select aspects of the comm-panel were known only to himself. The four techno-teams that had worked on it were unaware of all its functions.

He pressed the shiny surface, choosing tactile over voice command until he became more comfortable with the new system.

"Ms. Layne." He didn't bother to raise his voice. The microphones could relay his words from anywhere in the room to her station down the hall.

The holographic image of his administrative assistant flickered into view beside him. She leaped from her comm-station as though he'd suddenly stalked out of his office. *Good.* Already he liked the new setup.

"Yes, Dr. Barkley?" Her voice quavered.

"Jamaican coffee." Ram rose and sauntered to the windows. Fifteen-foot square, tinted security glass separated him from the vast open sky. Seattle glimmered in the distance, Puget Sound rippling under the noonday sun. On the fifty-first floor, nothing passed by his viewport, the airspace secure from any maniac hoping to make a political statement. Police had quelled the demonstrations during the dedication of the new building, but overall the attendance disappointed him a little. City officials, congressmen, and anyone else eager to be his friend had made an appearance. Unfortunately, the president and his wife had sent their regrets. Ram smiled sourly. The fools wouldn't make that mistake again.

With the quick steps of a man devoted to jinm-su, he tapped out a code on the imbedded computer keys. A few quick modifications brought Kelli Layne into focus.

She poured coffee into his engraved mug, speaking to someone out of sight of the micro-camera. "...makes me nervous."

"Just play along." Gloria, his other assistant spoke. "Ram'll get bored, then leave you alone."

He smirked at the advice she was giving. Trouble was, he didn't intend to get bored.

"I—I don't know," came Kelli's hushed response.

"Whatever. I'm only trying to help."

Keep on helping.

"I don't like the way he looks at me." Kelli leaned toward her listener. "It's like he's...he's..."

"Hungry," Ram said aloud.

"I'm sure you're imagining things." Gloria sounded bored.

Liar! She knew the *look* to which Kelli referred. His interest in Gloria had started with that. At an office party, he'd gotten her tipsy and one thing led to another. Quickly. Their affair had been stormy, brief, but satisfactory. Gloria's admin promotion had been enough to keep her happy and her mouth shut.

"I have to deliver this." Kelli turned toward his office.

Ram pushed another code to view the brightly lighted corridor. Exotic, alien plants lined the walls, providing a living path alongside the mauve and taupe

Orienz carpeting. The entire floor had been decorated with costly artifacts from a dozen worlds. However, he saw nothing but the woman who traversed the distance, gracefully balancing the hot beverage. He admired the muted aquamarine skin-suit, which molded her slim form and flattered her blond hair and blue eyes. Someday, he planned to dictate a dress code for SARC. When he got his way, Kelli would be in a skirt. She had long, beautifully shaped legs, perfectly proportioned for her height of five feet ten.

Moving with the grace of a ballet dancer, she passed the first hall camera. As she approached the double doors, Ram put the system in sleep mode. Some things even a personal assistant shouldn't know. Before she could sound the chime, he commanded the doors to open. He caught her startled expression before she smoothed it out of existence.

Seated again, Ram activated the communications screen behind her. Global news snapped on.

"Here is your coffee, Dr. Barkley." Kelli's fingers trembled as she set down the mug.

He nodded, focusing on the panel that depicted a serial killer's execution. Ah, so that's why his dedication was not better attended. While SARC got a demonstration, the execution got riots.

"Stay." He didn't even look at the young woman who'd begun to edge away. When the dedication came, Ram leaned forward to watch his speech. He liked the touch of gray at the temples along with his full head of hair, complimenting his crisp dark suit and pristine white shirt. Over two decades, he'd perfected his image and commanding voice. He listened to himself make a speech about pioneering new frontiers and all the politically correct crap everyone wanted to hear. *Perfect.*

"Get me a copy of the news coverage."

She started at his gruff tone. "Yes, Dr. Barkley."

"The unedited copy."

"Yes, sir."

"What's my schedule for the rest of the day?"

Half closing her eyes, Kelli took a deep breath. "Lunch with Senator Sherman at one, a meeting of the associate directors at three. Your wife called to remind you of your son's six-month checkup."

Ram smiled to himself and leaned back in his chair. Oh, yes. His son. Becoming a family man was one of the best decisions he'd made in the last two years. Not only that, his wife was well connected. The news coverage had been all he'd hoped for. Reporters predicted his "child bride" would rejuvenate his pursuit of a new and exciting chapter of space exploration.

Though he hated to miss the appointment, something more pressing weighed on his mind.

Ram steepled his fingers. "Call my wife and tell her I won't be able to make it. Apologize and all that." Leaning forward, he touched a smooth, lighted outline on his desk.

Kelli started when the doors quietly *whumped* together.

Placing his hands on the desk, he studied manicured fingernails. "After this afternoon's meeting, I'll need your help with the notes. It'll be a late night for you. I'm sorry." He waited until the obvious registered. They would both have a late night.

"I could work on them myself, Dr. Barkley. You could still make that appointment."

He added what he hoped was the right touch of sadness to his face. "Oh, no. My presence was never really expected…" He sighed. "Or wanted."

She fidgeted, her polished nails twitching. "But your wife specifically asked that you go."

He molded his expression to contain only regret. "I know. That's her way of making everything appear congenial between us. But, never mind. I'm sorry to have involved you in my private affairs."

Her hands tightened.

Ram prided himself on his patience. Calmness and persistence had gotten him everything he'd wanted out of life. So far. He could wait for Kelli Layne because he'd learned the art of seduction. Start with the emotions, cloud the issue, make the morality hazy. The plan rarely failed with someone like her.

He passed a weary hand over his brow. "That's all for now."

Don't press the issue. He had plenty of time.

"Yes, sir," came her whispered reply.

Not until she exited did he key in the sequence to spy on her as she moved toward her workstation. She stared at his office door with a perplexed frown. Perfect. He'd gotten under her skin.

He sat back. Kelli's bio and private life had been scrutinized by his head of security. A girl of high morals, she broke off her engagement when her fiancé strayed. She dated few men and rejected intimate relations. Even the charming Sean Reese had failed to seduce her.

Just the kind of woman Ram sought.

It had been a long time since someone like Aric Lindquist had come along. However, he wouldn't allow his impatience to ruin months of preparation. Never again would he blow it like he had with her.

Aric...

He straightened in his chair. When was that info-beacon due to arrive from Empusa III? He accessed the galactic calendars. Less than a month, according to Earth's time calculations. In it, he fully expected to hear from ex-Lieutenant Reese that Aric had "accidentally" met her death. With Ram's pressuring, the board would reclassify Empusa III as unsafe, like that other unfortunate planet where the science teams died. As a "good friend" of the deceased, Ram would vote for Empusa III to revert indefinitely to pre-phase one.

As he imagined the future, he let out a breath of contentment. Soon he would have total control of SARC and no longer be hampered by protocols. His meeting with Senator Sherman was the first step in securing the power to guarantee that.

Getting rid of nuisances like Aric Lindquist would be much simpler.

The power station's light flashed, jarring him from

his dreams. He rose and opened the door to the secret compartment, revealing communications equipment.

The computer relayed the message, alerting him that this was an info-beacon only, not a live transmission. Words printed across the screen, the letters scrawling slowly because of the great distance. He read it, then read it again.

Aric was still alive?

His cool facade nearly crumpled as the full meaning hit him. Reese failed? Why?

Since dispatching a ship would take time to arrange, he quickly prepared a reply. Even if the amateur eavesdroppers on Earth intercepted the report, they wouldn't know its destination or understand the content.

He typed, "I trust your judgment. IIDWTO."

As Ram contemplated sending more detailed instructions, a muted chime and Kelli's voice interrupted. "Senator Sherman is here, Dr. Barkley."

"Tell him I'll join him..." What was the name of that dining facility dedicated to the deceased scientists? "In Laotis 12."

"Yes, sir."

He relayed the communication, then secured the secret compartment. Content with his decision about Empusa III, he checked his appearance before leaving the office. His *If In Doubt, Wipe Them Out* message would ensure a genocide that included Aric and Reese.

Chapter 18

The ache began behind Aric's eyes, like the onset of a viral attack. Except this wasn't a simple headache.

Over breakfast, she shared the news. "I believe I'm coming down with Empusa III's one known illness."

"What do you mean?" Sean set down his juice.

"I've had this several times before." She massaged her forehead. "We called it jungle fever."

"What are the symptoms?"

"A stabbing pain in my head. I get feverish. Like a bad case of the flu."

"How long does it last?"

"About twelve to fifteen hours." She set down her

cup of juice. "And I always relapse in a couple days. The second bout is more severe."

His mouth pursed. "Any way to circumvent this?

"No."

"Do meds help?"

"I'm not certain. Regardless, I'm out."

He digested the news, then leaned forward. "What can I do while you're indisposed?"

"Garden, clearing. The usual." She sighed as she contemplated the helplessness that came upon her. "I'm sorry you'll have to do all the work."

"That wasn't what I was asking." Sean touched her wrist. "What can I do for *you* while you're ill?"

She chewed her lip. "Keep me hydrated."

"That shouldn't be too difficult."

Her cheeks grew warm as his fingertips lingered on her skin. Pulling away, she ran her hand across the back of her neck.

"I have only one other question." Brow wrinkling, Sean folded his hands. "Does this mean I have to cook?"

"Afraid so." She chuckled. "Perhaps it's better I won't be hungry."

His grin faded. "You did look a little pale yesterday."

"I thought I was just tired."

"Don't worry about anything." He reached over and squeezed her wrist. "I'll take care of you and the place."

"Thanks." She rose and backed away. "If you'll excuse me, I've got some chores."

By afternoon, she had trouble concentrating on her journal entries. With a sinking feeling, Aric realized this was going to be the worst bout she'd had. Her head throbbed while the pencil between her fingers refused to cooperate.

From what sounded like a great distance, Sean came into the room. Neck screaming in pain, she turned her head. He seemed to be walking toward her at an angle, voice interspersed by a buzzing sound.

"I don't feel well." At least that's what she thought she said.

He took the pencil from her. "Bedtime."

His words battered her head. She felt herself being lifted and carried, the room tilting. The bolts of her hammock creaked as she floated down upon it.

That was the last thing she remembered.

"Sean?" She croaked his name. Her tunic felt clammy with perspiration. When she struggled to sit up, the hammock swung crazily. "Are you there, Sean?"

No answer. Was he working in the garden?

Aric slid her feet until they dangled, then she gingerly lowered herself. The room swayed. After the dizziness lessened, she tottered into the common room.

He was neither there nor in his bedroom. Where

was he? She staggered to the door and looked out. The garden was empty. Before she made the trek to the shed, she rested against the doorframe.

The suns' position revealed it was about noon. Had she slept around the clock? Crossing the uneven ground, she felt as though her legs would give out any second. Before she reached the shed, she called, "Are you there?"

Nothing.

She couldn't squelch her building panic. Had he vanished like Julian?

"Sean!"

The kawyas paused their noisemaking. In the hush, Aric listened, desperate for a sound—any sound—that would tell her he was nearby. Slowly, the creatures began clacking again, even louder in the unnatural silence.

Loneliness clutched at her. She returned to the common room and slumped on a chair.

Had Sean only been a dream, a figment of her imagination? Closing her eyes, she couldn't stop the tidal wave of fear.

I've been ill a long time and only dreamed of him. She began to quiver uncontrollably as her imagination filled the void. Julian left a long time ago. SARC abandoned her. Ram finally had his revenge. Did he find out about Ella? What was he planning?

"Stop!" She ended the insanity by digging her fingernails into her palms.

Determination giving her strength, she staggered to

Sean's room. One of his shirts lay across the suspended nylon rope. Tears of relief stung as she shuffled to his hammock. Pressing the material to her face, she inhaled the lingering scent of his aftershave.

I have not lost my mind.

The moccasins she made for him sat on the floor. But her original worry returned. Where was he?

Clutching the shirt, she crawled into his hammock.

"Please, God, let him come back." Exhaustion pulled her into an abyss.

Confident she would be safe as she slept, Sean ducked out. He jogged to the cave where he'd hidden his equipment, then beelined for the Edenoi village. When he reached the jungle's edge, he activated the sophisticated scanner.

Calibrating the device, he focused on the settlement. He picked up the life forms that roamed the area. Dog-sized mammals, birds, rodentia. All of them were identified according to mass, movement, body heat, and heart rate. The noisy kawyas overloaded the microphone so he shut it off. For some reason, a cluster of them found him fascinating this morning. They settled in a nearby umbrella tree and gossiped.

Sean tuned the instrument to detect mineral readings only. The equipment started pouring out data about rhodium, platinum and ruthenium, all within a two-mile radius. Seriously? In all the reports he'd read about Empusa III, none of this information had been in them. Had it been deliberately withheld?

The planet appeared to be bursting with wealth.

Stupid of him not to have scanned the area for more than a decaying human body when he'd first arrived. He had been so focused on his orders that he'd ignored a personal rule to always verify the facts. How could he have so blindly believed the information SARC fed him?

I've been deep undercover too long.

He focused the instrument on one item—the shiny stones he'd seen. And it came up.

The numbers were slightly unusual, but when Sean keyed a command to identify and elaborate, the computer didn't lie. The Edenoi possessed unremarkable crystal called tazpan. Fairly worthless. What they symbolized interested Sean—the presence of "Angel Gold." The inhabitants of Empusa III probably ignored the soft, gray metal they found with tazpan. Neither they nor Aric would know about the substance that had become more precious than Terran gold.

Could this be the missing piece of the puzzle? If so, Aric was a hindrance to Barkley. He obviously would keep a discovery of this magnitude quiet. No survivors, no witnesses.

Including me.

Chapter 19

"Aric?" Sean panicked when he found her hammock empty.

Was she wandering through the jungle in a delirious daze? Adrenalin pumping through his body, he bolted from her room.

He had to find her before nightfall. The image of a tereph ripped through his mind.

As he rushed through the common area, he caught sight of his open door. A bare leg dangled from his hammock. By the stars, how...?

He crept into the room and stared at a sleeping Aric. Peaceful oblivion cradled her, no longer the restless incoherence that had consumed her for too many hours. As she clutched his shirt, a pale smile graced her lips.

His throat tightened. Was it only yesterday she was screaming at the height of delirium? He would never forget her wild-eyed terror as she begged someone to stop hurting her. Until the nightmare passed, he could only hold her. *No, it wasn't a nightmare.* She'd relived an event of a man assaulting her.

Who? Sean thought she'd said a name, but couldn't be sure. Impossible to quiz her in her state. She'd not spoken of him again.

When Sean returned to Earth, he vowed to hunt down the perpetrator. *Oh, yeah.* After he was done, whoever harmed Aric wouldn't do that to any woman again. He clenched his fist, impotent fury wrenching him as he thought of her being molested. It explained much.

When she moaned softly, he caught his breath. Very gently, he stroked her cheek. Her eyes fluttered open. They widened as she gaped. She grabbed his hand.

"Where've you been? I..." A breathy sob caught in her throat.

"Worried that I disappeared?"

A small squeak of assent escaped her.

"I couldn't leave you." He spoke softly. "We have too much fun together."

Her chin quivered as a tear trickled down her cheek. He swept a strand of hair from her forehead. "You've had a rough time. But you're better now.

Right?"

A shaky sigh escaping, she nodded.

He cleared his throat. "Listen, I thought about cooking lunch, but didn't want to spoil your first good day."

Her lips trembled into a tenuous smile.

He squeezed her hand. "How about some coffee? I saved some for special occasions. And this definitely is a reason to celebrate."

Her shoulders relaxed as her sigh echoed in genuine relief.

"But you can't drink it lying down."

As she tried to sit up, the hammock swung wildly. Without giving her a chance to protest, he scooped her into his arms. She relaxed in his hold, one arm wrapped about his neck. When he reached the common room, he didn't lower her to the chair right away.

For endless moments he held her, lost in the green of her eyes. They reminded him of the waters off Hawaii, teal and rimmed with blue. Her lips parted, expression full of trust.

"Down you go." He lowered her to the chair to hide his husky tone. "Coffee will take a minute."

He spooned out the dwindling grounds at the bottom of the container.

Her chair scraped as she shifted her weight. "What did you do while I took a vacation?"

"Same old-same old. Water, weed, work. The three W's. My favorite letter." He paused, enjoying her smile. "Did some digging around the clearing earlier.

Actually went berry picking, but didn't find anything. Guess the tereph got everything edible."

Aric listened attentively, gaze following his every movement. Her silence made him babble all the more. Funny how he'd picked up her nervous habit. He told her everything except the most important accomplishment.

She didn't speak until he poured the coffee. "How long was I out?"

"Twenty-two hours."

Shock etched her face. "A whole day? I thought I'd only imagined it."

"That good or bad?"

"Bad. Usually my first bout lasts half a day. And I remember more."

"So you don't recall everything I did while you were ill?"

"Not much."

"That's rather ungrateful of you." Sean teased with a smile.

"Sorry." She sipped her coffee.

He held his breath at the sight of her trembling hand. When she set the cup down with a *clunk,* he released the air.

"You're not having any?"

He grinned. "I already drank my two gallons this morning."

"Liar." Her tone contained only good-natured ribbing.

You have no idea…

"I washed two of your outfits yesterday." He sat across from her. "They're drying now."

"Thanks."

He could see a question poised on her lips. Let her believe he hadn't undressed her when perspiration drenched her clothing. If it preserved her modesty, he was content.

"I added to what you'd written about our Edenoi excursions." Sean hoped the new topic would distract her. "You're welcome to review it."

"I'd love to. Maybe later."

He rose, an uncomfortable need to do something pressing him. "I'll go harvest some lunch. Call me if you need anything."

A tired smile on her pale lips, she merely nodded.

"I'm sure I'll be fine." Leaning on the flimsy garden fence, Aric raised a hand to shoo him away. "Go. And don't worry about me."

"Okay, then. I'm going to pretend the stream has warm water today." Sean slung a towel over his shoulder, walking backwards as he spoke.

"Enjoy your bath." The lunch he'd prepared, which hadn't been all that bad, revived her. Or perhaps it was the reassurance that he hadn't abandoned her?

No gardening needed to be done even if she had

energy. The plants appeared to flourish. Her throat tightened as she thought of how good he had been to look after everything. Even while ill, she remembered more than she'd let on.

Images of his bending over her, the gentle hands that held her, his quiet voice calming her delirious fears. As tears welled, the garden blurred.

She wiped away the wetness on her cheeks, glad Sean wasn't around to see her crying like a baby.

Thinking she might fill the reservoirs for the irrigation system, Aric looked for the bucket. After shuffling to the shed, she rested against the wall. The trip from the garden had taken more out of her than she thought.

Surveying the small enclosure, she promised herself that she'd clean it when her strength returned. The end of a rope, gently swaying outside the shed's window, caught her attention. Aric wobbled around the small building to confront this new mystery. It was her other trap—sprung—but now empty.

Bemused, she stared up at the dangling end. Had Sean accidentally stepped into it? Peering at the tangle rope, she could see it had been cut or possibly gnawed by some creature. Too high to reach, she gave up the idea of examining it more closely.

Looking down, she noticed the partial imprint of a boot. She recalled his moccasins in his room. So, Sean *had* been behind the shed. What had he been doing? She pushed away the questions. Thinking took too much energy.

She made her way back inside, exhausted by the

time she reached the cabin. Too tired to climb into her hammock, she lay underneath it. As she drifted into sleep, the slashed rope continued to bother her.

Chapter 20

"No." Sean planted fists at hips. "You can direct me, but you're not doing any work."

Even though she claimed she had a good night's sleep, Aric's pale face and shaky walk proved how weak she still was.

"I can at least fill the bucket."

"No way. If you stand for very long, you'll fall over."

"Well, then I can sit and weed."

He frowned at her stubbornness. Well, he was more stubborn.

When she drew herself up to all of her five feet four

inches, he nearly laughed aloud.

"I'm the Team Leader—"

"I'm not listening." He covered his ears, pretending to be back in junior high. Which wasn't too difficult. "I'm not listening. La, la, la..."

She repressed a smile.

Good. "I'm not letting you do a thing, and that's final."

Her softening expression blinked out of existence. "I'd like to see you stop me, Sean Reese." Her jaw appeared set in concrete.

Ridiculous, considering he outweighed her by at least eighty pounds.

"Okay," he said slowly, "I'll *let* you weed."

Her lips twitched. A good sign.

He added a stipulation. "If you hold my arm while we walk." That was a huge concession, considering yesterday he'd carried her. And when he'd returned from his bath, he'd found her napping on the floor. Because she was too weak to climb into her hammock?

Extending his arm, he slowly led the way. She did seem a little stronger, but he wasn't taking any chances. Besides, he liked the way she leaned on him. After he got her settled in the garden, he hurried to fill the water bins.

At first, Aric weeded vigorously, but soon, she slowed. He joined her, pulling up the ones that were out of her reach so she wouldn't have to move too much. Row after row they worked. He was amazed at how quickly the invaders grew. They had all been cleared the day before.

She sighed and brushed the dirt from her hands. As she sat back on her heels with drooping shoulders, he could tell weakness still plagued her.

"Aric, would an antibiotic help?"

With a limp hand, she brushed back her hair. "Perhaps. A med-scan of my blood would determine that."

He pondered her statement. "Aren't antibiotics routinely included in supply shipments?"

She leaned forward to pluck a small weed. "Yes. But the last one was never delivered."

According to her, she'd never gotten it. According to SARC, she had. Someone was lying.

"Julian said it was accidentally destroyed."

"Why didn't...?" He broke off what he was going to say. *Why didn't SARC believe you?* Realizing she was waiting for him to finish his sentence, he said, "Why didn't they have me bring replacements?"

She studied him with a peculiar expression, head cocked to one side. "That did cross my mind."

Obviously Barkley had a hand in that oversight.

No wonder Aric had been suspicious. And resentful. He'd arrived with the luxuries she lacked—like soap, shampoo, new clothing. She had received no fresh supplies for a long time. What if she hadn't learned to live off the land? What if she'd caught an illness that killed her?

"That ba—!" He clamped his mouth shut.

"I'm sure it wasn't his fault."

"Who?" No excuse for Barkley.

"Julian."

Aric obviously hadn't made the connection between Barkley and the shipment not being replaced. Sean couldn't tell her. It would only cast a suspicious light on him. "Whatever."

"I've managed." She reached for another weed. "Sometimes simple things are overlooked when dealing with grander projects. I'm sure SARC has been busy with all their new contacts."

Yeah, right. His resolve to stop Barkley suddenly became personal. And when Aric's next attack came, Sean would be ready.

I can't go on like this.

Sean rolled out of his hammock. Time pressed upon him. Options—or the lack of them—ricocheted in his mind. In a couple weeks, the quarterly info-beacon would go out. As Aric's assistant, he would include his own report and an encoded dispatch to his deep-undercover contact in the communications department.

As soon as SARC received it, Barkley would know Aric was alive. He'd dispatch a ship.

Who would arrive first—the henchmen or the rescue posse? That is, assuming Sean's contact received the message and acted on it immediately. However, he couldn't sit around, waiting to see.

In six weeks, both Aric and I could be dead.

When he'd first departed for Empusa III, his friend and colleague had pressured him into bringing forbidden equipment. Jayden called it a *just in case.* In the cave where Sean hid his stash was a radio for emergencies. However, he had no emergency.

Besides, what could he tell Jayden? Barkley had been responsible for planetary sweeps eleven years ago—*so what?* SARC had either lied about Aric or been misled—*big deal.* Barkley falsified her bio—*mere speculation.*

Sean had no proof that the director even knew about Angel Gold. The fact that Barkley concealed the truth of other precious metals could mean he was merely protecting Empusa III.

Across the dark bedroom, Sean paced. He had been trained to be proactive. Time to start acting that way. The presence of the priceless metal was tangible, enough to justify a communiqué. And soon.

At last, a plan he could live with. He sighed, mind leaping to the future. In about a month, he'd head back to Earth. This planet would be behind him and...

What about Aric? He stared at the black floor beneath his bare feet as though the answer was written there. She would refuse to leave. The Edenoi were her sacred responsibility. Until she was certain they were protected, she wouldn't abandon them.

Not only that, she'd ask questions. Lots of them.

Once she knows who and what I am, she'll never speak to me again.

He strode from his room and flung open the exterior cabin door. As he stood bare-chested with only a pair of shorts on, the coolness soothed his agitation. Gulping the refreshing air, Sean braced his hands on the doorframe. Stars shimmered through the opening in the trees, but the night was eerily silent. He didn't even hear the moans of the tereph on the prowl. But the quiet had a price. His thoughts yelled loud and clear.

Someday she'll find out. Everything.

He shook his head. No, she wouldn't. He'd melt into his other life. His *real* one. Far away from SARC. Far away from Seattle. He'd never see her again.

I can't...

An unusual sound interrupted. Tensing, Sean tuned into the creak of a hammock, the soft padding of feet, and the almost noiseless opening of a door. What would Aric do when she saw him?

The nerves on his back prickled. He pretended not to hear her, giving her the chance to retreat.

When hesitant steps drew closer, he turned. "Can't sleep?"

"No." She stepped beside him.

He caught his breath. *She's wearing my shirt.* One he'd given her. Both sleeves were rolled up, proving how huge it was on her. The pale green fabric shimmered in the starlight. Aric smoothed the hem at her thigh, drawing his gaze to her slim bare legs. Sean gulped. *Keep it cool.*

As she relaxed against the doorway, he forced himself to stare into the jungle. The silence grew heavy.

"They're spectacular, aren't they?" Her soft voice caressed him. "The stars, I mean. I don't remember any of the names. Astronomy wasn't my forte."

He said nothing. In his peripheral vision, he watched her turn toward him, arms pressed behind her. His insides coiled under her scrutiny. He felt like the spring in Gigi's antique clock. When he was a boy, he used to wind it too tightly.

"I'm glad you're awake." She paused.

What could he say that wasn't foolish or forbidden? He clamped his mouth shut.

"I wanted to thank you for all you've done since you've been here."

"Don't mention it." He couldn't help his clipped tone.

She responded slowly. "But it's important that I do."

"You've already thanked me several times." Fighting not to sound so abrupt, he clenched one fist. The hard decisions that soon would have to be made battered him.

All I have is now.

"I really needed to tell you." She touched his arm.

Sean twitched away from her warm fingers. "There's no need to say anything. You'd do the same for me, right?"

"Well, yes." Her eyes glittered in the faint light.

"Then forget it."

He stared stonily ahead. Out of the corner of his

eye, he saw her furtively wipe her cheek. Her small sniff weakened him further.

"You don't understand." Aric's voice shook. "The last time I was sick, Julian did next to nothing. I almost lost my entire garden. So I had to tell you how much I appreciate you."

If you knew what I was—what I am, you wouldn't be so appreciative...

She grasped his fingers. "Honestly, Sean. I do." She raised his hand, pressing it between her own.

A spark snapped between them, expanding to a jolt that ripped through him. Without considering the consequences, he jerked her into his arms. The next second, he was hungrily kissing her.

In the moments he held her, he burst with the realization that she didn't stiffen or pull away. She felt so warm, so alive. The universe fled as he became aware of nothing but the sweetness of her lips trembling against his. Her mouth softened as she slowly entwined her hands behind his neck.

Groaning, he crushed her against himself, his passion-induced fever spiking to an impossible temperature. The longer their embrace, the more she leaned into him.

Sean grasped her hair, pulling her head back so he could drink of her lips more deeply. As he murmured her name, his mouth found the hollow of her throat. She must yield. She *must*.

His shaking fingers found the top button of the shirt while his other arm kept her pinned.

"No." The word was uttered against his lips. Aric suddenly arched away from him. "No." Stiff-armed, she pushed against his chest. "Sean, stop." Her rising voice broke through.

He couldn't understand, wouldn't believe her rejection. Not after the way she kissed him.

"Aric." He slipped his other arm about her waist. "Please don't..."

"I can't—no." She strained all the harder.

He took a firmer hold. If she'd give him a minute to explain, she'd know he wasn't going to force her into anything.

"Let me go."

The shrill note of panic pricked him. "If you would just..."

She struck his solar plexus, knocking the breath from him. The next second, her knuckles made contact with his jaw.

That did it.

Protecting himself from her thrashing legs, Sean lifted her from the floor and fumbled for a chair. While she fought and screamed, he held her. Taking her abuse, he waited for her to calm.

Then he understood. Did she fear this was a replay of her past?

"I'm not going to force you, Aric. Do you hear me?"

Instantly, she stilled. Her eyes were pools of water, dark, shimmering in the dim light.

A name—*the* name she had cried out in her delirium—suddenly hit him.

"Was it Barkley? Was he the one?"

Blanching, she sucked in an impossible amount of air. But no words came. She didn't need to say anything.

"I'm not Barkley," he ground out. "I'd never hurt you."

Releasing her breath, she shuddered and went limp. From the depths of her soul, a wail rose as she crumpled against him. As he gathered her more closely, she pressed her face to his neck and yielded to racking sobs. Sean clenched his jaw so hard, his teeth felt as if they might break. Impotent fury raged inside him. Right now, he could kill Barkley with his bare hands.

Eventually, her weeping subsided to shuddering gasps. Finally, she grew quiet and sat up.

"I'm sorry." He gingerly touched her back. "I didn't mean to frighten you."

A small hiccup escaped, her only answer.

With a determination he didn't feel, Sean set her off his lap and stood. "I'm going back to bed."

Without waiting for her response, he went into his room, hoping sleep would ease his torment.

Sean had guessed. How?

Shame hounded her. She'd never told anyone what

had happened that night in Ram's office. Not even the division manager who'd interrupted them. He had threatened to call the police if Barkley didn't open the door and prove everything was all right. Those moments had given her a chance to slip away. Gratefulness for him again washed over her. As far as Aric knew, he had never told anyone either.

Then how had Sean found out?

Curiously, she felt relieved by his knowing. The burden that once overwhelmed, now seemed easier to bear. He hadn't asked for details. Hadn't insisted she tell him everything. Hadn't implied Barkley's actions were ultimately her fault.

Sean held me while I cried.

Not only that, he'd walked away when she was the most vulnerable. He could have waited until she had finished crying, then gently seduced her. Isn't that how some men operated? Her ex had used that ploy. Many times.

No, Sean was different.

Yet, he had made assumptions about her. Assumptions she must clear up.

Tomorrow. If she wanted him to be part of her future—and she desperately did—she needed to open up. Even if her confession drove him away.

Chapter 21

After arising late, Sean took his time dressing. As soon as he entered the common room, Aric rose and poured him some coffee. Her cup of mathoke was half consumed. An invitation for them to converse?

Fine. She could start.

Sitting, he averted his gaze from her tightlipped paleness. Last night had made him feel like a eunuch. No, worse because he still wanted her. And she would continue to reject him.

Aric cleared her throat. "We need to talk."

"Okay." He slurped the hot brew. *She's going to tell me she can have nothing to do with me. And that'll be that.*

"Are you listening?"

"Yeah."

As she lowered herself to the seat across from him, he stoically stared into the black coffee. The stuff tasted terrible.

"Then would you have the courtesy to look at me?"

He couldn't help grinning at her scathing tone. "All right, you've got my attention." He put down his cup, deciding to forgo the rest.

Gray circles shadowed her eyes, making them appear more intensely green. That little furrow of worry creased the space between her brows, tugging at his heart.

"I wanted to apologize for my behavior last night." She drew a deep breath. "You were right. About— about Ram."

"No news flash there."

Her bloodshot eyes betrayed her weariness. "For a minute, I forgot that all men aren't scum."

Sean toyed with the cup's handle. So, Barkley had raped her. His stomach twisted, setting his teeth on edge. "Okay. Finished?"

"No." She grabbed her drink, released it, then strangled it again.

While he waited, she rose and paced away from him. He steered his gaze away from her shapely form, remembering so vividly how she felt in his arms.

Shoulders rigid, Aric pressed her hands to the windowsill. "You'll call me odd or—or hypocritical. But..." She stopped to draw a deep breath. "I cannot get involved with you."

"I figured that part out."

"Because I told you 'no' last night?"

"Well, yeah. That was the first clue."

Her neck muscles tightened. "I need to tell you the reason."

"I get it. What Barkley did—"

"This isn't about him."

Staring at her inflexible back, he tried to piece together what she was saying. "Oh, I see. Everyone else can ignore the directive about no relationships, except you."

She wheeled around. "No. This has nothing to do with the directive. Although I agree with it."

He pressed his fingers to his forehead. "Then what're we talking about?"

She spoke slowly. "Intimacy should be reserved for marriage."

His jaw went slack.

She clenched and unclenched her hands. "I believe in the standards with which I was raised. Not because of fear of punishment but because it was designed that way."

His mind remained blank.

"If you hold me in any regard, please accept that."

"I don't believe it." The words popped out of his mouth before he realized what they might mean to her.

"You think I'm making this up?" Her eyes burned darkly.

"No. That's not—"

"Obviously, I'm lying." Aric stalked toward him.

"You think I have no feelings?"

"No, I'm—"

"Don't you know it about killed me to refuse you last night? You've no idea how I wanted to..." Her neck muscles tightened as she strangled the remainder of her sentence.

While he sat glued to his seat, she stood before him, panting from her passionate speech.

I love her. I have for a long time.

The simple confession rocked his world. He loved her more than ever—for her strength of character, passion for life, commitment to standards. They made her what she was.

He looked at her with new understanding as he rose, towering over her. "I had no idea."

"That I'm so old-fashioned?"

She seemed so childlike, yet strong in ways that always surprised him. When Sean grasped her arms, she shivered. Pulse pounding in her throat, she slowly raised her eyes.

For once, he abandoned the urge to joke. He spoke with a sincerity that he rarely could indulge. "You are a special kind of woman, Aric."

Her furrowed brow melted into contrition. She opened her mouth to say something, clamped it shut, then took a deep breath. "I'm sorry I shouted at you. I just wanted you to believe me."

"I believe you."

"I couldn't bear the thought of your not believing me."

"I said I do."

"Laugh if you want." Her chin quivered, as though she expected a verbal slap.

"No." He rubbed her arms before releasing them. "As I said, I'm not Barkley."

Her head snapped up, expression rippling with confusion. And pain. For endless minutes, she scrutinized his face as though seeking proof there. Finally she said, "I know." She bit her lip. "I guess I've always known."

"Friends?" Holding out his hand, he waited.

Again, that odd expression passed her face, as though she didn't know what to expect. Hesitantly, she raised her small hand. As his closed around hers, he grew aware of the calloused palm and slender fingers. Instead of shaking it, he drew her closer and kissed her cheek. "Thank you for opening your heart to me," he whispered in her ear.

Resisting the temptation to do more, Sean strode away.

For sanity's sake, Aric had to avoid him. She left whenever Sean entered the room. Or the garden. Or the shed. By evening, exhaustion rippled through her. The silence of their meal became an almost unbearable torment. She rose immediately afterwards to clean up.

Before she could take Sean's bowl from the table, he was already holding it out to her. However, he didn't release it. Baffled, she tugged. Their gaze met, the deep look in his brown eyes paralyzing her. Her heart started to pump wildly.

"You don't need to do penance, Aric."

She knew he'd probably meant to tease, but the effort failed. The edge in his tone could draw blood.

He took back the bowl. "I'll clean up."

No need for another invitation. Aric fled to the edge of the clearing. As the violet sky decayed to gray, then black, she reveled in the veiling darkness. If only she could hide from her swirling emotions. Not until the first tereph moaned did she rebuke herself for being so foolish.

She retired to her hammock, afraid to undress, afraid to sleep. Though she tried to read, her concentration broke every time she heard Sean in the next room. A chair scraping, a cup clunking, or his firm step.

Very late, he paused by her door. She tensed. What would she do if he entered her room?

"Goodnight, Aric." His voice came low behind the barrier.

"G'night." She thought she spoke, but nothing came from her tight throat.

The void of silence pressed against the door, battering her heart.

He moved away and shut his bedroom door. Heart sick, she clutched the journal to her chest.

"God...?" she whispered as she stared at the ceiling. No easy prayer rescued her from anguish. She didn't know what to ask. Though her eyes burned, no cleansing tears came.

Her gaze strayed to the shelf in her room. For the hundredth time she wished she still had her little New Testament. But that disappeared the same time as Julian. She wanted so much to read the Psalms included in the book. They always comforted her.

When she climbed out of her hammock, the journal she'd been studying thumped heavily to the floor. Before she could think, she was kneeling with her hands clasped so tightly they hurt.

"Lord..." Still no petition came. Instead, questions. Questions she had not dared voice in years.

Why did you let Mitt abandon me?

Why do I have to be so far away from Ella?

Why have You allowed so many difficult things in my life?

A dozen more thoughts tumbled in her soul until she stretched herself face down on her floor. And when all the old questions had been asked, her soul grew still.

Finally her heart whispered, "Why did you let me fall in love with Sean? I never intended to, Lord. You know that."

Self-recrimination tore her, taking away excuses.

I should never have kissed him...or even touched his hand.

The second I saw him, I should've gone back to bed.

Guilt crushed her until she could hardly breathe.

An eternity passed as she pressed her forehead against the floor. "Forgive me, Lord…"

He has, reassurance soothed the turmoil inside her. *Completely.*

Rolling over, she inhaled the peace that passed all understanding. She was forgiven. Condemnation need not pretend to be the victor. God's grace covered all.

The solar lamp flickered, its light competing with the twinkling stars in the skylight. One in particular glimmered and danced, swathed in white and blue. The turmoil of unanswered questions evaporated.

She couldn't change the past. Couldn't take back anything that she'd done. However, she could guard her future.

"But…"

No excuses. As long as she remained on Empusa III, she not only had to follow SARC's directive, but her personal standards. No matter how difficult.

Give me strength, God. I have none of my own.

When she stretched out her arms, her hand bumped the journal, still on the floor. She sat up and pulled it onto her lap.

As she reviewed the entries about the Edenoi, she smiled. She'd written about their well-developed society, their orderliness, their peaceful existence. In the last entry, Sean had recorded his thoughts.

"…we witnessed a beautiful wedding. The innocence of the bride and groom at the feast afterwards was a joy to watch."

She caressed the sprawling handwriting. For many

minutes, she stared at the blank space below. Finally, Aric retrieved her pencil and scribbled a last line. "Holding to values contributes greatly to happiness."

Anyone who read the entry might find the addendum odd.

But Sean would understand.

Chapter 22

Days later, her relapse hit. Sean recognized its imminent arrival in her haggard face, weakness and disorientation. A fever made her shiver during the hottest part of the afternoon. With eyes of trust, she regarded him.

He didn't dare go for the antibiotic yet. When he was away, she might wander into the jungle. No, she had to be completely incapacitated. He watched and waited, miserable while she suffered.

After wrapping her in a blanket, he seated her in the common room where he could keep an eye on her. She accepted only water that he had bolstered with softened pieces of a food packet. While she worked on that one small glass, he settled across from her to polish the latest journal entries. He couldn't concentrate as her teeth chattered and limbs jerked uncontrollably. Hating his helplessness, he gathered her onto his lap.

Focused on the war within, she didn't protest. While he held her, his gaze lit on the entry about the Edenoi wedding and Aric's last scribbled line.

Values. She was indeed a woman of high standards.

What if I marry her? The idea hit him square in the forehead. Matrimony would solve a plethora of challenges.

SARC and its director didn't worry Sean. *They* did. The ones who were ultimately responsible for sending him to Empusa III. With a marriage contract, Sean could invoke the spousal privilege. Not only to protect himself, but Aric.

His mind raced to the proper procedure.

For those who lived off-world and without an official available, couples had the option of a "writ of marriage." The document was legal and binding, as long as the contract was registered with the department of licenses on Earth within one year. Or an authorized person performed the ceremony.

Sean inhaled slowly, thinking through the ramifications. And risks.

This is to protect Aric. Once she recovered from her illness, he wouldn't tell her about the arrangement until he could tell all—who he was and why he was there. At that point, she could tear up the contract. No one would be the wiser.

Or—his heart hammered with hope—they could register the document when they returned to Earth.

Setting her aside, he leaned her head on the table so she wouldn't fall. He tore a blank page from her journal and wrote up a marriage contract. It stated that they both entered into this agreement willingly. He stopped a few times to rack his brain for the words to the ancient, but revered ceremony. *For richer or poorer, in sickness and in health...* The added words weren't necessary for legality, but Sean wanted her to see he was serious.

That would do. He hoped.

"Aric, I need you to pay attention." He rattled the paper.

"Hmm?" She didn't move.

"Look at me."

Eyes glazed with fever, she lifted her head.

"Do you want to marry me?"

"Sure." She smiled softly. "Love to."

His heart swelled. So far so good. "I wrote up a marriage contract. I need your full name."

Face screwed in concentration, she slurred the words. "Aric Morning Sky Lindquist."

"Great." He wrote it on the contract. "You need to witness my signature."

She blinked. "Why?"

"So it'll be legal." He scrawled his signature next to

his printed name, then dated it. "There."

Again, she lay her cheek against the table's surface.

Now to have her sign it. She seemed barely able to hold up her head.

She agreed to the marriage. Later she can contest it...or register it.

As he looked at her limp hand draping the table, he couldn't do it. Couldn't trick her into a marriage that might outrage her.

Ethics.

Very well. He'd done his part, but the option would be hers. After folding the paper, Sean put it in his shirt pocket. This would be his secret.

For a while, anyway.

By morning, she was completely out of it. As before, she babbled. He learned what a jerk her ex-husband was and heard about someone named Ella. Then she slipped into a sleep that resembled death. Time to get the antibiotics. Before Sean left, he wedged a shovel against the door, shoving the end deeply into the soil. If Aric did wander, she wouldn't be able to get outside.

He hurried to the cave and set up the radio. The power packs only allowed a one-way transmission so Sean sent a short, cryptic message. "Target healthy.

Place heavenly. Boss AAD." He hoped Jayden understood from the message that not only Aric was alive, but mentally stable, nothing like SARC painted her. "Heavenly" was the closest he could get to mentioning Angel Gold without risking marauders picking up the message. Jayden would understand "boss" meant Barkley. The letters were an acronym for "armed and dangerous."

Problem was, he had no idea if or when his friend would get the communication. He wasn't sure what Jayden could do to help, but Sean's gut told him to send a message now. That accomplished, he took the med-kit and his neuro-gun back to base camp.

When he returned, Aric lay on the floor under her hammock. Sean injected the antibiotic pellet plus a nutritive supplement. She didn't even flinch. Then he put a pillow under her head and covered her. She would be safer on the floor.

Now, to hide the equipment. He wanted everything on hand in case Aric needed another dose.

He saw no improvement over the next twenty-four hours. Instead she seemed to grow worse. To pass the time, he read her journals, looking for information. Sean found the entry that told of her first bout. She didn't know where she'd picked up the bug or what it was. No one else got sick. With no other recourse than to ship her back home, they shot her up with antibiotics. Happily, she improved.

So, it sounded as if the antibiotic *would* help.

The next happened shortly after her second assistant arrived. Without a medical lab, Aric couldn't be certain why the illness reoccurred. The strange thing was, the assistant also became ill, but at a different interval.

The third time was after Geoffreys came. He'd been at the base for two months before Aric became indisposed. And he didn't get sick.

Sean shut the book with a snap. Geoffreys wasn't affected. Why not? And why hadn't any of the original team fallen ill? Sean went back to the second incident and reread the account. The assistant had gotten mildly ill. If the contaminant was airborne, more than one other person should have been afflicted. If it was carried another way, then why did only the second assistant get sick?

This time Aric had succumbed, but not Sean. The pattern eluded him. As he considered possibilities, she called his name.

Though pale and haggard, she looked remarkably better. By all accounts, she should have been deathly ill for another two to three days. Or—the grim reality had to be considered—dead.

"How are you doing?" Crouched by her, he felt her forehead. It was damp and cool.

"Like a tereph mauled me." She croaked the words.

"You look it."

She managed a wan smile.

"I think your fever has broken."

"Good sign. Is there any coffee?"

"Unfortunately no. How about mathoke?"

Aric was still awake when he returned with a cup. Steadying her while she sipped the juice, he was pleased she was able to drink nearly all. Did he imagine it or did she lean against him?

He couldn't tear his gaze away. While she wore his shirt, he had absolutely no control over his thoughts.

By evening, she felt well enough to totter about the room with a blanket about her. "How many days was I out this time?" She slumped in a chair.

He discarded his first inclination to lie. "Day and a half."

That's all?" Her expression betrayed surprise. "I thought that's about how long I was sick the first time."

"Maybe you're finally building an immunity."

"Not possible." She studied him. "It wouldn't improve on its own."

He shrugged. "It's probably all that water you drank. Or the food bars I dissolved in it."

"Seriously?"

"Glad I saved them for a rainy day."

She weakly smiled.

Then he sobered. "Tell me, don't you wonder about your illness?"

"I've racked my brain a dozen times."

"What'd you conclude?"

She shook her head. "Nothing. This is the weirdest thing I've ever heard of. Even the first team didn't have a clue. I figured it was a new, uncatalogued disease."

"Didn't they take a blood sample for analysis?"

"Sure."

"And no medicine or immunizations arrived to combat it?"

"No. I guess a cure hasn't been found."

Doubtful. He recalled the battery of hypos he endured before leaving Earth. "Doesn't it strike you odd that only one other person got ill besides you?"

"Of course. But I know little about bacteria or viruses or whatever I had." Aric pulled the blanket about herself more securely. "If it was merely a bacteria I picked up, I would have built up antibodies. Or if not, the infection should have killed me. I think. A virus, on the other hand, shouldn't be something that spontaneously reoccurs."

"Antibiotics wouldn't affect most viruses, right?"

"Not unless we've run across a whole new type." She rubbed her forehead. "If I had a microscope, I could do some tests."

Or a bio-scanner? The one he stashed in the cave could be converted to medical use with the press of a button. If he could sneak back and get it, he could do his own testing. But drawing blood from Aric wouldn't be as easy as having her witness a document. Perhaps he could do testing on the grounds about the base. That might be where to start.

He *would* find answers.

Chapter 23

"This is too soon for you to make a trip into the jungle." Sean's jaw jutted as he pushed tangle rope out of their way. "Mathoke bulbs can wait."

"You're acting like a mother hen." Though Aric teased, his concern pleased her.

"Oh, is that what they call common sense nowadays?"

She pressed her lips together to hide her smile. "I feel a lot better today. Honest."

In the last two days, she gained strength every hour. She had no explanation besides his confession of dissolved food packets in her water. Their secret ingredient must be awesome.

She chose the closest whippet patch. The labor wouldn't be difficult. However, that didn't appear to make Sean happier.

"You could've stayed at base camp."

He made a sound of derision. "Like I'd let you do this yourself."

Sucking her lower lip, she again disguised her smile. What had come over him lately? He acted as if he was taking personal responsibility for her. Protective.

When they reached the spot, he went into full-bore mother-hen mode. First he cleared a place for her to sit, then made sure she had a bag within easy reach.

Before he let her harvest anything, he had one more admonition. "Don't overdo it."

"Yes, dear." Then realizing what she'd said, her cheeks burned. She ducked her head.

Did he snort?

For a while, they worked in silence. Aric moved slowly to preserve energy for their return trek.

Sean cleared his throat. "If you had a chance to leave Empusa III, would you?"

"What a way to begin a conversation."

"Well?"

"My tenure isn't over until the end of next year."

"If you were able to break it, would you?"

She stopped working to stare at him. Intent on picking mathoke, he kept his head lowered. What did he want to know exactly?

Finally, she answered. "I'd have to have a pretty good reason. Why do you ask?"

"Merely speculating." He plucked a handful of bulbs. For many minutes, silence again reigned.

Aric fingered a knobby root. "If the Edenoi were in danger, and my giving evidence on Earth would help protect them, then, yes. I would."

Sean's head shot up. Then as quickly, he looked away.

"Something to think about," he finally said.

What did he know? With her communications equipment on the fritz, Aric's information was spotty. Sean had left home mere months ago. He would be much more informed about SARC's policy regarding the Edenoi.

Best to be blunt. "Does SARC plan to make Empusa III phase three?"

"Not that I'm aware of."

"You sure?" Her voice tightened.

He took his time answering. "To be honest, I'm not sure of anything anymore."

His defeated tone surprised her.

Sean's brown eyes met hers. "If push came to shove, Aric, would you testify against Barkley? About what he did to you?"

She recoiled. "I—I couldn't." Publicly broadcast her shame? The mere thought made her ill.

"What if it came down to protecting yourself or protecting Empusa III?"

She sucked in a deep breath. "How can you ask

that? How can I choose between…?" She flung out her hand.

In two strides Sean closed the gap between them. Squatting, he grasped her fingers. "I need to know if you're willing to do whatever it takes for the sake of justice."

"Justice? For what?"

His grip tightened. "Barkley is deviant and corrupt. His hurting you is the tip of the iceberg. If you had a chance—by your testimony—to put him away, would you be willing to tell what he did to you?"

She tugged on her fingers. "I don't—how do you know about him? And—and why do you care?"

He opened his mouth, then clamped it shut. Finally he shook his head. "Trust me when I tell you that his days as director are coming to an end." Face set in granite, he released her hand.

She stared at him.

As Ram's opponent, whatever Sean had put into motion would come to pass. Aric had no doubt.

Relief flooded her. "Is that why you wanted to know if I'd leave Empusa III?"

He glanced away. "Mainly."

Just as quickly, relief fled before a greater worry. "Are you—are you leaving early, Sean?"

His gaze met hers. For once, he didn't have a ready answer.

Her heart froze into a block of ice. "How soon?" She could barely squeeze the words out.

A mask seemed to slip off his face. Raw emotion

etched his expression. His mouth worked and he swallowed several times. "Aric, I..."

She wanted to yell. *Don't go. You can't leave, now that I know...*

Know what? She saw it so clearly. He loved her.

A mask snapped back into place. His brow cleared and Sean sat back on his heels. "Whatever happens, whatever you find out, believe that I will do anything—and everything—to protect you. However, I cannot forget for one moment that my ultimate mission is to take down Barkley."

"Mission...?" A chill gripped her. SARC didn't send people on "missions."

Not the organization she knew.

Before she could ask more, Sean shot to his feet and walked away.

Neither of them said another word the rest of the harvesting trip.

One question burned in her heart. *How can I stay if he leaves?*

"That should do it." Sean studied the neat rows of mathoke laid out on the ground. The suns would soon peep over the umbrella trees and begin the curing process. Not a bad day's work, even if he worried more about Aric than the bulbs.

"Great." However, she wasn't looking at their harvest, but at him.

He forced his thoughts back to work. "Seven hours or so enough time?"

"Yes." Her expression softened. "Thanks again for your help."

"Hey, we're a team."

Her cheeks turned a pretty pink. However, the look of pain he'd recently seen, flashed across her face. She hadn't brought up their discussion from the day before. Would she go with him when he left? He had no right to ask. "I'll get busy watering." He walked away.

Coward.

In light of the marriage contract, he should ask her soon. He pressed his shirt pocket where he stored the document.

Later. He'd tell her later that evening.

She weeded while he filled reservoirs. As he poured the water into the bins, he watched her. Today she seemed much stronger. Knees smudged gray with dirt, she squatted to scrutinize the plants. The way her braid fell across her shoulder captured his heart anew. Never had she looked more beautiful. When she caressed the soil into place, he caught his breath.

He congratulated himself for giving her the antibiotic. But what if she got sick again? What if next time the meds didn't help? Sean needed to find out for certain what caused her illness. Today.

"Aric, I need to make a little excursion. Be gone about an hour."

Panic flashed across her face. "Where are you going?"

"Around. Don't worry."

If he hurried, he could return before she was done tending the garden.

"See you, sweetheart." Before she could react, he bent and kissed the top of her head. "Be back by lunch."

Without another word, he hurried away. When he reached the edge of the clearing, he glanced behind. Her mouth still puckered in a little "o." He waved, then pushed through the spongy foliage.

The trek to the cave wouldn't take long. Finally acclimated to the planet, he jogged most of the way. Across the spongy undergrowth he hurried, planning what to do when he returned with his scanner. He slowed to a walk. The time for a partial confession had arrived. At least about the equipment he brought. And why.

All of a sudden, he stopped. The kawyas that had been clacking minutes ago were silent. Danger crackled in the air. Squatting, he listened.

A high-pitched whine came from directly ahead. The sound seemed muffled, but it wasn't coming at him. *Not a neuro-gun.* Sean recognized the tenor of a blaster. Only it made that particular sound as it shredded particles into nothingness.

Keeping undercover, he crept forward. Who were they and what were they shooting? His first thought was marauders. They'd discovered the metal and were already fighting among themselves. The firing stopped. Sean paused as well, listening. Where were they?

A metallic *crack* punctured his hearing. The sound came from the cave ahead. *His* cave. They'd found his stash. Sean's heart sank as he thought of the loss—extra food, medicine, communication equipment. Had they destroyed the scanner with the evidence he'd recorded?

He inched forward. From the thick foliage, he looked into the small clearing near the mouth of the cave.

Some of his things lay heaped at the entrance. He took quick inventory, noting only food and meds. A blaster again whined from inside. Were they destroying his radio, barrier beacons, and everything else? Booted feet tromped toward the mouth of the cave. His mouth gaped when he recognized the lone man with dark hair, lean frame, medium stature.

Julian Geoffreys. The missing assistant.

Not dead after all. He looked in remarkably good shape for a man who'd traveled alone through dangerous, alien territory. His clothing appeared new and his boots untarnished by Empusa III's black dust. Standing above the equipment, Geoffreys surveyed the lot. Choosing some items, he crammed them into a bulging knapsack.

After he tore open a food packet, he ate with relish. Sean noted the string that hung about the man's neck. Crystalline tazpan dangled from the end.

Thoughts snapped through his mind.

He knows about the Angel Gold.

He can't be working alone.

He wanted Aric—and SARC—to believe he's dead.

Did something change? Why return now? Unfortunate that he'd stumbled upon Sean's supplies. Or had he been looking for them?

The conclusion followed quickly—*we're his next stop.* Geoffreys likely would kill them.

Sean considered the distance from his hiding place to the cave. Too far. Geoffreys would have plenty of time to draw his weapon.

If they wanted to survive, he had to grab Aric and go. *Now.* Backing away, he made certain he was well out of earshot before plunging headlong through the jungle. If the man had used the scanner on his belt, Sean wouldn't have escaped undetected.

Sweat soaked his shirt by the time he arrived.

"Aric?" He battered the cabin's door and crashed into the common area. Empty.

He hustled back outside. "Where are you?"

As she rushed out of the shed, he ran into her.

Sean took a quick breath. "You have five minutes to get together what you need. We need to clear camp."

No response to his panted command. Her expression grew tight. With anger? Suspicion?

"Come on. I'll explain later." He reached for her.

She avoided his swipe. "Explain these." From behind, she pulled out the hypo and medi-kit he'd hidden in the shed.

Without speaking, Sean grabbed the items. Good thing he brought them to camp. Otherwise, Geoffreys would have destroyed them too.

One item was missing—his gun.

"I'm still waiting, mister."

How long did they have till Geoffreys arrived? Hour? Ninety minutes?

"Julian Geoffreys is alive. I saw him thirty minutes ago. He's working for Barkley, Aric. The two of them unearthed a vast amount of wealth. They plan to plunder Empusa III."

Some was speculation, but he had to convince her.

Aric crossed her arms.

"You're a threat to Barkley," Sean continued. "Geoffreys destroyed all the evidence that could lock them both up. He's coming here to finish us off."

"Why should I believe you?" Her voice rang with distrust.

"I'm telling you the truth."

Still nothing.

"And because—because I love you."

Amazement melted some of the anger from her face.

"If we work together, Aric, we have a chance to nail Barkley. But if we linger, we're dead. And I need you to live."

Precious seconds ticked by as her expression softened even more.

He tugged on her arm, leading her inside. "Take

only what's necessary. Food, water..." Sean grabbed his knapsack and stuffed in blankets, the remaining food bars. When he returned to the common room, Aric held her science books and journals.

"We can't take those."

"I know," she said, face white. "But if I don't hide them, Julian will destroy my work." She wrapped them in a buffalo-hide tunic. "I'm going to put them in a spider tree fold."

Would anyone come to Empusa III to look for them? Sean couldn't let himself doubt he and Aric would get off this world. They had to survive.

He grabbed a bowl, then wedged it between the radio and the transmitter, snugly against the wall. With the volume down, he turned it on so that it would continually broadcast an emergency signal. A faint crackle was barely audible. Sean flung a towel over the equipment, hoping his contact at SARC's communications department would pick it up first and not allow Barkley to dismiss the beacon as malfunctioning equipment. A long shot, but Sean had to try.

A short time later, she returned.

"I need my gun, Aric."

She retrieved it from her room. After taking the weapon, Sean checked power levels. Everything appeared to function properly.

Brow drawn, Aric stared at him. "You handle that like a pro."

"That's because I am one." He set his jaw. "Let's go."

He's a pro? At protecting people or killing them?

Aric had no chance to ask. Not at the nearly impossible pace Sean set as they jogged through the jungle. Always several steps ahead of her, he pushed through the foliage. She knew she held him back. Her illness had drained any reserves.

Does he really love me? Or did he say that merely to persuade me?

In a short while, they reached the ridge where they'd hiked during his first weeks there. In record time, they climbed to the top. Her lungs burned and her legs felt like lead. But he wouldn't allow them to rest.

"Where...where are we going?" She panted so hard, she could hardly speak.

"Unexplored area."

Her heart pounded harder. From exertion or fear? She wanted to ask how they would survive with only knives. Yes, he had a gun, but how long could that keep the tereph at bay? Soon enough, she saw that he meant for them to stay along the top of the ridge. Did he trust that the predators would remain in their jungle habitat?

Traveling became more difficult. Huge boulders rose up endlessly before them. Aric lost count of how many they climbed over, how many times they backtracked to find passage across chasms. Her feet grew sore and her sunburned skin stung.

Sean moved tirelessly while she dragged. More than a few times, he waited at the top of a boulder, holding out a hand to help her. Never once, though, did he admonish her to hurry. Or voice disapproval for her stopping to bend over to gulp air.

At one point, while they took a breather, she asked, "Think Julian will follow us?"

"If I were him, I would."

Something about the way he said it—with cold certainty—made her shiver.

"If we get far enough from base camp, we'll be safe?"

"I'm not counting on it." Her expression must have betrayed her because Sean added, "He has a scanner. It's an older model with limited range, but we're not going to test it."

Aric clenched her teeth. A scanner? *But they're forbidden.*

Not only Julian, but Sean possessed prohibited equipment. Ironic that it once would have upset her. But not if it would save their lives.

Face set, he turned toward her. "Ready?"

She nodded. The test of endurance resumed.

Darkness finally compelled them to stop. He found an overhanging ledge under which to spend the night.

"Wait." He kept her from entering the space. After grabbing a couple rocks, he tossed them into the depths. When nothing emerged, he crawled in. Sean came out, brushing off his hands. "All clear."

Weary beyond words, she crept under the ledge. While she was deep within the black hole, his silhouette stood out in stark contrast with the starry sky behind him.

Aric cast about for something to say. "This should be fairly safe."

"Good. I didn't plan to become tereph fodder when I took this job." He sat next to her, then pulled the knapsack towards them. In the blackness she couldn't see much except his shadowy form. He shoved a blanket at her. Awkwardly, she draped it across her shoulders. Already the temperature had dropped enough to be uncomfortable. She pulled bare legs up and wrapped her arms about her knees.

Say something. Anything.

But Sean remained silent. A stranger.

Had she ever really known him?

"What...what did you do at SARC?" She forced out the words.

"I was a security officer."

She drew a quick breath, then released it. "That makes so much sense now."

"I wasn't a very good scientist, was I?"

"Actually, you were."

She caught the gleam of his smile. "What gave me away? I'd like to do better on my next assignment."

His next one? She chewed her lip. Once he'd used the word "mission." Did they mean the same thing?

"The first week you said some odd things. But over

time, you improved."

"Huh. I thought I made a ton of errors." He was silent for a few moments. "Maybe your judgment was colored."

"Colored? By what?"

"Your interest in me." He quickly added, "Or perhaps my interest in you."

Hands shaking, she pushed hair from her face. What could she say? Everything was topsy-turvy. She felt like she was hanging upside down in one of her own traps. No way down. No one to help except this man beside her. But could she really trust him?

She drew the blanket more tightly around herself. "So what's next for us?"

"First order of business—survive."

"How long do we have to keep running?"

"As long as necessary."

That didn't sound promising. Aric couldn't imagine spending an indeterminable amount of time dodging a phantom—one who most likely was better equipped and had more food. How long could they last?

"What exactly were your orders before you came to Empusa III?"

He took his time answering. "Find evidence of Geoffreys' fate. When you sent out the next info-beacon, my report would contain information about what I'd uncovered."

"Anyone could have done that. Why someone from security?"

He took so long to answer that Aric thought he wouldn't.

Material rustled as he repositioned the backpack. "SARC was convinced you were mentally unstable. That you destroyed your own supplies and murdered Geoffreys."

That still didn't satisfy. "Security is under the domain of the director." The next question *had* to be asked. "Did...did Ram send you?"

Sean's silence answered for him.

She pulled her knees more tightly against her chest.

"By now you should've figured out that I don't blindly obey Barkley." His voice was icy.

"I know." Her reply barely breached a whisper.

Unshed tears burned. She was hungry, scared and in desperate need of a good night's sleep. She couldn't think clearly. Questions pummeled her but couldn't be voiced because she feared the answers.

What did Ram order Sean to do?

Aric squeezed her eyes shut as possibilities bombarded her.

Don't think. Don't try to guess.

"As I've mentioned before, I want to take Barkley out."

She swallowed the dryness in her throat. "Didn't you say that was your mission?"

Again, he took his time answering. "Yeah, that's my mission in life."

That was not how he'd put it a few days ago. *He's a pro.* She had no doubt that at SARC he'd been a security officer. But she knew—to the depths of her being—Sean Reese was much more than that. He kept secrets. Lots of them. Secrets that would die with him before he'd betray those to whom he'd given ultimate allegiance. Whoever "they" were, they weren't in the employ of SARC.

She felt as though she'd swallowed too big of a khatseer stalk. She fought to take a slow, deep breath.

"My mission now is to keep us alive," Sean spoke softly. "Keep *you* alive. No matter what."

Why? The word would not pass her lips.

God, how can I ever believe him about anything again?

She pressed her forehead to her knees.

"Aric. I need you to trust me. If we're going to survive, you need to believe we're a team."

She raised her head. "Are we?"

"You tell me."

She thought over the last two months. No matter how hard she tried, she couldn't dismiss everything he'd done for her. Things that went beyond merely doing the job SARC had given him. Or his mission...whatever that might be. He'd tirelessly thrown himself into work. In hundreds of ways he'd made her life easier. He'd cared for her during her illness.

Did he really love her? Or did he say that to get her on his "team?" Every word he spoke was suspect. But if he could avoid questions, so could she. "What do you want me to do?"

His sigh whispered in the night. He knew she shied away from answering the real question.

"We need to put our brains together and uncover all Barkley's dirty little secrets. Fill in the gaps of what I already know. What the connection is between him and Geoffreys. Then we'll be able to take them both down."

"How?"

"I don't want you to spend your energy worrying. Please trust me on this."

Tempted to protest, she clamped her mouth shut. She wasn't the Team Leader anymore.

After reaching into his pocket, Sean held out a piece of paper. "I want you to hang onto this."

"What is it?"

"A marriage contract."

She stared at him, but in the darkness, she could see nothing of his expression. Slowly she reached for it. "Who got married?"

"No one. Yet." He spoke slowly. "This is your insurance policy."

"Please, Sean. Speak plainly. I can't understand innuendos and half-truths right now."

"I wrote up a marriage contract for me and you."

"You want to—to marry me?"

"I wrote it and signed it. I printed your name, but your signature is missing." A stone rattled as he shifted. "It's called 'spousal privilege.' This document— should you need it—will protect you."

Her heart burned. *He didn't answer my question.*

She gulped. "Protection from whom?"

"I can't answer that right now."

"If I signed this, could you tell me?"

"Possibly." He sucked in a slow breath. "But sign it only if you have to. Or..."

Or want to?

"As a last resort. If necessary." His words came out in a rush.

She fingered the folded paper.

"I wrote it up when you were sick. The second time." Sean spoke quietly. "I considered having you sign it—but couldn't. I didn't—didn't want you to..."

She wouldn't try to guess the remainder of his sentence.

As he stretched out his legs, he grunted. "We'd better rest. We have a long day tomorrow. Do you have the first watch or me?"

"I do." Her tone sounded as empty as she felt. "You sleep."

"Take this." He shoved the gun into her hand. "If no tereph come—or Geoffreys—you can always use it on me."

Without waiting for her response, Sean turned to his side. After pulling a blanket over himself, he seemed to go right to sleep.

Despite her weariness, Aric felt painfully awake. She clutched the marriage contract he'd given her. Was it to protect her? Or him? Fear from more than the immediate danger rippled through her.

Chapter 24

"Sean."

He smiled at the sensation of warm fingers on his shoulder. Aric? The sweet dream lingered. He imagined her soft body pressed against him. Murmuring her name, he reached to pull her closer.

The rocky ground, scratching his face, jarred him from sleep. Cursing reality, he opened his eyes.

She leaned over him. In the predawn light, exhaustion marked her features.

"You let me sleep too long." He sat up.

"You needed it."

He rubbed his face and stretched, puzzling over the warm spot on his back. Maybe that hadn't been a dream. Then he remembered her enmity of the night before and reasoned she merely shared heat. Nothing more.

"Take my place. You'll be more comfortable." Sean moved so she could crawl over. "The knapsack makes a great pillow."

Staring into the gray night, he rested his arms on his knees. Attuned to her, he heard every sigh, every breath she took. In a short while, she slept. Then he scooted closer to keep her warm.

Sean listened to night sounds. This planet resembled Earth in only the broadest sense. Tereph and their prey roamed nocturnally. The predator hunted in the deep jungle, far from the barren ridge. Aric had once told him if they smelled blood, even human blood, they'd go out of their usual boundaries. Otherwise, they disliked open spaces. She'd never seen them venture out onto the plains, but what about the ridge?

With thoughts consuming him, the night passed slowly. For the thousandth time he berated himself for stupidity. And for sitting around waiting for Geoffreys. As soon as Sean found evidence of the Angel Gold, he should have known the lost assistant wasn't dead.

I allowed myself to be blinded by emotion.

He shoved away the self-recrimination. What was done was done. He wasn't going to waste energy on the what-ifs. Time to concentrate on the what-now. *Survive.* Keep ahead of Geoffreys and they had a chance to live. If Sean's contact in SARC's communication department picked up the emergency signal, he'd send a rescue ship.

Two, maybe three weeks. If they could survive that long.

However, if his contact didn't pick up the signal, that meant staying ahead of Geoffreys longer. When SARC didn't get the quarterly info-beacon they'd investigate. He hoped.

Another plan flashed through his mind. Find Aric a safe place for her to hole up and then go after Geoffreys alone. Considerably more dangerous, this second plan involved some risky assumptions such as Geoffreys taking over their base and staying put. Chances were he would set up some sort of early warning device that would alert him if anyone approached. Though Sean had seen no such equipment, the enemy must have some barrier beacons to have stayed alive in the jungle. At any rate, Geoffreys was equipped with a much higher level of technology than them.

No, Geoffreys will do everything to kill us—and quickly. No witnesses.

Back to the first plan—wait for rescue. But for how long? By the time a ship arrived, he and Aric could be dead.

After climbing a boulder, he scanned the area. The man was out there, drawing closer with each passing hour. Sean felt it in his bones.

Roaming the ridge, he noted how the jungle widened in the unexplored area. The trek to the plains would take considerably longer than the one they'd taken many weeks ago. Eventually they would have to cross the jungle. But not yet. They needed to get as far from base camp as possible.

The morning grayness forced him to return to Aric. He surprised her when he bent down and peered under the ledge. She hastily shoved something under the neckline of her tunic. Had she been reading the marriage contract?

As he crouched at the entrance, he pretended not to notice. "Sleep well?"

"No."

With practice, she'd learn to block out worry and get better rest. "Let's eat and get going."

This day was like the last. Then they endured another, traveling along the ridge. The further they got from base, the more inclined Aric was to chat while they rested. Sean reminded himself to remain detached. When this mission was over, he'd be reassigned and probably never see her again. Then he inserted the word "if." *If* they survived.

Their fourth night, Sean took the first watch. Aric was beginning to look exhausted. Before she lay down, he gave her another hypo-spray of antibiotic as well as a high-nutrition injection. As she curled up against the steep cliff wall, he reconsidered their choices. Food packets were about gone, fresh vegetables and fruit consumed. They would have to plunge down into the jungle soon and scavenge. Perhaps even find an Edenoi settlement and steal food.

"Do you think we'll make it?" Aric's quiet question broke into his thoughts.

He refrained from a flippant answer. "Would take a miracle."

She sighed, turning over to face him. The light from the stars reflected off the white rock, providing enough light by which to see her expression. "Thanks."

"For what?" His tone turned scathing. "Being a greenhorn? Not having brains enough to see trouble coming?"

"No. Thanks for being one of the good guys."

Nicest compliment she could have paid me. He felt himself grinning. "I suppose you believe the guy in the white hat always wins?"

"Absolutely," she said without any hesitation.

"Thanks for the vote of confidence."

Sitting up, she extended her hand. "Can we be friends again?"

Sean held his breath as he took her warm, slim fingers in his. Then he withdrew his hand, realizing he'd begun to caress her skin with his thumb. "Get some sleep. I'll wake you in a few hours."

She didn't react immediately, but studied him for an impossibly long moment. With her loosened hair and wistful expression, Sean thought she'd never looked so gorgeous. His heart spasmed.

Sign the contract, Aric, he wanted to say. *Not because you have to, but because you want to.*

But he wouldn't allow the words to pass his lips.

In the morning, Aric opened a food packet. The last one lay in the bottom of the knapsack with trash, personal items and hypo-spray. They needed to make some drastic decisions about another food source. After breaking the bar in two, she held out the bigger piece to Sean. Before she could react, he swiped the smaller of the two and popped it into his mouth. Her protest was too late as he chewed and swallowed.

"Please have some more of mine." She broke off another portion. "I don't need much."

"I don't either." He stalked away from her outstretched hand.

Aric stared after him. What sort of man was he? With his dark blond whiskers, he looked all the more dangerous. In the last few days she'd seen a part of him that was cold, deadly and aloof. This man who stared into the distance was nothing like the light-hearted Sean she'd come to...

To what? Respect? Love? She was no longer certain of her feelings. Or his.

If the old Sean was gone, as well as his facade of being a mere scientist, then who was this man? He allowed her a greater portion of food though he needed it more. He let her sleep longer during his watch.

Sean could have done a dozen different things than swoop down and carry her away from danger, putting a bounty on his own head. Ram would find out. He'd kill them both without hesitation. The one thing J. Bertram Barkley hated above all was not getting his way.

Though the morning air grew warm, she shivered.

Sean turned. "Ready?"

After collecting their things, she slipped the knapsack onto her shoulder.

He tramped over and lifted it from her. "I got this."

Any protest faded. With wonder, she pondered the evidence that her companion wasn't a complete stranger. The man who'd lovingly cared for her while she'd been ill was still there. Though the images were blurry, she would not forget his gentle hands. How he'd tenderly held a cup to her lips as he'd urged her to drink.

"Aric, I asked if you were ready."

"Yes." She pushed the memory away.

After they traveled a short distance, he spoke. "We're going to have to cross over the top and see what's on the other side. As soon as we can find a good spot."

The ridge had grown into a mountain. Dangerous and inhospitable, the peak loomed above them. Looking across the jungle, she could see no plains, only miles and miles of trees. She shuddered to think of spending even one night there, vulnerable to the tereph. When Sean had asked her how they might fare and what the creatures' numbers were, she didn't have an answer. She'd never been this far from base camp.

In the afternoon, they found a place they could climb without too much difficulty. By evening they reached the top and started their trek down the other side.

Sean pointed out a possible Edenoi settlement in the distance. "If we hustle, we could make it there by tomorrow night." Though he spoke with confidence, Aric detected the forced tone.

"We should stop soon so we can get an early start." She too pretended she believed the sham. The plains were very far away. With the insignificant food, water and rest they'd had, she doubted they'd make it.

Again, they found a small cavern. After he scouted out the area, he announced he found water. Eagerly, she followed him to a gushing stream that tumbled over a pile of rocks. Cupping her hands, she drank until she thought she'd burst. The water tasted so good. Then she replenished both canteens.

Sitting on a rock, Sean merely watched. Feeling self-conscious, she rose and brushed away the pebbles from her knees. She caught a glimpse of his face, a soft smile playing on his lips.

That's what I've missed. His look of love.

How could she have not seen it before?

A mask slid back over his face as he rose. "While you wash up, I'll get our sleeping spot ready. I'll wait for your return."

Delight filled Aric. "Thank—"

Without waiting, he strode off. When he was out of sight, she placed the marriage contract in a safe, dry nook. Then she stripped and splashed the chilly water over herself. She longed for a bar of soap. But in their haste to leave, she'd forgotten one. She scooped up gritty sand and scrubbed herself raw. Then she rinsed her hair. When she could take the cold no longer, she stepped out of the stream.

After she washed out her clothing, she put them back on wet. Aric couldn't stop grinning when she returned to their shallow cave. Her smile widened when she realized Sean reflected her happiness.

"If that's what a bath can do for you, I can't wait for mine." Leaving the gun, he walked away.

She mentally followed him as she settled to sleep. For many minutes, she allowed herself to dream of resting in his arms.

When he returned, she noticed that he'd butchered himself hacking off his beard with a knife. Then his bare chest drew her attention. He'd taken her lead and rinsed his clothes as well, but he'd only put on his pants and moccasins. Face growing hot as his eyebrows rose, she looked away. How could she have stared at him like that? She busied herself with moving the knapsack and looked in desperation for something to do. Nothing. Camp was simple. Whoever slept first got the knapsack for their pillow.

He shook out his wet shirt and laid it over a rock to dry. Then he crawled into the small space beside her. "Tired?"

"A little."

"No dinner tonight. We should save the last bar for breakfast."

"Agreed." Aric couldn't help shivering, not so much from the cold as the stark reality that faced them on the morrow. They would be crossing the jungle, the domain of the tereph.

He moved closer. A magnet drew her nearer to him. His arm came about her shoulders. *We are merely sharing body heat.* Savoring his warmth, Aric snuggled closer.

"You sleep first." His soft baritone fell on her ear.

She doubted she could. Every atom was acutely aware of him beside her. He dragged the knapsack closer, propping it behind her back.

"There." His arm returned to its place across her shoulders. "Lean your head against me."

Without protesting, she let her head sink against his relaxed chest muscles. She closed her eyes, but even with them shut, she knew he was looking down at her. Her imagination saw his lips, parting in a soft smile.

She singled out every muscle and commanded them to rest, confident that eventually she would fall asleep. Slowly, she succumbed to the deep pull of oblivion. Her reliable trick worked again. Except her heart refused to cooperate. Wide-awake, it relished his nearness. In the space between sleep and consciousness, she felt Sean's hand softly stroke her shoulder before settling across her back. More thrilling was the tender pressure of his lips on her forehead. Against her skin he murmured, "I love you, Aric Morning Sky Lindquist."

Sleep swaddled her more snuggly in its embrace. She must rest, though every ounce of her being wanted to share a tender moment with Sean. *No.* They had to conserve strength. She must not distract him. And now

that she believed—without a doubt—he loved her, Aric
desperately wanted to live.

Chapter 25

They set out in the predawn, feeling their way down the steep mountain. When they reached the base they plunged into the jungle. The kawyas were barely starting their early morning clatter. Once Aric was relatively sure it was safe, they pushed into a jog through the dense foliage. Shoving through the heavy brush drained any strength she had recouped during the night. Sean stopped occasionally to rest. His nod signaled when it was time to go. Neither of them had the energy to talk.

As the morning brightened, the kawyas' volume increased. Banwoks, zeheeks and other creatures scurried about. Intent on crossing the jungle, she ignored everything. They had to reach the plains before night. One word pounded in her mind with each step. *Hurry.* Before the suns rose, perspiration drenched her.

The morning ticked by miserably. Aric wouldn't allow fear to cripple her. Forcing breath into her overinflated lungs, she fought to ignore her burning muscles. On they went, her tired arms no longer able to keep the smaller tree branches from slapping her. Heat built into suffocating heaviness. She gasped at the damp, thick air. The umbrella trees trapped the stillness, strangling any breeze that might give relief.

Both suns crawled into the sky, playing tag in her imagination. Which would reach the horizon first? Through the haze of endless running, she envisioned the Alpha sun losing. Weariness made her mind wander until pain thrust her back into reality.

By mid-afternoon, her confidence flagged. If they couldn't make it to the plains, where could they hide in the jungle? Any number of tereph could hunt them. She plowed through tangle rope vines while her tired legs struggled on. A handful of yellow berries, snatched on the run, provided them with a miniature respite. Sean grasped her fingers and pulled her alongside him. His shirt was soaked with sweat and his face flushed with weariness.

One sun went down. Neither commented on the brilliant violet sky visible through the canopy of trees. The setting of the sun brought an omen of death. The noise of the kawyas diminished, an audible reminder that time was running out. *Clatter, croak, shriek. Clatter, croak, shriek*. The creatures were winding down for the night. The next moment, Aric pitched forward and fell, dragging Sean with her.

For a second she lay dazed. He regained his feet and lifted her by the yoke of her tunic. "Come on," he panted. "You haven't earned rest."

If she'd had energy, she would have pushed away his hands.

"Aric!" He shook her.

Somehow her legs kept pumping. The ground flew under each step, impossibly long for her length of stride. They crashed through a thick wall of vegetation, clawing their way through the compact foliage.

She cried out when she ran into a scraggly spider-tree branch. An ordeal of unending succulents closed upon her, grasping her with fleshy fingers. Her muscles shrieked in protest. *This isn't worth it.* She'd rather lie down and die.

I can't.

A living atrocity would stalk them. Five-inch claws would rip through layers of flesh, seeking tender organs. The image spurred her on.

The second sun descended, snuffing out the kawyas' noise. Above the pounding of her heart, she heard Sean's rasping breath. Each tortuous step was accompanied by gasps of air. When she tripped again, he caught her. He put his arm about her as they pushed on, his other hand on the gun, tucked at his waist. With him at her side, heart pounding next to hers, she could go on. She anchored her fingers in his belt. Step for step she matched his gait and somehow found the stamina to keep running.

Aric heard the first cry of a tereph, voicing its territorial claim. The sound was echoed by another, somewhere deeper in the jungle. The moan of the first changed mid-cry to a snuffling rasp. It had caught their scent.

"Faster!" Her legs screamed in pain.

His pace somehow increased. The blackness of night settled over them, making it harder to see. As vision became limited, her hearing grew more acute. A second rasp came, like the snap of a naked electrical current. The sound changed to a guttural growl. The creature was zeroing in. Branches crackled as the lumbering beast stalked them.

Somehow they pushed on. Was the foliage thinning? Whippets interspersed the spider trees.

"Almost...there." She hoped Sean understood her reference to the plains, not the proximity of the tereph.

"Will it follow?" panted Sean. "Out...t'plains?"

"Don't. Know."

Five-inch claws...

The beast shambled closer, succulents squishing in protest under its weight. Aric could almost smell the stench of its rotten breath. Its moan rose to a shriek as it sensed them. The sound reverberated through her.

White. Slug-like. Folds of overlapping flesh.

The clearing had to be nearby. It *had* to be. The whippets grew thicker until finally, she and Sean stumbled onto the grassy plain. Simultaneously they fell. The pale mass of a tereph broke through the jungle, opposite from where she'd heard the first predator.

"Sean!" She scrambled to her feet.

He drew his gun and fired. The thing screeched and wheeled about.

Dragging her by the arm, he ran. She could hear the other tereph, gaining ground.

Down the hill they ran at an impossible speed, away from the nightmare. The growls of the tereph intensified as the two beasts clashed at the jungle's edge. Chilling, banshee-like screams rent the air as they fought.

Stars lighting their way, they continued to run. The short grass-like growths were easy to traverse compared to the jungle. Finally, Sean stopped. Aric plowed into him. *We're safe.*

"Enough." He collapsed.

Shoulders bowed, chest heaving, she kept silent vigil.

He finally spoke. "We made it."

Spent, she could only nod. He mirrored her weary smile.

They sat for what seemed like hours, cooling and resting. Aric's cramping stomach forced her to rise. Legs protesting, she wobbled. Sean stood and put his arms about her while she buried her face against his chest. Feeling the firm pounding of his heart, she wished she could stay there forever.

"Let's find a place to sleep." His weary voice fell on her ear.

"You mean, eat first then sleep."

"Yeah. Whatever. Anything around here edible?"

"Maybe." She staggered in the direction they'd been going, desperate for something quick.

Sean linked his arm through hers. "Where can we hide?"

"I'll let you know as soon as I do."

He plodded forward. "I don't think I can outrun anything else. You?"

She shook her head. They needed somewhere safe. That's all she wanted. "Look for a mound of dirt. Like what a Terran mole makes. But a big one."

They traveled for what seemed like hours. Relying on him to steady her, Aric dozed. She succeeded in imagining she was asleep when her feet suddenly gave way, sinking into soft soil.

"What—?" Sean beat her to the question.

"You found one." She chuckled. "The opening can't be far."

They followed the convex path to the entryway of a large burrow. Aric dropped to her knees and felt the rim of gaping blackness. "Perfect."

"Isn't the creature inside?"

"Probably. And his family. But they'll leave by the back door."

Sean squatted and peered into the hole. "You sure a tereph isn't in here?"

"Positive." She roused enough energy to tease. "I'll go in first if you're afraid."

"I think we'll have to go in together, side by side."

He looked at her quizzically.

"I don't care about anything except sleep. And this place is best."

"What about food?"

With a wave of her hand, she dismissed that thought.

Together, they maneuvered into the small opening, his legs and arms tangled in hers. Pulling the knapsack, he closed off the entrance. She swiveled until her back pressed against his chest, cheek resting on his arm. Finally, they settled.

His breath tickled her neck. Though not uncomfortable, it drew attention to the rest of him. His tautly muscled stomach and chest molded against her back.

"You want first watch or...?" She battled exhaustion.

"I..." Sean never finished his sentence.

The last thing she remembered was his lips nuzzling her neck.

Chapter 26

A stomach cramp gripped Aric. She groaned, trying to draw up her knees. Before fully awake, she thrashed to escape. Claustrophobia hemmed her in.

"Whoa, *whoa*. Take it easy!" Sean's voice sounded overly loud in her ear. "Aric. Wake up."

Then she remembered. They were squeezed into a burrow, stretched side by side like two snakes.

"That's better." Humor laced his voice. "I thought for a minute you were going to unman me."

Her face burned. Good thing she faced away from him. The view of her world was limited to black dirt, mere inches from her nose. Light gleamed through the den's opening, partially blocked by the knapsack. She sneezed. When her elbow hit him, she apologized.

"I suppose we should get up." Sean sighed. "You cooking breakfast this morning?"

"I wish."

"Let me leave this cocoon first." With a lot of grunting, he wiggled out.

He crouched at the entrance, peering over the mound. "I don't see anything except miles and miles of plains."

"Good. I was afraid we ended up right next to a settlement." After squirming out the rest of the way, she stood. She couldn't help groaning in pain.

"Legs hurt?"

"That's not the half of it." She bent and stretched her back, to one side then the other. But when she caught sight of Sean's grin, she stopped. "What?"

"You." He swiped her cheek with a finger. "You're covered with dirt."

"You're not all that clean either."

A film of black shrouded him from head to foot. His blond whiskers were swarthy, transforming his visage into a pirate's. Aric moaned when her abdomen spasmed.

"Come on." Sean held out his hand. "Let's find something to eat."

Hesitating a second, she placed her palm against his.

Dew drenched her moccasins. Slowly, the peacefulness of the morning enveloped her. She sighed in contentment. The grassy-like blades bent under their weight, but sprung up after their passing. No hint of their footprints would remain once the drying suns rose.

They soon found a bush, loaded with stringy pods. With their knives, they sliced off the fruit.

Sean made a face. "They look like giant green beans. Except bright orange isn't that appealing."

"But they're delicious. Peel it like a banana." She demonstrated. The sweet fruit melted in her mouth. "They're high in carbs, protein, and vitamins."

He grinned. Because she talked with her mouth full? Or because of her scientific explanation? After his first bite, his face lit up.

Juice ran down their arms as they gorged themselves.

"I'll take some along." Sean stuffed several into the backpack.

She hadn't the heart to tell him the fruit would soon destabilize and lose much of its nutritious properties. As they walked across the open field, she kept alert for Edenoi. They encountered tilled ground, proving a settlement wasn't far. But strangely, no one worked the lands.

"I don't understand." Aric stared at the weed-choked fields.

"What?"

"This is their primary food source. Why would they abandon it?" A chill rippled through her.

They continued walking. From the position of the

suns, she determined it was mid-afternoon, but she had seen no activity from the Edenoi. They came across field after field of immature crops. Frightened now, she quickened her steps. A clump of buffalo hide trees stood directly ahead of them. Beyond that, she was certain, they'd find a settlement.

"Let's hide in there." She crouched and peered ahead, Sean following her lead. Seeing no one, they moved forward, then ducked into the grove. Except for older, toppled trees, all vegetation had been cleared from the center. A living wall surrounded them, fifteen feet in diameter, ten feet in height.

"Are they safe?" Sean pointed to the nearest tree.

She nodded, smiling in anticipation.

With a hesitant hand, he touched the smooth hide-bark. He suddenly leaped back. "By the stars...it moved!"

She laughed. "What do you expect when you pet an animal?"

"Animal?"

"I told you it was alive."

He shuddered and made a face. "Yeah, but I thought you meant like Terran coral. Something that doesn't move perceptibly fast."

"Sorry I wasn't more specific."

When he made a sound of disgust, she chuckled. "Let's wait until the first sun goes down. Then we can check the village. I'm sure they'll have plenty of food drying."

As they waited, they took turns napping. Finally,

the first sun dipped on the horizon.

Sean pulled out his gun.

"Is that really necessary?"

"Just a precaution." He adjusted the weapon. "It's on the lowest setting with the widest spread. Should only stun to give us a chance to escape."

Aric reluctantly nodded.

In the gathering dusk, they made their way towards the village. Were the Edenoi taking some sort of holiday? Perhaps attending a feast at another settlement? Staying behind the cover of bushes, they crept forward.

From behind a mound, they peered into the small village. Buffalo-tree hides stretched over large poles. When Sean glanced her way, his smile told her he too thought of their last trip to a settlement. She watched for any sign of the humanoids.

As they waited, she neither heard nor saw anything. Unease grew.

He touched her arm, voice low. "Isn't anyone there?"

"I don't know."

"Perhaps they've gone traveling. Maybe another wedding?"

Puzzled, she shook her head.

Again they maintained a silent watch.

Impatience filled his sigh. "Wait here. I'll be right back." He handed her the gun and knapsack, then army crawled forward. Puffs of dirt rose, the fine black dust glittering in the dying sunrays. A breeze blew the dust away from her.

Filled with anxiety, Aric watched, then gasped when he stood. Any Edenoi in the village would see him. The next moment, he strode boldly into the settlement. Hunkered below the mound, she lost sight of him.

What possessed him to do that? Still he didn't return. Then she knew.

Something's wrong.

Leaving their things, she ran after him. Sean was coming out of the nearest tent, face etched with fury.

She focused on him. "What's going on? What's happened?"

"Go back, Aric." He spread his arms to ward her off.

"No. I need to..." She looked beyond him.

A body lay nearby.

His hands clamped onto her arms. "Don't look, Aric. *Don't.*"

Too late. A small cry escaped her. She struggled in his grasp, unable to comprehend what she was seeing. Finally she wrenched from his grip. Corpses drew her gaze like a magnet. They were all over.

Avoiding his attempt to recapture her and unheeding of his cry, she ran into the center of the village. As she swiveled, she saw another body, and another. What could have caused such carnage? Nearby, a child's remains lay in the black dirt. Empty, human-like sockets stared without seeing.

Her mind screamed as she looked for evidence of

war, famine, animal attacks. The torn tissue, sightless eyes, ghastly grins of death, the stench of brutally stolen life, eerie silence, decay...

She retched.

"Come away." Sean's arms wrapped around her.

Strength gone, her knees buckled.

He lifted her. Across the expanse between the hill and the village, he carried her.

"And I was worried they would see..." She squeezed her eyes shut, but couldn't block out the nightmare.

After he set her down inside the grove, he chafed her hands as though she were cold. She trembled uncontrollably.

"Those beautiful people," she whispered. "Lost."

The picture of their rotting flesh burned into her mind, the stench engraved indelibly into her senses. Flopping to her side, she dry-heaved. Then she cried, a deep wail taking hold and wringing her dry.

She didn't know how long she wept, but finally realized Sean held her. As sobs racked her, he stroked her back. Helplessness and horror consumed her until she was utterly spent.

He finally spoke. "Geoffreys did this. I figured it out. The missing link."

The only word she could manage was, "Why?"

"Greed. I found this in the settlement." From his shirt pocket, Sean pulled out an object.

Aric stared at it. "I've seen that before. On the Edenoi."

257

"It's called tazpan. Totally worthless to Terrans."

"I—I don't understand."

"It's like kimberlite. Find it and you sometimes find diamonds. Tazpan is worthless, but what is found with it is vastly precious."

"What is?"

His mouth tightened. "It's called Angel Gold because after processing, it's iridescent. The metal has some of the properties of gold but it's lightweight. The technological uses are only now being discovered."

"I've never heard of it."

"Angel Gold was located about two years ago on the Keelias IV Colony and has become the rage on Earth. It is so versatile that it can be woven like cloth. And it contains a harmless, radioactive compound that makes the wearer feel like a billion dollars."

"And it's here?" Aric still couldn't comprehend what he said.

"This planet may be filled with it. That and other priceless minerals."

She shook her head. "How is Julian involved?"

"Barkley used to monitor the preliminary surveys done on phase one planets. Once the price of Angel Gold skyrocketed, I'm guessing he went back to the early scans and found the evidence on Empusa III."

She nodded. Yes, Ram had been the division coordinator.

"My guess is he hid the findings. But you were already ensconced here so he sent Geoffreys to check everything out."

Aric shivered. "But the—the people." She had trouble saying the words.

"They're a hindrance. If this is a two-man deal, they don't want any conflict. No witnesses."

Aghast at the evil plan, she remained silent.

"Aric, remember how curious I was about your illness? I think I figured it out."

She waited.

"You got sick the first time after you'd arrived, according to your journal. No one else did."

"Right."

"But your second assistant *did* get ill. And Geoffreys didn't get sick at all."

She nodded, still uncertain where this was leading.

"What if someone in that first team put something in your food or drink? In the case of the second assistant, I think she accidentally ingested it. But with Geoffreys—now this is the clincher—he was here for weeks before you got ill."

She clutched Sean's shirt as his explanation fit the facts. "So the first infection was a trial. What about the second and third?"

"You didn't say it exactly in your journal, but you did tell me that each time you became more ill. Do you think Barkley was trying to learn how much you could tolerate before it killed you?"

"But my last bout was under two days."

"That's because I gave you a hypo of antibiotics. It took twenty-four hours to knock that bug out."

"I was Ram's guinea pig." Before thinking through

what she implied, she asked, "But Julian was gone for weeks. How'd I get sick this last time?" Wide-eyed, she stared at Sean, the only other person who had been at base camp.

His face hardened. "Why would I infect you only to turn around and cure you?"

She met his glare, ashamed she'd doubted him for even a moment. "I never believed that."

Then a memory struck. The sprung trap—the one she stumbled upon after she'd recovered. "Julian was at base camp."

"How do you know?"

"I saw a boot print behind the shed. I thought it was yours because you weren't wearing your moccasins one day."

Sean nodded, his face relaxing. "Obviously his research paid off because he found the right amount to kill the Edenoi."

Her stomach contracted. "They'd have no immunity..." Fresh tears stung. "They must've been in agony."

He gently took her hand. "You see now why Barkley can't let us live. I'm convinced Geoffreys has been communicating with him all along. Obviously he knows you are still alive."

"Why not send a ship from SARC? To track us down? Or arrest us?"

"Barkley's bound by protocols. And he wants to keep all this quiet."

Aric leaped up to pace. Anger replaced sorrow. "We've got to stop them."

He rose as well. "The best way is to return to Earth as soon as possible."

"How?"

"Wait for SARC. Or..." His gaze flickered. "For my contact to send a ship."

His contact? One of *them?* She didn't ask. "We can forage enough food on the plains or along the ecotone. As long as necessary."

"Great." He nodded. "Okay, you need to tell me everything you know about Geoffreys and Barkley."

They sat together, Aric giving him every bit of information she could about her one-time assistant. Then she shared, for the first time, all she knew about Ram.

Except the details of that one horrible night.

Sean absorbed all she'd told him, but he had a speculative look. *He knows I'm holding back.*

She relaxed when he said, "Did you know Empusa III is loaded with precious minerals?"

"Not just Angel Gold?"

"My cursory scan showed platinum, rhodium and other metals. I wish I'd checked for other commodities." He grew pensive. "They're after more than just gold. I'm sure of it."

"I've always maintained this planet is a paradise."

Nodding, he gripped his knees. "When did Barkley molest you?"

She physically recoiled. If he hadn't leaped to his feet and grasped her arm, she would have bolted.

"Don't run away. Let me help."

Heart pounding, she drew a deep breath. *I can't face*

those memories. I can't!

"I know it's hard, but I must know." Sean took both her hands. "Did he rape you?"

"No." The word burst from her. "Almost." The air pained. "We were alone one evening at the Center. Ram invited me to his office. I thought—thought he was my friend. He'd been so understanding. When we were alone," she clenched her teeth to stop them from chattering, "he pinned me on his office floor…" Her stomach roiled. "But we were interrupted."

"By whom?"

She stared at him. "A friend."

"Who was it? I need a name."

"B.J. Matheson. A division manager." The remembrance came back to her—a fist banging against the door. A voice yelling, "Are you all right, Dr. Barkley? What's going on in there?" With Ram's hand about her throat, Aric had agreed to remain silent about the incident. She'd never revealed everything to B.J., but suspected he knew the truth.

Sean's mouth tightened. "Thank you. You confirmed a long-held suspicion." She hadn't a chance to question him because he suddenly turned. "You need to eat."

"I can't."

He peered at her, brow wrinkled. "You've got to try." He reached into the knapsack and brought out the fruit.

Squelching nausea, she dutifully ate. She wanted to ask questions, but his bowed head betrayed he was deep in thought. His face was a mask of cold deliberation.

She'd seen that look before—his first days on Empusa III.

When she finished, she found a place to lie down. She wanted so much to slip her hand in his and ask him about his thoughts.

He seemed so far away, not even responding when she said, "Good night."

She squeezed out the brilliant light of the stars. Torment ate her.

I'm alone. Again.

Chapter 27

A black curtain shrouded the night. Even the stars couldn't dispel the darkness in her soul. Aric lay rigid, unable to sleep. Loneliness gnawed her, more terrible than her recent hunger pains.

Where are You, God?

Nothing. Even the plains creatures moved without sound. A void of silence filled the universe, making the desertion all the more terrible.

"Sean? Are you still awake?"

He lay facing away. When he didn't respond, she sighed deeply.

"Yeah." He rolled onto his back. His eyes glittered and reflected pinpricks of light. Though solemn, his brow remained smooth, mouth relaxed.

"Will we win?"

He flashed a brief smile. "You told me the good guys always win. Since we're the good guys, the answer's obvious."

"Tell me the truth." Elbow bent, she propped her head up on her hand. "Please."

She needed to hear that soon, they'd be heading home. Ram and Julian would pay for their crimes. In safety, Ella would grow up.

I want to be the one who raises her.

Sean continued to stare into the sky. "Look up there. With the trees around us and the stars glittering, it's like we're gazing through a giant microscope. Don't you think?"

Her throat tightened. *He didn't answer my question.*

Though she didn't have the heart, she glanced up. "I guess."

"You know; those buffalo trees are going to give me nightmares." He tucked one arm under his head. "They're waiting until we're asleep. Then the blanket critters will creep down and suffocate us."

"That's nonsense."

"Think about it." He faced her, mirroring her body position. "A couple hundred years ago, humanity dealt with bedbugs. Now we have to fight off bug-beds."

How could he joke at a time like this? She squelched tears of frustration. "Oh, never mind. Go to sleep." She flopped on her back.

When Sean suddenly scooted closer, she froze. For

several moments, he did nothing but scrutinize her.

"Good," he said quietly. "You're so worried about what I'm going to do that you've stopped being overwhelmed about our situation."

She blew out a breath. "How do you always seem to know what I'm thinking?"

"Because I know you, Aric. I've studied you. And…" His voice grew unsteady, "I've grown to love what I found." He looked away, face clouding. "But you won't let me in. I find out what you're thinking by tricking you."

Her throat burned. *How true.* Barrier beacons guarded her mind, heart, and soul.

Sean lay back, sighing deeply. In defeat?

Closing her eyes tightly, she fought with herself. Everything said to keep him at arms' length. Protect herself.

She inched closer and rested a trembling hand on his chest. Inhaling deeply, he put his hand over hers. That was all.

But that was enough.

Aric forced herself to relax. *It's okay,* she kept telling herself. *Sean's safe.*

No sooner had she started to feel comfortable, when he said, "Tell me about your beliefs."

She lifted her head. "Why?" When he frowned, she knew she was pushing him away again. "Are you serious about asking?"

"Yes. I want to know."

She chewed her lip. A test? Sean had bumped

against one of her barrier beacons. But why delve into the secrets of her soul? He could not have chosen a more private topic.

Never had his expression been so solemn. "I'm thinking, Aric, that if we don't make it—hypothetically, of course—I'm not ready to die. Hypothetically."

Emotion rose in her throat. He wasn't the invincible warrior with a heart of rock and the mind of steel. He was flesh and blood. He had fears.

This wasn't only about her letting him into her soul, but an invitation into his.

She didn't know where to start. And because she didn't, she merely began. "I feel like I've always known about God. We did the church routine when I was young. But by the time I went to college, I kind of drifted away." She paused, introspectively.

"What happened?"

She sat up, trying to recapture memories. The painful ones barged to the forefront. "I came to the end of my rope. Daddy had died. I was in the middle of my master's degree and my marriage had fallen apart. I found myself wondering why I existed." She ran her hand over the dark soil, the admission painful. "I discovered I was pregnant. Kind of awkward since I no longer had a husband. Many knew of my moral standards and would obviously conclude I was a hypocrite."

Again she paused. "On top of that, I'd signed a ten-year contract with SARC. Stupid of me. But Mitt pushed me into it. Before I knew I was going to have a baby."

"You gave birth?" Sean, too, sat up.

"Yes. She—she's seven. I haven't seen her in four years."

"Ella?"

Her head snapped up. "How did you know?"

"When you were delirious, you talked about her. I put two and two together."

"Yes, Ella." Aric lowered her head. "One night—while I was pregnant—I went for a walk. I remember feeling trapped. Hopeless. With no future. It was snowing. I traveled down this long dirt road until I was numb. I think...I *know* I wanted to die."

Sean remained quiet.

With difficulty, she continued. "I was freezing, but figured it would be over soon. So I sat in the snow. And waited." Tears ran down her cheek as she spoke. "Then I started thinking of the little life inside me. That I wasn't only going to kill myself. But her."

Awash with the guilt of that *almost,* she stopped.

He took her hand, gently, carefully.

"What I was doing was wrong. But I saw no way out." She exhaled. "I remember saying, 'God if you're really there, do something.' And...and He did."

Sean's grip tightened. "How? What happened?"

She looked at him. "It's hard to explain, but I heard this voice. No, that's not exactly what it was. I think I heard this voice inside my head. It wasn't audible. But it was real."

"What'd it say?"

The memory felt too sacred to explain. "I heard, 'Trust Me.'"

Aric expected scorn, or even mild derision, but his expression didn't alter. If nothing else, he grew more pensive.

"I can't prove it, but I know God spoke to me. I got up and made it back home. Like—like—inside I was glowing with warmth and…" She struggled for words. "Those words thawed my heart. I wasn't afraid anymore. I needed to live. I *could* live." She stopped, sniffing away her tears. "I don't know how else to say it."

Again he squeezed her hand. "Sounds perfect to me."

She met his gaze. "You mean it?"

He nodded.

"I think that's why I am so passionate about life. I was on the brink of throwing away two. God redeemed mine and Ella's. I am forever grateful."

Brow etched with emotion, his mouth puckered, then relaxed. "Do you think He would redeem a worthless junk pile like me?"

Aric sandwiched his hand between hers. "You aren't worthless. You are precious to Him. Talk to Him, like I did. Better yet, trust in Him."

"Trust…" His voice broke. "I remember Gigi—my great-grandmother—praying when I was a kid. Is that what you mean by talking?"

She nodded.

"I don't know how. To pray."

"Talk to him, like you said. Tell Him what you

think. Tell Him your fears. Ask Him for help."

"Aloud?"

"Or silently. Doesn't matter."

He pursed his lips. "Gigi prayed a lot. And she prayed over me—her hands on my head. There were two prayers, in particular, that she had me say."

Aric waited while he struggled with a memory.

"I don't recall much of one—except I agreed that I was a sinner. And I remember saying I needed a savior. After that, she asked me a lot of questions. I guess I answered them correctly because she told me I forever belonged to God."

Her heart swelled. "What about the other prayer?"

"We said it more often. She had this plaque in her parlor. The Lord's Prayer?"

"Do you remember it?"

"Some. Not very well."

"Do you want me to say it for you?"

He nodded.

Aric began, slowly leading him through the traditional prayer. At first, Sean stumbled over the words, but spoke more confidently as his memory prodded him. When they uttered "Amen" together, her throat tightened when she saw his wet lashes.

"Do you think...?" He stopped, looking away. "Do you think Gigi was right? That I've belonged to God since I was five?"

Aric carefully chose her words. "The prayer merely expresses what happens in your heart. Once you're His, you never stop belonging to Him."

"Even though I forgot about Him...abandoned Him most of my life?"

"He never abandoned you. You were completely forgiven that moment—not just for your past, but for everything in your future. Do you believe that?"

Head low, he seemed to reflect on all she told him. Finally Sean nodded. "I do. I have no doubts."

They settled back onto the ground, his arm around her while she curled to his side.

After a long moment, Sean said, "Thanks." He squeezed her shoulder.

"Good night, my love," she whispered.

"Good night." He added softly, "We're going to win, Aric. Even if I don't own a white hat."

Contented, she sighed. Everything would turn out right.

Chapter 28

Sean's sweet dream shattered when footsteps grated nearby. First he saw the blaster pointed squarely at his face, then the grim visage behind it—Julian Geoffreys.

"Don't try anything, Reese."

"Wouldn't dream of it." Mind racing, he slowly sat up.

Stupid to have not assumed their enemy would predict they'd end up there. As soon as they found the dead Edenoi, they should have gotten as far away as possible.

Sean took in the man's appearance, noting the

awkward way he held his shoulder. The scratch on his cheek. The way he favored one leg. How had he been injured?

"Aric," Geoffreys raised his voice without taking his eyes off Sean. "Wakey, wakey."

With a cry, she sat up.

Arms resting on crossed legs, Sean didn't move. He wouldn't do anything to risk her life.

"J-Julian," she stuttered. "I thought—thought you were dead."

"How sweet of you." His voice rasped with sarcasm.

"I kept hoping you'd turn up."

"So why were you checking out those animal carcasses? To see if I was among them?"

She stiffened. "They're sentient beings, Julian."

"Spare me the lecture. If you weren't so stubborn, we would've cut you in on the deal."

"I want nothing to do with blood money. You're a—"

"Could you lay off the high ideals for a few?" Sean drew the man's attention before the situation escalated. "Personally I'm sick of them."

A smirk crossed Geoffreys' face. But the camaraderie between them quickly vanished.

He motioned at Aric. "Tie him up. Hands where I can see 'em."

With studied nonchalance, Sean yawned and stretched before holding out his wrists. She took the proffered tangle rope and did as instructed.

"Make it tight. You don't want me getting rough with you." Geoffreys scrutinized her while she worked. "Now go over there." He pointed to the edge of the buffalo hide trees.

While Geoffreys watched her comply, Sean tested the tangle rope. As he feared, the smallest movement made the rope tighten.

Geoffreys spoke to Aric. "Turn around and get down on your knees, hands behind your head." After she obeyed, he limped forward and checked Sean's binding. Satisfied, he backed away, then holstered his gun. To Aric, he said, "Get up. You two have been more hassle than you're worth."

She rose. "What do you intend to do with us?"

"Nothing yet. I need to make a call."

Sean shifted his weight, working to loosen his bindings even a little. Was that why Geoffreys didn't kill them? Because he needed Barkley's approval? *Once they talk, we're dead.*

"I know about the Angel Gold." Sean purposely steered away from including Aric. "Cut me in and I'll do your grunt work. You could move into upper management and get off this crummy planet."

Geoffreys' lip curled. "I would've been already if you hadn't messed this up."

"I had my reasons."

"I'm sure." He tilted his head in Aric's direction. "Even I got a little distracted by her—"

"Are you kidding?" Sean sneered, sticking to what the man probably knew. "She wasn't selling and I wasn't buying." Before the conversation degenerated further, he got to the point. "Whatever deal you have with Barkley, I can sweeten it. Before I left Earth, I learned USF is keeping tabs on him, so he can't fence as much Angel Gold as he thinks. That's where I can help." He gauged the man's reaction. Nothing but contempt.

Ignoring him, Geoffreys turned to Aric. "Come with me." He walked unevenly to the perimeter of the trees and pointed. "My stuff is a few hundred yards from here. I want you to bring just the radio, canteen and food pouch. Got it?"

"Yes." She looked at Sean. Because their captor watched, he didn't react.

"I can see you from here, so don't try anything."

"Where exactly are—"

"That way." He waved impatiently. "Go."

She hurried off. If Geoffreys' possessions were fifteen minutes away, the jungle was only another half hour to an hour beyond that. The smartest thing would be for her to disappear into the jungle.

Be smart, Aric. Don't come back. Even for me.

After rifling through their knapsack, Geoffreys dumped everything out, again favoring one arm. However he'd hurt himself, Sean knew it wasn't an act. Why else send Aric for his things?

Slowly Sean tucked his legs. This was the perfect time to act, while she was out of danger. How far away was she? He raised his voice. "So what'd'ya say?"

"I say you should've done what you were told and

killed her."

If he knew about Barkley's secret orders, then Geoffreys was in this deeper than Sean imagined.

He noted the man's belt with a scanner and Aric's knife. Where was the other knife? How about the neuro-gun? Sean wouldn't waste energy being upset for not keeping his weapons at hand.

The scanner isn't mine. The one Geoffreys possessed was an older model. Limited range. The blaster seemed older as well, but still capable of killing. Easily.

Sean tossed his head. "I could help you fence the gold. Get you a bigger cut. I'm sure you already have a lab to process it. But with my connections, we could make this operation very profitable."

"It already *is*. And we don't need a security guard."

We? He and Barkley were that tight?

"I've not always been just a security guard." He tensed, ready to launch himself.

Geoffreys smirked. "Yeah, I know all about your one-time military career. Betting you didn't share that with Aric, though." He limped to the edge of the trees as though to look for her.

Too far away. Before Sean could get on his feet, his enemy would have plenty of time to draw his weapon.

Keep him distracted. Keep pumping him for info.

"I knew Barkley never intended me to leave after I did his dirty work. So I had a contingency plan."

"You leave a note in a safety deposit box or something?" Geoffreys snorted as he rested his sore foot on a tree stump. "Uncle Ram knows what he's doing. He picked you for a reason."

Uncle Ram? Stupid of his colleagues to have missed that. Sean discarded his original idea of driving a wedge between the two men.

"Didn't know, huh? Guess you're not as smart as you think." Geoffreys suddenly wheeled, weapon drawn.

Aric? No!

She came into the circle of trees a minute later, chest heaving. Had she run the whole way?

Forcing his muscles to relax, Sean delayed his plan to attack.

Geoffreys holstered the blaster. "Put the radio on that toppled trunk. Then go sit. Not too close to him."

She did as ordered, glancing in Sean's direction. Before he could mouth, "Trust me," their captor's head swiveled around.

"We gonna make a deal?" Sean asked.

"You have nothing we want, so no deal." Geoffreys repositioned the radio.

He raised his voice. "I left Aric alive for a reason. You should probably ask yourself why."

"Uh huh." He powered up the equipment.

"She is worth more alive than dead. To you, if not Barkley. And believe me, she's worth a lot."

Geoffreys glanced between them. "Oh? Let's hear it."

He concentrated on their captor, aware of Aric's widening eyes. "Something she kept secret."

"Sean." She sounded breathless. "Don't..."

"And what would that be?" Geoffreys now gave him his full attention.

He smiled. "If I told you, then it wouldn't do me any good, would it? Do we have a deal?"

"Tell me what you know. We'll see if it's valuable enough to trade for your life."

"Sean." Expression stricken, Aric panted his name. Did she fear he'd tell Geoffreys about Ella? Although Sean would never reveal her secret, it pained him to use her that way.

"Must be something to get her all riled up." Geoffreys looked between them.

"Get us off the planet. Then we can talk. You have a ship nearby, don't you?"

The man's cheek muscle twitched ever so slightly. *Nope.*

"Or one on its way?" Sean studied him. *Yes. Ship not too far out.*

Mind made up, Geoffreys said, "Okay, I'll see what Uncle Ram has to say."

Aric's face blanched. "Uncle—?"

"Why?" Sean challenged. "Can't take a pee without his approval?"

Geoffreys' jaw tightened. That stung, but didn't dissuade him. Without answering, he returned to the radio.

Sean strained to hear his low voice. He picked up the words, "Paradise... captured... new info... instructions."

How soon before Barkley replied? Though Geoffreys had the latest technology, the transmission and response would take time. And no doubt, the two men feared any listening ears between Empusa III and Earth.

Sean glanced at Aric, careful not to let their captor see him. How to communicate with her? How to convince her to run for it if the chance came? Time was running out.

As Geoffreys pulled a food packet from the pouch, Sean's stomach growled. Their enemy grinned as he held it up. "Thanks for extras. They're fresher than mine."

Sean played dumb. "You found my stash?"

"Yep." His expression rippled with superiority.

"Aren't you the least bit curious why I hid them?"

"That's easy." Mouth full, he nodded toward Aric. "It would've been fun to watch her starve."

"Not exactly."

"Aren't they a thing of beauty?" He held up the wrapper, its silver glinting in the twin suns. "I like the new packaging and logo."

Unable to follow the change of topic, Sean merely frowned. *This guy's psycho.*

Catching his expression, their captor laughed.

"So Barkley..." Sean pressed. "How'd he manage to keep your identity under wraps?"

"Like I said, he's smart. His half-sister adored her little brother. Didn't you know the 'J' in his name stands for Julian?"

"I thought it stood for 'jerk,'" Aric finally spoke.

Geoffreys smiled sourly. "Still can't think outside the box. Can't you understand that no one is what they seem?"

She shot a glance at Sean.

"Especially him." Geoffreys sat on a toppled tree as he unscrewed his canteen. "Did you know ex-lieutenant Reese caused the death of two Rangers under his command? Uncle Ram found out he killed them. Cold-blooded murder."

Sean twisted his lips into a grimace. "No one proved anything."

"He was supposed to kill you too, Aric. Oh, didn't know that either?"

She turned a frightened look toward him.

Their captor sputtered in mirth as he leaned back against a buffalo hide tree. Seconds later, he bolted to his feet, swearing as he glanced behind. Obviously, he'd forgotten about the trees. "Everything in this place gives me the creeps."

His beeping radio caught his attention. As he turned away with one headphone pressed to his ear, Sean watched.

"Sean," Aric whispered.

He shook his head as he concentrated on Geoffreys' body language.

Whatever their captor heard didn't bode well for them.

After setting down the headphones, their captor turned. "Good news. Uncle Ram wants to hear what you have to say, Reese, since Aric isn't going to give anything away. We'll head back to base camp immediately." His gaze didn't waver as he spoke.

Liar.

Sean relaxed his shoulders and smiled as he held out his bound hands. "Great. Untie me."

"Uh, not so fast."

He shrugged. "Okay. Let me carry something. Least I can do."

Geoffreys' eyes narrowed. "Take the knapsack after you put everything back in it. Aric—radio." Hand on his blaster, he stepped back and watched them obey. "Reese, lead on."

Of course Geoffreys wouldn't risk any of his equipment getting damaged. Behind him, Aric followed with their enemy at a safe distance.

What did Barkley tell him to do with us?

Every step brought death closer.

Chapter 29

In silence, Aric trudged between the two men. Several times she nearly asked Julian why he was limping but changed her mind when she saw his jutting jaw. It didn't matter at this point. She stared at Sean's tall form, their knapsack dangling carelessly from his bound hands. Obviously he had a plan, but what was it? She began to tremble. From lack of food? Or did worry crawl into her soul and devour all hope?

When they came upon the remainder of Julian's things, Sean slowed. "Hey, how about something to eat?" He nodded toward the bulging backpack. "I'd even take one of the older food bars."

Julian glanced at the position of the suns. "Sure. But we can't dawdle. A ship's already on its way."

Was he really expecting one? The knot in her stomach tightened.

"Great." Hands still bound, Sean fiddled with the knapsack's bindings while she lowered the radio.

"Front section." Maintaining a safe distance, Geoffreys glanced between them. From all appearances, Sean seemed completely at ease. Everything in Aric wanted to scream, *"Don't trust Julian."*

Sean flopped to the ground, leaving her on her own. With a grunt of satisfaction, he bit into the bar.

Her mouth watered while uncertainty dogged her. "May I…?"

Julian shrugged.

She moved toward the knapsack and knelt beside it.

"Mind if I have another?" Sean spoke with a full mouth as he tossed his empty wrapper to the ground.

"One more. Then we've got to go."

Before Aric rose, Sean strode to her side.

"Run when you can," came a whisper.

Had she merely imagined it? Still crouching, she glanced at him.

Suddenly he scowled. "Hurry it up." Pushing her aside, he yanked another bar out of the pack and stalked away.

Open mouthed, she stared after him as he reclined a few yards away. Julian smirked.

She'd barely sat to eat when Sean rose. "Ready to

go."

Julian pointed. "Reese, you take the big knapsack. I got the barrier beacons."

"What about the solar collectors?"

"Leave 'em. Don't really need them anymore."

Don't need them? Confused, Aric glanced at her one-time assistant. Though the radio had appeared charged when she'd retrieved it earlier, those transmissions to and from Ram had to have drained much of the power supply. It would be nearly useless now.

"Whatever you say." With a smile, Sean set out.

As she grabbed the radio, she hurried to finish her food bar. It stuck in her parched throat. She gagged, then swallowed until the dry bar slid down.

Glancing at her, Sean chuckled. The two men exchanged looks like they enjoyed her discomfort.

Did he really believe Julian would let them leave the planet? Fear coiled more tightly with every step they took, especially when she observed they weren't heading directly to base camp. Sean apparently didn't seem to notice as he hummed some inane tune.

When they reached the jungle's edge, Julian stopped them. "I want to camp here for the night. I twisted my ankle sliding down the mountain and need to rest it."

Though his injury appeared real, his words rang hollowly. Aric looked between him and Sean.

The whippets were mere feet away. Wouldn't it make more sense to travel as far as possible? The power supply of barrier beacons couldn't be good for more than one night. Not without the solar collectors.

What did Julian plan for them?

"Why not go on?" Aric asked. "We've still got several hours of—"

"Just do as he says." Sean's tone scathed as he lowered the knapsack. "Why do you have to argue about everything?"

"I...I'm..."

"You're not Team Leader anymore." He turned to Julian. "This where you want your knapsack?"

"That'll do."

"How about the barrier beacons? Need help setting them up?"

"Sure."

Sean's lip curled as he glared at her. "Why not be useful, for once. Go pick berries or something."

"No." Julian countered. "I want her close."

Aric sucked in a slow breath as understanding dawned. Was this what Sean hoped for? That she would appear so beaten down Julian would discount her?

But what about you, Sean?

"I could harvest some mathoke." She spoke in a small, apologetic voice as she pointed. "There's a patch right there."

"Whatever. Just stay in sight." Julian busied himself setting up the beacons, then turning them on. To keep tereph away? She gulped as suspicion clawed her mind. Did he intend to stay inside the small safety zone? *What about us?*

She swallowed bile as her imagination conjured up terrifying possibilities.

As casually as her shaking legs would allow, she sauntered toward the whippets. One look behind revealed the two men busy setting up the beacons in a rectangular pattern. The equipment hummed with life.

Sean glanced up, their eyes meeting. Tension flashed across his face. "Run," he mouthed before ducking his head and saying something to draw their captor's attention.

Without hesitation, she plunged into the jungle. Seconds later, Julian shouted.

Which way to go? She crashed through the whippets and stumbled across the roots of a spider tree. A thousand options crowded her mind, but she could give thought to only one.

He told me to run.

What choice did she have? Blindly, she pressed on. But where should she go? Couldn't Julian still track her? Breath coming in gasps, she pushed onward. Head toward the ridge? Base camp? Or deeper into the jungle? Whichever direction she chose, she couldn't run too far. She had to be able to backtrack and find Sean.

The next thought pounded in her head.

What would happen when the tereph emerged?

With a shout, Geoffreys drew his blaster. Hands still bound, Sean rammed him with a shoulder. With a yelp, the man fell. The weapon flew into the jungle. Was that metallic crunch from the scanner? Momentum pitched Sean sideways. He staggered, then regained his feet. As Geoffreys scrambled for the weapon, Sean vaulted himself toward him.

I need to end this. Quickly.

At the last second, Geoffreys rolled. They wrestled. Hands unhindered, his enemy deflected blows. Shielding his throat, Sean diverted jabs to his face and torso. When Geoffreys' knee caught him in the gut, he lost his hold. Again, they both went for the blaster as it lay glittering among the tangle rope.

They grappled. Geoffreys blocked his grip from tightening around his neck. As he reached behind, he wrenched Sean's bound hands, then jerked with a slashing movement. Shock ripped through Sean. Crimson blossomed across his forearm. A blade gleamed in Geoffreys' hand. Sean avoided another swipe. Averted a third. With renewed determination, he fought but it was only a matter of time before his enemy gained the upper hand. Lack of sleep, food and now an injury began taking its toll. Red dripped onto the man's chest. Sean felt the effects of every lost drop.

Geoffreys struck him, dazing him. As Sean wrested for the blade, he realized the man was going for the blaster. The knife slipped from his blood soaked grip. Already several seconds too late, Sean scrambled up and kicked Geoffreys' injured leg. The man howled in pain. It slowed him. But only momentarily. His groping hand connected with the gun. He fought to free it from the tangle rope.

Sean tumbled into the jungle.

A high-pitched whine made the hair on his neck stand up. He ducked and rolled as part of a nearby tree disintegrated. Deeper into the foliage he ran. Another whine. Goop from the succulents splattered him.

"Nice red trail you're leaving," Geoffreys yelled, voice growing increasingly faint. "Tereph will love—"

Clamping a hand over his wound, Sean kept running. As he pushed through the succulents, he felt blood pounding through his body—and out his arm. Finally, he stopped and crouched. Had Geoffreys given up? He tore his shirt and bound the material over the wound. The pain was agonizing, but he forced his thoughts to redirect.

Where was Aric? How could he find her? He listened as denseness closed around him. Nothing could be heard but the clatter of the kawyas. Deeper into the jungle he ran.

Mind growing fuzzy, he forced himself to push on. He could only hope that in the scuffle, Geoffreys' delicate scanner had been damaged. Without it, he wouldn't be able to track them. Not only that, he would have to go back for the solar collectors. His equipment needed to be recharged.

Again Sean stopped, noting with alarm that his bandage was nearly soaked. The suns, filtering through the trees, told him he had about six hours until nightfall. Six hours to find Aric. How could he contact her?

The answer came in the clatter above him. Kawyas were engaged in their never-ending cacophony. Sean had grown so used to the noise that he scarcely heard them. The one thing that would shut them up was if they were disturbed. He located a large gaggle. They hung upside-down as they buzzed around each other, huge wings flapping like automatons with missing microchips.

Sean threw a rock into the group. Immediately they stopped clattering. Some fluttered to avoid being hit, but settled down into the same tree when the missile harmlessly passed. They glared at him with beady yellow orbs.

In silence he waited, aware that with the noise of other distant clusters, Aric may not hear the void of this one bunch. For many minutes the kawyas above him were quiet. Gradually they resumed their clatter.

When they got noisy enough, he hoisted another rock. Again, silence. Stubborn creatures, they hadn't the intelligence to move out of their tormenter's range. They hung and glowered. Time crawled by while the kawyas' volume increased.

Once more he disturbed them. He was feeling weak, drained of energy. Every time he released his injured arm, it began bleeding again.

I have to rest...

He leaned his head back against the thick branches

of a spider tree.

"Sean!"

He started awake. Gentle hands raised his head while Aric crouched beside him.

"Did my phone call work?" He was hazily aware of her softness as he rested against her.

"Beautifully. Until you fell asleep. I think the kawyas planned you for their afternoon snack."

"Glad you chased them off."

Aric stroked his face. "What happened?"

He leaned into the gentle touch of her hand. "I became irresistible to the tereph."

"Let me look." She carefully pried his hand loose from his arm, then gasped. "We've got to stop the bleeding."

"Betting Geoffreys has a mender. Think he'll share?" He again clamped his hand over his wound.

"No, but tahor will help. Come on." With a strength he'd only begun to comprehend, she helped him stand. Her arm gripped his waist. "Lean on my shoulder."

He stumbled beside her. The sound of rushing water soon met his ears.

"This is the stream we encountered in the mountains a few days ago," she said. "The plant grows beside the water."

They walked along the streambed, Aric searching the muddy bank. "Ah, there."

Sean squinted, oblivious to whatever she spotted. Dropping to her knees, she dug in the wet, black dirt and pulled up what looked like fuzzy brown eggs wrapped in thick spider webs. She pulled the orbs from their netting and laid them on the ground.

"These are what give the Edenoi their silver markings." She untied his crude bandage. "I'm afraid they don't smell very good." She paused as she looked up. "And it's going to hurt."

"Go for it, doc."

She peeled one orb then split the membrane with her fingernail. The odor made his nostrils burn and eyes water. It smelled of ammonia, rotten eggs and garbage that had been in suspension too long. She squeezed the glistening gel onto his wound.

The sensation of acid crawled across his flesh. The torment intensified until he clamped his jaw to strangle a primeval cry. It felt as though the gel burned into his bone and crawled up his shoulder. Panting and shaking, he fought to resist plunging into the cool river.

Sean waited to speak until he could control his voice. "And the Edenoi purposely smear themselves with this?"

Face pale, she didn't even crack a smile. Her tender heart must hurt for him.

"We should put more on. Just in case."

"All right." He gritted his teeth in preparation. "You sure you aren't getting even with me? For the way I talked to you earlier?"

This time she managed a small grin. "I knew you were faking it."

When she split open the second egg case, it burst,

splattering them both with silver. This application didn't hurt as much. Was the wound already sealing?

"Now what?" He gingerly placed the bloody bandage over his arm.

Her expression filled with anxiety as she retied it. "Keep moving. And pray we can reach safety."

"Let's head to the ridge. I don't want to run into Geoffreys." Sean wouldn't chance going toward the plains.

"I'll take extra tahor." As she spoke, she slipped four pods into the neckline of her outfit. They made an interesting picture as they slithered inside her tunic, stopping above her belt.

He had to ask one crucial question. "Is there anywhere safe from the tereph?"

"Perhaps in a spider tree, but I've never tested my theory." She pointed to the squat vegetation. "They could easily break these lower branches. We might find a root fold higher to hide in, but they can climb as well."

"Okay then." Taking a deep breath he said, "Let's go."

They stayed beside the stream where travel was easier. Did the water run on a direct path to the mountain ridge? He'd not glimpsed white rock through the thick trees.

When he slowed, Aric slipped her arm about him.

I'm weaker than I thought. With every step, his feet grew heavier. More than once, he found himself drifting, unable to jog a straight path. She tried to hustle him into a faster pace, but Sean was unable to maintain the speed. Finally, he stopped.

"What's the matter?" Her brow wrinkled with concern.

He had difficulty forming words. "You go on. Find somewhere to hide. Survive."

Her face hardened. "If only one of us gets out alive, it should be you."

If he let her, she'd do something foolish like sacrifice her life for his. "Then we're in this together."

Her face relaxed. "That's right. And don't you forget it."

More slowly now they progressed as the day wound towards dusk. Sean was ever aware of the fleeting hours.

"I gotta rest a sec." The words rasped from his throat. If he didn't, he'd have no energy when night came.

Without answering, she tugged on his arm.

"We're not going to make the ridge." His own negativism surprised him.

"Yes, we are." She literally pulled him along.

He marveled at how well they complimented each other. When one of them was down, the other was full of confidence. Because of his injury, Aric had become the strong one. But she couldn't possibly carry him through the jungle. He forced her to stop.

"I can't go on." Legs wobbling, he slumped against the trunk of an umbrella tree.

Face twisting in fear, she helped him sit. "Stay here.

I'll see if I can find some food."

He melted onto the moist ground as weariness claimed him. Thinking became too difficult. He didn't regret the loss of his own life, but Aric's. She deserved better. His mind wandered, landing on fragments of memory before hazing.

From what seemed a great distance he heard, "Sean. Open your mouth." He tasted something soft and sweet. They were like grapes, or cooked tapioca, huge and melting on his tongue.

Aric knelt beside him. "I hit the jackpot. These are related to the fruit you watched me pick the first day we met."

He smiled. "You knew all along."

"I suspected. Have more."

He ate what she offered. Soon they were gone.

"Sign the contract and register the marriage." Sean gripped her hand. "My money. Everything. It's all yours."

"Don't talk that way. You need to live."

"My parents will love you."

Surprise flit across her face. "They're alive?"

"Siblings too."

"I can't wait for you to introduce us." She tried hauling him to his feet.

"Aric, wait."

She crouched before him. "What is it?"

He grappled for energy. "You're beautiful."

She smiled. "Flatterer. I'm covered with filth and smell bad."

"And I need to tell you that I love you. In case…"

Her lashes grew wet. She touched his cheek. "We've got to go."

She slipped her arm about him and helped him rise. Together, they staggered on. The first sun slid under the horizon. A short time later, the second sun followed. The kawyas fell silent. In a matter of minutes, a tereph's guttural growl told him it was already looking for them.

Chapter 30

Sweat stung Aric's eyes as they stumbled through the jungle. *Please no.* If she prayed hard enough, nothing bad would happen. The first cry of the tereph filled her with horror. The last time they'd crossed the jungle, they'd started out early and Sean hadn't been injured.

She refused to let Ram and Julian win. *We have to survive.* Her breath ripped through her lungs with each step. Sean sounded worse as she urged him to a stiff jog.

The moan came again, closer now. Then a snuffling rasp. The beast had picked up their scent.

"The stream," she panted.

The fading light couldn't disguise the pallor of Sean's face. Sweat-laden hair plastered his forehead.

They plowed through cold water, stumbling over uneven stones. In the middle, the stream leveled out at a little more than knee height. She dared not let Sean's arm get wet, fearing the wound would bleed again. If only the water were higher and faster, it could have transported them out of the jungle.

Trembling with exhaustion, they waited. A white form soon emerged from the trees. Aric recoiled. In the early evening light, the tereph appeared to glow, like a gargantuan slug. Hairless skin folded on top of itself and hung down the creature's sides. It stood on all fours, olfactory glands under its fangs twitching. Clearly it hesitated to plunge into the water.

Leaning in to Sean, she spoke low. "Don't move. They have poor sight and hearing."

The tereph paced along the bank, stepped into the water, then backed out. It raised its muzzle high, testing the air, returning to the spot closest to them. Snuffling changed to a pitiful whine. In the distance echoed another guttural growl. She couldn't help but shudder as her imagination conjured up a dozen tereph lining the banks. *Don't panic! Don't move!*

A second, larger predator came into sight, noticed the first, and immediately attacked. As they clashed, their screams echoed through the jungle. Slashing with huge claws and fangs, the beasts mauled each other.

The smaller one broke away, but the other didn't follow. It took up the loser's post.

This one snuffed and paced, but seemed less intimidated by the water. The beast took a couple steps toward them before retreating.

"I have a feeling this one won't give up easily," Sean whispered.

Again the creature stepped into the water, moving closer. And again, it backed out.

Her mind raced for a plan. "Take off your bandage. Behind me. Slowly."

She feared that the creature would charge if Sean moved too quickly. Once on a rampage, the tereph wouldn't let water hinder it.

Sidling behind her, he did as she bade. Aric could feel him struggle to undo the bandage and heard his grunts of pain.

"Okay. Off."

"Ball up the material. Fling it as far as you can."

Aric waited, gaze never leaving the beast. The predator stared in their direction, its limited vision unable to see what its nose sensed. Behind her, she felt Sean tense, then catapult the bloody bandage away.

The tereph let out a shriek, stepped toward them, then followed the wadded up material as it sailed overhead. In seconds, the beast pounced on it.

"Come on." He grabbed her arm.

While it was distracted, they plowed to the other bank. They plunged through the wall of vegetation, back into the jungle, leaving the gurgling water behind.

"Over here." She grabbed Sean, pulling him toward a huge spider tree.

Behind them, the beast splashed through the water. The taste of blood had made it brave.

She helped Sean navigate the stiff root system, aware the growls of the tereph grew louder. "Hurry. It's coming."

Up high, she found a pocket between the dense roots that was large enough for them both. "Get in." She broke off a dead root to use as a weapon, then wedged herself into the small space next to Sean.

God, please...please help.

When cold wetness crept down her belly, she shuddered. What new horror lived there? As odor burned her nostrils, she understood. Two tahor orbs broke when she squeezed between the roots. Gel oozed down her thighs.

"If the tereph has any problem finding us," Sean said, "I think you just set off the red alert."

Aric didn't reply. Any words of hope stuck in her throat. The tereph was close. At the base of the tree? She tried to slow her panting. Heart racing, her grip tightened on the stick.

But for some reason, the predator didn't climb the root system. It made its way around the base. Moans turned into guttural whines.

"Something's wrong," Sean whispered.

The beast continued to circle the tree.

"Of course!" The answer suddenly came, filling her with elation. "It's this dye. The odor obscures our scent."

"But it still knows we're here."

"Maybe because of the blood. Quick, your shirt!"

He struggled to remove it. "What are you—?"

She grabbed the material and squeezed out of the space.

"Aric!"

She ignored his cry. This was her one chance to make certain he survived. Since the tereph would zero in on blood, she could lead it away with Sean's shirt. As long as he smelled of blood, he remained vulnerable.

She leaped down the root system while the tereph was on the other side. A sharp snuff told her it picked up the scent. Flapping the fabric, she raced away.

Behind her, guttural sounds grew in intensity. Aric found a spider tree and flung the shirt as high as she could. Then she ran off. She had to get back to Sean. Two dye eggs still remained unbroken in her tunic. She would use them as insurance.

Knees trembling, she gave the beast a wide berth. In the dark, she had trouble finding which tree they'd climbed. Finally!

"Sean?"

"Here!" He stuck an arm out of the folds of vegetation.

Aric climbed up quickly. After she squeezed inside, he enveloped her in his arms. Holding her, he buried his face against her shoulder. With difficulty, she slipped her arms about him.

"Don't ever do that again." His voice caught. "I thought—"

"That I'd lost my mind?" Euphoria edged out fear. "No, Mr. Reese. You can't get rid of me that easily."

He squeezed her tightly.

We can survive the night. If they were careful to avoid Julian, they could return to base camp in time to send a live info-beacon. Help would soon be on its way if it wasn't already.

Now they had a chance to stop Julian Geoffreys and Ram Barkley.

Chapter 31

The clacking of the kawyas worked like an alarm. Aric jerked awake, agonizingly aware of her cramping muscles. Beside her, one arm still draped about her, leaned Sean.

"Good morning." Bleary eyes focused on her. "I never thought I'd be so glad to hear the kawyas."

She moaned, head flopping back. Every part of her body ached. She longed for a comfortable, sturdy hammock. After a bath. Didn't matter if the water was cold.

When he rested his forehead against hers, she

smiled.

"We did it," he murmured. "We found the secret of living in the jungle. It's a miracle."

"It *is* a miracle. I prayed and God..." Emotion overcame her.

Sean awkwardly stroked her hair back from her face. "I prayed too." His face was full of wonder. "And—and we lived."

Humbled and grateful, she could only nod.

They climbed down the roots. In spite of his injury, he reached solid ground first, then helped her. When she slipped, he caught her. She remained in his arms, in no hurry to rush into the day.

His lips moved against her temple as he spoke. "When we get back to Earth, I'm going to teach you the right way to climb trees."

"I'd actually like that." She smiled. "Let's find some food." They'd slept longer than she thought. If she could call the hours they'd been wedged in the spider tree *sleep.*

"And we need to find some more dye eggs. Then we go after Geoffreys."

"Do we have to? Can't we—"

"No. I'm certain Barkley already sent a ship to pick him up. I have to get his radio equipment so I can send a message to intercept."

"How?"

He shook his head as though unwilling to explain. "First things first—food, water."

After she located more fruit, they sat together on

the cool jungle floor. They quickly consumed the berries, but found no more nearby. Her stomach grumbled. Sean must be starving. If only they could return to the plains with its abundance of food. When she mentioned that to him, he shook his head.

"No time," was all he'd say.

No time for what? If Ram sent a ship and it left Earth yesterday, that gave them a good two weeks. Why the hurry all of a sudden? Sean was planning something. His expression had regained a grim determination that frightened her.

She led the way back to the stream where they both drank. All the while, he surveyed the area, never letting down his guard.

"If only I had the vegetables in my garden." She sighed, trying to lighten the mood.

"Probably dead by now." He didn't look at her while he spoke. "We would be too if Geoffreys had his way. But I'm not giving him another chance."

Dead. Death. She gazed at Sean's fierce expression. Did he mean he was planning Julian's death? Sean would show no mercy.

"We need those dye eggs."

She merely nodded. As they walked down the streambed, she looked for the signs of the buried plant. Again she was successful. Splitting one open, she smeared Sean's back with it.

"Phew!" he complained. "Makes my nose run."

"The tereph will steer clear from the amount you're wearing." She smoothed the silver across his chest.

"But Geoffreys will smell me a mile away."

She spoke slowly. "Then it's a good thing we'll be many miles away. On the plains."

"No, Aric." His mouth settled into a hard slash. "It ends here. Tonight."

Her throat constricted. "Are you going to kill him?"

When Sean didn't answer, she looked into his face, hand resting above his heart. His expression grew so unyielding she withdrew her fingers.

"Aric, I've got to finish the job."

"Job? You said your job was to get evidence. Right?"

His answer came slowly. "True."

"What does killing Julian have to do with that?"

Sean grasped her fingers, his grip tight. "You really want to know?"

Did she? The grim set of his jaw made her gulp.

"I'm an operative for the Universal Security Forces. My mission was to infiltrate SARC. Specifically, to befriend Barkley, then take him down. By any means at my disposal."

"USF?" The lump in her throat expanded. When she'd left Earth, USF was already a formidable organization. What was it now? "So Julian was right. You are a killer."

She shivered at the flinty look on Sean's face. Who was this man? Recently she'd seen a side of him that shocked her—a man that could become anything. He'd so successfully fooled Julian that he'd let down his guard, giving her a chance to escape.

"Did you believe what Geoffreys said about me? About my murdering two men under my command?"

She drew a deep breath. "Not—not entirely. But I don't understand."

"It's not true, at least, not the way he said it. Two men did die. I was the fall guy. But I didn't kill them."

Kill them? She heard the emphasis on the second word. Not *them*, but others. Government-sanctioned killing wasn't really murder, right?

She was going to be sick.

A mask of impassiveness slid over Sean's face. "I am a hired killer, though." He spoke in a matter of fact tone, his fingers moving against her hand. "USF doctored my bio so I could get into Barkley's good graces. Lucky for you, I came here instead of someone else who may not have had any qualms about carrying out orders."

"To kill me?" Aric's thoughts flitted through the puzzle pieces. Julian's words. Sean's confession about Ram sending him.

"Yes."

"Did you ever plan to carry it out?" She stared into his face, praying he wouldn't lie. His grip tightened almost imperceptibly.

He took his time answering. "Yes. At one point, I did."

Though she'd already guessed, the shock of hearing him speak the truth still made her stomach spasm.

Infiltrate SARC...by any means. That's what Sean had said. Any means? Including assassinating an innocent person? Her throat burned.

"Only if I was convinced you'd murdered Geoffreys." Sean's mouth pulled to one side. "I was going
to be judge and executioner."

Aric licked dry lips. "So that now gives you the
right to murder Julian?"

"I tend to think of myself as an enforcer of the
law." The muscles in his cheek flexed. "If you put me
in the same category as Barkley and Geoffreys, you've
got a warped sense of morality."

His tone and tight grip on her fingers hurt. Lack of
sleep and food as well as the dangers of the last week
pressed upon her.

I need to get alone. Go someplace I can think. And pray.

Her knees quivered. The shivering crept up her
body until she feared she would collapse.

"Sean, please—*please* don't kill Julian." Her throat
grew so tight she could hardly speak. "Capture him.
Let him be tried for his crimes, but don't—please don't
murder him. I couldn't bear it if..." She bit her lip
when Sean's jaw jutted.

He spoke through clenched teeth. "You ask too
much."

Her soul shrank. Had she only imagined his softening? Their conversation about God? Could this fierce
man with a relentless determination to extinguish life
really be the gentle giant who had tenderly cradled
her? Julian wasn't the issue. The thought of Sean planning his demise, then coldly carrying it out pained.
What would happen to her love for him?

He released her. "Put some dye on yourself, then we'll go."

Numb to her soul, she did as ordered. She dug up extra eggs, then followed him. Though full of questions, Aric didn't dare ask one, afraid of the answers.

Along the way, she found other edible plants. A small patch of whippet trees by the river provided mathoke.

He pointed to a huge spider tree. "We'll rest there."

Without a word, she climbed the root system and found a fairly large fold. Together they sat side by side. After leaning back his head, Sean appeared to doze. Taking his cue, she folded arms across drawn-up knees. But she couldn't sleep. She longed for his arm about her. Breathing inaudible, he remained motionless.

Later while he slept, she crept down to hunt for more food. A few overripe honeypods were the only things she could scavenge. When she returned to the tree, he started awake. Wordlessly, she gave him the fruit, then settled back into the cramped space. The afternoon rushed toward evening, then a sun blinked out beyond the hidden horizon.

The second sun melted away. The cries of the tereph began. Though she was confident of their security, Aric couldn't help trembling. She rested her head against the tree, listening, thinking, praying about her future. *Their* future. Darkness spread across the sky.

Stirring, Sean rose.

She reached toward him. "Where are you going?"

"I'll be back in a few hours." His tone carried a heavy secrecy. "Give me one of those dye eggs."

She dutifully pulled one from her outfit.

"Get some rest, but don't go anywhere."

"I won't."

The grayness of the sky outlined his form, but his face was a black void. "If I'm not back by morning, stay away from the base. Return to the plains. Keep moving. Don't stay too long in one place."

"Can't I wait for you?" Her question burst in a rush of air.

He didn't answer. Aric wished she could see his expression.

"Goodnight." He turned to go.

"Wait," she cried.

He immediately stopped.

"Please." Her throat constricted. "Please be careful."

"Always." He disappeared.

"Sean..." But he was oblivious to everything but the course set before him. The spider tree creaked under his weight. Then, silence.

Burying her face, Aric wept.

Through the night she dozed. Every time she thought she heard Sean, she jerked awake. Time and again, the moans of the tereph made her shiver back into consciousness from the dark abyss of sleep. Never had a night seemed so long or so lonely. If only he would return, take her in his arms and…

Tell her what?

He said he was an operative. The word was synonymous with killer, phantom. That Sean belonged to their ranks, she had no doubt. Everything made so much sense now. Under the layers of masks, she saw the true man. He was an assassin, trained and molded into an instrument of vengeance, sabotage or whatever mission they deemed necessary.

What would happen if they survived Empusa III and returned to Earth? What if he truly wanted her to be his wife? She imagined herself sitting in some metropolitan home, waiting for his return. Could she welcome him with open arms if he had blood on his hands? The idea made her ill. What if her daughter fell in love with Sean—a father she'd never had—then she learned the awful truth about him?

Thoughts and emotions collided. Sleep forced the pain deeper. Reality and reverie blurred. All night, she fought nightmares. Her mind filled with corpses and a faceless man with red hands.

With a shriek, she awoke. Soaked with perspiration, Aric shuddered as she grew more wakeful.

Sean didn't murder the Edenoi. Julian did.

Though she reminded herself of the haunting truth, she couldn't block other thoughts. Would Sean have killed them if USF had ordered him? Sniffing back tears, she massaged the knots in her neck.

As the morning brightened, a new nightmare awaited. He had not returned.

Chapter 32

In the darkness, Sean vacillated about which direction to take. He climbed the nearest umbrella tree and peered over the endless jungle. The night settled into eerie silence, the moans of the tereph absent for now. Very little light filtered through the foliage. The stars were not yet shining their brightest. He slid back down.

After taking out a dye egg, he broke it and smeared the gel over his wound. He rubbed the rest over his chest.

Aric's distressed face hovered in his mind. *"Don't kill Julian."*

How could she ask that? Did she want Geoffreys to take another shot at them? No way. The man should be tortured. Did she forget the Edenoi he'd murdered? Who knew how many other settlements the man had wiped out.

As Sean planned his enemy's demise, a number of possibilities flickered through his thoughts. He'd string up Geoffreys, then let the kawyas at him. They'd kill him slowly.

Out of the blue, words from the Lord's Prayer seared his mind. "Forgive us...as we forgive our debtors..."

"After what he's done?" Sean looked upward.

Then he realized he'd spoken aloud. To the One who listened.

He dropped the empty shell. No, Julian Geoffreys deserved to die.

Okay, I'll give him a quick, clean death.

Again, he wrestled with that one line. Sean wiped his palms on his pants. They suddenly felt clammy.

Aric's green eyes shimmered into his memory. *"That gives you the right to murder?"*

If he killed Geoffreys, she'd find out. Their relationship would never be the same.

Sean struck off in a direction, not even aware of where he was going. His plan once seemed so simple. Not anymore. Technically, he'd not been ordered to eliminate Julian Geoffreys. He wasn't disobeying orders by not killing him.

Then what motivated him? Personal vengeance?

Sean leaned a hand on a tree. *She's right. In good conscience, I can't do it.*

But could he capture the man and bring him to justice? His colleagues at USF were experts in prying truth from an unwilling party. The information they got could cement their case against Barkley.

However, he knew the danger of attempting to apprehend Geoffreys.

Sean had to try, even if it cost his life.

But he wouldn't risk Aric's. If he failed, he had to ensure she lived. Never would he put her life in danger again.

He had to attempt this alone.

Up another umbrella tree he climbed, peering across the vast jungle. In the distance an artificial light flared. *Gotcha.* From the location, he ascertained Geoffreys was returning to base. Because he believed them dead?

Sean clambered down.

Though he was sure he remained on track, he climbed trees several times to verify the distance. He didn't want to overshoot the campsite. As he drew closer, a plan formed in his mind. Sneak into camp, grab a gun, then hold Geoffreys hostage. A breeze was blowing toward him, which would keep the dye odor from announcing his arrival.

Sensing he was close, he did a half-circle sweep. Where were the barrier beacons Geoffreys had undoubtedly placed? If Sean crossed the invisible beam, he might trigger an alarm. The beacons made little noise beyond the muted snap of energy. In the darkness, their dull indicators would provide a little help.

He stopped when he heard snuffling nearby. A tereph? Apparently it hadn't picked up his scent. If it hunted Geoffreys, then the beacons had to be somewhere very close. As the creature advanced, Sean froze.

The predator came within fifteen feet of him before it rose on its haunches. Claws gleamed like slick, bloated termites. Sean tried to slow his rapid breathing. Sweat poured from his forehead while his heart felt like it was going to hammer out of his chest. In the black night, the thing was huge, pale, ugly. Opening its mouth, the creature revealed massive teeth in a wagging jaw. What appeared to be olfactory glands also twitched, testing the air, searching. The stench of rotting garbage swept over Sean. As bile rose in his throat, he clenched his teeth. With a *garumph*, the tereph lumbered off.

Stomach still heaving, Sean crept forward. He finally spotted a metallic gleam, braced against a tangle rope tree. Slowly, he approached the equipment, trying to determine what warning system it used. The type was unfamiliar to him, probably a new device that SARC had recently developed.

Barkley had been keeping more than a few secrets.

After examining the equipment, Sean grew confident that the configuration was very much like the beacons he'd brought to Empusa III. He pressed a switch and the equipment powered down. However, he didn't know if this one received or sent the beam.

Maybe both. To be certain, he would have to disable another one. And quickly.

The second was more difficult to locate. Sean searched, then backtracked when he decided he'd missed it. The hunt seemed to take hours. He suppressed a frustrated growl. All the while, he grew aware of time disappearing. Finally, he discovered the device, lashed to the root of a spider tree.

After he shut it off, he headed toward the light in the center of camp. Foot by foot, Sean crept forward, crouched, then listened for any sound that might betray Geoffreys' location. He hoped the man was sound asleep by now. As he drew closer to the lamp, he fixed his attention on the figure that lay motionless beside it.

The site was well chosen, with a large open area for Geoffreys to spread his gear and still have enough room to comfortably sleep. Spider trees surrounded the small clearing, providing a wall of security. Besides the knee-high foliage, the fibrous strands of tangle rope trees drooped. Geoffreys had cut many of them so that his view would remain unobstructed.

His radio was set up, as though he'd recently used it. Sean noted the food supply, dangling high in the tree. His own knapsack lay a few feet from the lantern. With his gun and knife in it? He fixed his attention on the pale green canvas.

Geoffreys appeared lost in sleep, bedding pulled over his head. Even with that assurance, Sean moved stealthily forward, stopping often to listen. If the man made a move, he would duck out of sight. But Geoffreys seemed to sleep like a rock.

After stepping from behind a spider tree, Sean made his way toward the knapsack. The succulent growth squished quietly under his moccasins. *A few more feet.* Gaze glued on the form, he reached for the knapsack. He froze as he imagined the slumbering man twitched. From his distance, he could hear Geoffreys' soft breathing.

Sean waited, paralyzed in a half-crouch. With no sign of the man awakening, he lowered himself more. The lamp momentarily blinded him as he got on the same level of the glowing beam. Learning forward, he went down on one knee.

At last! The rough material was within his grasp, his fingers tightening on the flap as he quietly edged the sack toward him.

From behind Sean came a soft, wet protest from a succulent plant being crushed. Still kneeling, he hadn't the mobility to swivel about quickly. He turned his head. Nothing. The sound stopped. Then a whispered movement in front of him drew his attention back to Geoffreys. Too late! His enemy sat up, blaster pointed at Sean.

"You!" Geoffreys' eyes narrowed.

The next second, he looked beyond Sean to the sound of sloshing wetness. Without thinking, Sean vaulted himself at the distracted man. The blaster fired harmlessly past his shoulder. He dove for the weapon, but Geoffreys swiveled, using the momentum to his advantage. A knee in his chest catapulted Sean to one side.

The next second, a mass of white filled his vision. The stench of rotting garbage billowed through the camp. A tereph charged directly at Sean.

Chapter 33

Aric waited, spirit flagging with every passing hour. Where was he? A torturous conclusion assailed her—Julian had killed him. Despair cascaded over her.

Sean had ordered her to go back to the plains. Until when? Until Julian or someone else hunted her down? Without Sean's testimony, USF wouldn't know what he'd found. Julian and Ram would go forward with their carnage because no evidence of their heinous crimes would be brought against them.

I have to do something.

Determination elbowed sorrow aside. She had to get back to base camp. Back to the radio still there. Had to contact B.J. Matheson—the one person who would believe her—and tell him everything.

But what if Julian was waiting? He would kill her. Without hesitation. Aric shuddered violently at the thought, then grew calm.

I can't run away and hide any longer. I have to do what is right.

Mind made up, she headed toward the mountain ridge. She walked with a resolute stride, but also with caution, aware that Julian could be somewhere close.

By the early afternoon she came across a shredded piece of material. Aric examined the fabric. From all appearances, it looked like a portion of Sean's shirt that they'd left for the tereph. Why had it carried the material so far away? She dropped the cloth and walked on. A short while later, she found another piece. Because of the amount of blood, she didn't pick it up.

A knot formed in her stomach. Something wasn't right. This couldn't be part of the shirt she'd flung as a decoy. As she stared at the evidence, she realized it was pant material. The world narrowed to a gray tunnel while her breathing came in gasps. Sean! How had he fallen victim to a tereph? She shut out the picture of a gruesome death.

Clenching her hands, Aric rose. She had to get to base camp to send the message. As she walked on, she found more proof of the tereph's predation. Rusty red smeared the ground. Something large had been dragged over the roots of a spider tree. A human body? Bile rose in her throat.

Following the grisly trail backwards to the point of origin, she soon came to what appeared to be a campsite. Had Julian spent the night there? As she stared at the crushed vegetation, she saw signs that a tereph had been within the area. Had it merely come and scavenged?

A portion of torn blanket draped the ground. The soil was gouged, vegetation pulverized, and...

She gulped when she saw more blood. Sean's?

Not like that. Please, no...

Pressing her palm to her forehead, she willed her world to balance. Aric again examined the camp, trying to understand what had occurred. But not enough evidence remained for her to do more than speculate. She found no clue of which direction Julian had gone. Did that mean he deliberately covered his tracks?

He must suspect she was following him. As she contemplated the journey back to base, her courage faltered. As long as Julian was unaware of her plans, she had a chance. But now...

A faint crackle reached her ears. She scrambled up the nearest spider tree. The soft whisper of a moving body came in her direction. She waited.

I was stupid to come here!

Holding her breath, she peered through the massive tangled branches.

A form stepped through the wall of foliage.

"Sean!" She shimmied down the root system, scraping knees and hands.

In moments, she was in his arms, crying and hugging him. He dropped the knapsack and embraced her.

"Little fool," he chided. "Geoffreys could've held me at gun point to flush you out."

"I feared you..." A ragged breath consumed her.

Sean stroked the tears off her cheeks with his thumbs. Then he hugged her tightly once more.

"Oh, my love." Her words squeaked in relief.

Again, he pulled back from her to look into her face. His smile vanished. "Geoffreys is dead. A tereph charged at me, but at the last minute went for him. I watched it drag him off..."

She took a deep breath. "I suspected."

Still holding her, he looked about. A shudder ripped through him. "Let's get out of here."

With her in tow, he pulled her along, a knapsack on his shoulder. After they were well away from the campsite, he pulled out a couple food packets and handed them to her. They trudged on. For over an hour, they traveled side by side without speaking. Aric noted his haunted look. What had he seen?

"We can't be more than a few miles from the ridge." Sean spoke without looking at her. "When we get there, we'll talk."

She then noticed he wore a shirt. Julian's? The fabric stretched across Sean's chest. Their green knapsack bulged with items. What had happened? He'd tell her when he was ready.

"Comfortable?"

"Sure." Aric pulled a rock from under her thigh and tossed it aside. In the early evening light, she examined her scraped knees. Then she looked around. Hadn't they camped here before?

Sean handed her a food packet and canteen of water. Brow perpetually pensive, he'd barely spoken all day. Her heart went out to him.

"I hope never to see anything like that again." The light of the setting suns glittered in his eyes.

"Julian's death?"

He nodded.

"Do you want to talk about it?"

Sean passed a hand over his face. "When I tracked him last night, I kept thinking about what you said. It would've been so much easier to kill him." He blew out a breath. "But I decided to capture him. So I disabled two of his beacons."

When he paused, she asked, "And?"

"I must have triggered a warning of some sort because when I reached camp, he was waiting."

Aric could guess the rest. "He didn't know they were out?"

"No. We struggled for his gun, but neither of us saw the tereph until too late."

"The dye must have saved your life." Or had God decided?

"I've never..." Voice faltering, Sean shook his head.

"I couldn't find the blaster. Couldn't stop..."

She already knew the horrendous details. Then she heard what he said. By his own oversight, Julian killed himself.

"Why are you looking at me that way?" Sean asked.

Pressing her lips, she didn't know where to start.

His brow lowered. "More importantly—why didn't you head back to the plains? I had quite a job tracking you down."

"You found me, though."

"That doesn't answer my question."

Aric studied him, the man she loved, the man she would do anything to protect. "When you didn't come back, I decided I had to stop Ram."

"Go on." It was Sean's turn to prod.

"My plan was to return to base camp and radio SARC. Even though it's early, the relays are about lined up. I had to try to get a live message through."

"It was a good one. And that's where we need to head." Without elaborating, he stowed his trash.

She handed him her empty food wrappers. "What's going to happen once we get there?"

His jaw flexed briefly. "I'm not a hundred percent sure."

She gulped. "Will Ram have men waiting for us?"

"Doubtful."

"USF?"

He didn't answer, but his tensing shoulders let her know that's exactly what he suspected. Or feared?

Why should Sean grow anxious about his employers waiting for him?

Unless...

All the reasons why *they* would be unhappy sprang into her thoughts. Because he hadn't done what they ordered? Because he deviated from the plan?

Or is it because of me?

She cast about for a safer topic. "What happened to the rest of Julian's equipment?"

"I hid it. We need to travel light since we have a lot of ground to cover."

She nodded, unable to come up with a reply.

"I used his mender on my cut." He rolled up his sleeve. A jagged white scar shone through the silver dye. "It's nearly healed."

"That's great." She managed a pleased smile.

Brow pinched with worry, he glanced at the sky as the Alpha sun ducked under the horizon. Sean let out a slow breath. "Let's sleep. I'm wiped."

She was more than willing. Before she lay down, he handed her two blankets. Without a word, he settled with his own bedding, back to her.

For a while, she lay awake, wishing he would open up to her. Soon, his breathing deepened.

As exhausted as she was, sleep eluded her. One question hounded her. Did he regret the rash decision of writing up a marriage contract?

Chapter 34

In the morning, they arose late. Food was plentiful, thanks to Julian's supply. However, Aric found herself constantly on edge. Disinclined to talk, Sean pushed them, almost as hard as when they'd been fleeing from Julian. What was the hurry? The future loomed ever before her like the jungle at night, shrouded in darkness, impenetrable, unseen dangers lurking.

One day passed, then a second and third, all alike in strained silence. By the time they stopped for the evening on the third night, she vacillated between wanting to sleep and wanting to scream.

"How much further?" She paced as she ate a food bar.

"We should reach camp before noon tomorrow." Biting off a hunk of the bar, Sean seemed to take excessive interest in the wrapping. Suddenly he burst into laughter.

Aric stopped in front of him, sure he'd lost his mind.

"Oh, don't mind me." He crumpled the wrapper. "I just realized I'm denser than a grav-ball in a tournament."

She frowned as she sat.

"I was admiring the wrapper." Sean held up an unopened bar. The metallic packaging was emblazoned with a name: *J-Bar*. "Hmm, I wonder what the 'J' stands for."

When he didn't elaborate, she shrugged off his odd comment. She rose again and paced. The question *had* to be asked. "Sean, I need to know what's going to happen once we reach base."

His brown eyes fixed on her. For the first time in days, a hint of a smile played on his lips. "What do you want to do when we get back?"

Confounded, she said the first thing that popped into her brain. "Water my garden?"

"Huh." He ran a hand over his cheek and chin. "First thing I want to do is shave."

She frowned, feeling more out of her league. "Tell me, why did USF get involved with investigating Ram? Isn't that a bit unusual?"

Sean's expression closed. "They've expanded their interests. Especially now that Intergalaxia is growing in power. Barkley is taking the competition very personal."

He took so long to continue that Aric said, "Go on."

"Remember my asking you who kept Barkley from raping you? You told me it was B.J. Matheson."

"Yes. But what does he have to do with all this?"

Sean put the wrappers in the knapsack. "Matheson died two years ago in a freak accident."

Her legs suddenly couldn't hold her. She sank to the ground. "B.J.? Dead?"

"Yes." His jaw tightened. "I didn't understand...I'm sorry."

"I still don't..."

He reached over and squeezed her fingers. "Barkley's name was loosely connected with the incident. USF launched an investigation but found no conclusive evidence. When Barkley stepped into the director's position, the suspicion escalated since Matheson had opposed his promotion."

"And B.J. would've talked." Aric lowered her head and stared at the uneaten bar clenched between white fingers. B.J. had been her friend, one of the kindest men she'd known at the Center. For him to die because of Ram...

Guilt washed over her. She should've said something. Should have revealed what kind of man Ram was. She'd been so ashamed, she never imagined where her silence could lead.

"I'm sorry." Sean released her hand. "Were the two of you...?" He too seemed to have trouble finishing his sentence.

"B.J. was a good friend." Hunger evaporating, she put away the rest of her food.

Scooting back, she leaned against the rough wall and stared across the expanse. The stars were beginning to shimmer through the sky's gray veil, white rock reflecting light. Behind Sean spread the black abyss of the jungle. High on the ridge, she couldn't even hear the moans of the tereph. The evening was utterly still, dead.

I'm so sorry, B.J. She should have renounced Ram back on Earth. Years ago. Her friend had a wife and two darling children...

Sean brought out the blankets, then settled against the wall beside her. For a while, they both looked out into the deepening dusk.

"Who is Ella's father?" His question ripped through the stillness.

She stared at his profile. Why ask that now?

"Was it Barkley?"

"No." The word burst from her. "I already told you—"

"I know what you told me, but I need the truth."

"You think I lied?" Passion fired the question.

"I merely want to know who her father is."

She looked away.

"Was it Matheson?"

"Don't ask me." She pressed her palms to her temples. "I can't..." Then she understood.

Did he believe her daughter was conceived by

some casual lover? No wonder he suspected her of deceit. The truth would preserve her honor, but also give her ex-husband a weapon he could use against her.

Sean spoke quietly. "Why won't you tell me?"

Rebellious tears burned. Why, oh why did he have to make this personal? Ella had come into existence long before Sean arrived on Empusa III.

"Aric." He murmured her name, the sound heart-rending.

"She's Mitt's daughter." She jumped to her feet. The story poured from her as she stalked away then back. "He abandoned me—abandoned us—before I discovered I was pregnant. He was tired of our marriage, tired of me. I didn't tell him, because it wouldn't have made a difference. He used me and my family. Then moved on."

The bitterness in her tone surprised even herself.

Sean's voice echoed off the wall behind him. "So you're punishing him."

"No. He doesn't want her. I know he doesn't. And I won't let him hurt her the way he hurt me." She scrubbed tears from her cheeks. "Ella means everything to me. I can't let Mitt take her. I won't let him."

He remained silent.

Finally, she looked at him, sitting so quietly.

He rose. "Pretty lame revenge if your ex doesn't even know he's being punished."

The truth of the statement hit her. Was she really punishing Mitt? Or herself?

When Sean's arms came about her, she stiffened.

"I'm not your enemy, Aric."

Still she couldn't melt. Her fists remained clenched as they pressed against his chest.

"I love you."

Her rigid defense started to relax a tiny bit. Her elbows bent a little as she stopped pushing so forcefully against him.

"Can't you trust me? Even if I smell bad?"

A nervous laugh escaped. "I probably stink worse."

"I believe that dubious honor belongs to me. After all, I was the last to rub myself with the dye."

"Then it's a toss up." Tension slowly began to ebb. "The last bath we had was on the same night."

"Aren't you getting tired of primitive living? Don't you wish for modern conveniences, even luxuries?"

The question was one she'd long ago ceased to ponder. Her life on Empusa III had consumed her, especially when she feared SARC had abandoned her. But now that she had choices...

"Well?" Sean tilted her head back with a gentle finger.

If she were to protect the Edenoi, she would have to leave. On Earth, she could fight most effectively for them. Most importantly, if Sean was going to depart, she couldn't stay. Her heart belonged to him.

And Ella...oh, to be with her daughter again. To no longer have to hide her little girl. To openly acknowledge her.

Aric's fingers moved restlessly against his shirt. "Yes. Will you take me home?"

The brilliant starlight gave enough illumination to see his soft smile.

"Absolutely." He gently caressed her cheek. "The next question is, do you want to go as a Lindquist or a Reese?"

Her pulse hammered through her as all her earlier worries dissipated. "Is this a marriage proposal?"

"Actually, my second to you."

"Second?" She shook her head, confused. "When was the first?"

His grin was sheepish. "When you were feverish."

"How did I answer?"

"You were delirious…with happiness. I think your exact response was, 'Sure, love to.'"

"Really?"

He took her hands. "Please believe that I want you to be my wife. And would you allow me to adopt El-la?"

Aric grew rigid. That meant Mitt would find out about their daughter. "No. I have to keep her safe."

"Won't you let me help?" Sean's hands slid up her forearms.

Not too long ago, she'd cried her heart out, yet he'd helped her to face the unfaceable. He demonstrated he was unlike any other man she'd allowed to get close. He loved her. How could she forget that?

"Can you trust me? To protect you both?" His caress grew mesmerizing.

She whispered, "Yes." She quickly added, "Yes, to the first question."

He smiled. "And the second?"

A picture of Sean and her daughter, meeting for the first time, flashed through her mind. Would he kneel so they could be on eye level? Aric imagined him picking her up so she could ride on his shoulders. Playing hide and seek. Even coloring.

How would her little girl react to having a father?

How will she react to me being her mother?

Aric gulped. "I'll have to think about adoption."

"Fair enough." He tilted his head. "By the way, where's the marriage contract?"

"Here." Aric fished the folded paper from inside her tunic. "It's probably ruined. The dye got on it."

He took the silver-streaked document. "You know, I just happen to have a pencil, thanks to Geoffreys. Would you consider signing the contract? It'll make great memorabilia."

"You want me to sign it now?"

He didn't answer, but strode to the bag and looked inside. With a flourish, he handed her the pencil. He carefully unfolded the document and spread it on the sheer wall. "This should work for a writing surface."

She glanced at his smiling face, then scrawled her signature. The writing on the rest of the sheet was barely legible. However that didn't seem to matter to Sean. He dated the document—ten days prior. Then grinning broadly, he folded the sheet and put it in his shirt pocket. "I plan to frame this someday—and hang it right next to the adoption papers."

Aric opened her mouth to protest, then shut it. She

hadn't the energy to argue anymore. Or desire.

When he again sat, she remained standing before him, suddenly uncertain. And nervous.

"Sit before you fall over." He held out his hand. "You look exhausted."

She slipped her fingers into his and settled beside him.

"Lean against me, my love."

She pressed her cheek to his shoulder, tension dissipating.

"Don't let worry keep you awake." His soft voice caressed. "It'll all work out. I promise."

She sighed. "Really Sean, you don't have to right all the wrongs of my past."

The low rumble of his laugh reassured her. "Well I can try, can't I? You assigned me a new role. I'm the hero in your story, remember?"

Chapter 35

Ram Barkley permitted a self-satisfied smile as he climbed the exterior stairs to SARC headquarters. Stopping halfway, he viewed the magnificent panorama behind him. Fluffy white clouds dotted the peaks of the Olympic Mountain range. Puget Sound appeared even more brilliantly blue. His bodyguards waited, faces tense as they too turned. The longer he paused, the more nervous they appeared.

Without speaking, he continued his way to the building.

All was going as planned. The second shipment of mathoke had arrived and was already being processed for the new J-Bars. The food industry was going nuts, raving about their superior nutritional value. Everyone thought the supply came from Gemena IV. As director of SARC, he would keep them believing that.

The stocks of the company he and Julian had set up overseas were skyrocketing with the exclusive rights to process the off-world food source. Not only that, but the secret plans to mine Empusa III's vast mineralogical wealth were progressing nicely.

Ah, Julian. The idiot child had finally proved useful. Only a few loose ends to tie up.

His nephew's last radio transmission said that Aric and Reese had been killed by predators. Their deaths would unquestionably be ruled accidental. The preliminary reports about the planet's safety would be reexamined.

How to word the announcement of their deaths? The report would have to contain the right amount of alarm so that the planet would be abandoned as a dangerous ecosphere. And the right amount of regret. After all, Ram and Aric had been good friends.

He nearly chuckled aloud at the thought.

On the second floor, his bodyguards left him. Alone, he traveled to the fifty-first floor in his private elevator. His mind was abuzz with anticipation. By that afternoon, he fully expected to hear from Julian. Now that Ram had successfully quashed the alarm over the unexplained emergency beacon from Empusa III, he anticipated no further problems with that planet. Or Aric.

Kelli Layne was waiting for him when he reached

his floor. He nodded to Gloria and the other assistant. What was his name? The young undergrad who was so hot to elevate his career? He abandoned the thought as Kelli's short skirt distracted him. *Nice.*

"Good morning, Dr. Barkley." She spoke with a little more warmth than usual as she followed him into his office.

Could she finally be softening toward him? The months of persistence were finally paying off.

"Good morning, Ms. Layne." He allowed himself a slow perusal of her outfit once they were alone. "I see you took my suggestion."

"Yes, sir." She blushed and glanced away.

He found the gesture sweetly innocent. "I'm pleased you take my preference seriously."

Her eyes shyly met his and her voice came out barely above a whisper. "I'm glad to do what you wish."

His heart skipped a beat. Did she recognize his life would soon make a dramatic turn? Perhaps the rumors about his deteriorating marriage had hit the gossip pages.

"What's my itinerary today?"

Kelli stated his schedule from memory. Such a sharp young woman.

"No meetings during lunch." She smoothed the skirt in a self-conscious manner when he stared at her legs. "Would you care to have a meal delivered to your office?"

"That'd be great." He preferred eating alone to entertaining simpering idiots who sought favors. A quiet lunch would be a welcomed change.

But Kelli seemed to have other plans. "If you like, I could bring the notes from the Xerxian file for us to go over before the meeting with Intergalaxia this afternoon." A bright pink stained her cheeks.

What was she asking? Ram sucked on his lower lip and pondered the implications. "The free time between lunch and the meeting should be plenty."

"Oh, I thought..." She patted a stray blond strand at her temple.

"If you believe we need more time, by all means, we should meet." He wasn't going to miss an opportunity since she suggested it. The office, after all, was soundproof.

"I'll have them ready." Without waiting for his dismissal, she hurried from the room.

Through the morning, he conducted business, rewrote the speech his public relations department drew up, confirmed appointments with government officials and argued with a department head about new contact protocol. Four hours disappeared in mind-boggling bleariness. At long last, Kelli escorted in the caterers who delivered roasted herbed prairie chicken—his favorite.

They laid out the meal on a table wheeled in for the occasion, two chairs accompanying the setup. The doors closed and Ram and his assistant were alone.

Kelli cleared her throat. "I'm sorry if I overstepped my bounds, Dr. Barkley, but I told Gloria she could take her lunch break now. She wanted to run a couple of errands too, which I said was all right."

"No problem." He detected a faint nervousness. What was this young woman planning? "Please. Help yourself."

While he seated himself, she served them both. As she leaned over, he tilted his head to watch her. "I'm sorry I've been preoccupied of late."

"No doubt you've a lot on your mind." She sat.

"Have you heard rumors about my private life?"

"Yes." She spoke in a low voice before nibbling on a wheat-sprout roll.

"What was your reaction?" He'd meant to be blunt.

Her hands shook as she set down the bread. "I think...perhaps your wife made a mistake."

"Mistake?" Anxious not to err, he let Kelli do the talking.

"I hope you don't mind my frankness, Dr. Barkley. But I've known you for almost a year. I don't understand why your wife would want a separation."

Pursing his lips, he allowed sadness to filter over his face. Kelli would never hear of their arguments, his wife's protestations of his affairs, her complaints of emotional abuse. She'd been too well paid not to spill to the press now that they'd separated. She wouldn't endanger the promised settlement once the divorce finalized. Lately he'd begun to think marriage had been a horrible mistake. Because of Kelli's softening toward him, he wasn't so sure. This was so good, he'd have to use it on one of his other conquests-in-progress.

"I'm sure you've been aware of our estrangement for quite some time." He paused, waiting for her response.

Kelli nodded, blue eyes wide with sympathy.

"My wife," he said slowly, so very carefully, "suspected that I am in love with someone else."

She sucked in a sharp breath, her lips puckering into a surprised "oh" at the obvious implication.

Examining her face, Ram leaned forward. "You knew that too, right?"

Her chest rose and fell, but she seemed unable to tear her gaze away.

"Can you guess who that is?" He inserted the right amount of huskiness into his voice.

The wetness that sprang to her eyes and her quivering lip surprised him. "I'm sorry, Dr. Barkley." She spoke in a strangled tone.

"Please. Call me Ram."

"I didn't mean for you to fall in love with me. I don't want to be the cause your divorce."

"It wasn't your fault." He patted her hand, allowing his fingers to linger. "Let me share something with you. Can you quiet yourself for a few minutes while I explain?" He didn't want her to dissolve into weeping.

She dabbed her lashes with a napkin.

"My wife and I married for political reasons." It wasn't often he got a chance to tell the truth. He repressed the urge to chuckle at the irony considering the plethora of lies soon to follow. He sought to relay them with care, mixing enough truth to make them believable. "Though I didn't love her, I hoped that something magical would happen between us. I didn't know it at the time, but she wasn't interested in me from day one."

"But—but you have a child together."

He shook his head, pretending to be ashamed. "The boy isn't mine. I know it might come as a shock to you, but she and I never..." He let the gargantuan implication sink in, averting his gaze as though mortified. "I did—and do—intend to raise him as my own, though."

"How noble."

"So you see, our separation means little. I couldn't handle any more of my wife's infidelities."

"So you...?" Kelli blushed.

"I couldn't even look at another woman." He paused, hoping the timing was right. "Not when I'm in love with you."

She shot to her feet, but she didn't scurry away. He too stood. Very gently, but firmly, he pulled her into his arms. *Proceed slowly.* He couldn't help his mind from leaping ahead. When he tried to kiss her, she broke from his embrace.

"Please. This is too fast." Holding up her hands, she backed toward his desk.

Consumed with the imminent conquest, Ram stalked her. "You can't stop this, Kelli. Admit it. You're in love with me as well."

She glanced behind her as though she'd find the answers on his desktop. "I don't know."

He grabbed her wrist. "Don't be afraid. You love me, don't you?"

She nodded slowly.

"Give in to your feelings. Let me love you."

She trembled, her lower lip catching in her teeth. "I can't." She glanced toward the windows.

"We're perfectly safe. No one dares enter without my permission. If you want, I'll lock the doors."

"No!" The suggestion alarmed her.

"You act as though you don't trust me. That you don't believe me."

"I do, Doctor—Ram." The look on her face was now pitifully tragic. "Please don't say that."

"Then give in to your feelings." He fastened his fingers around her arms, pulling her against himself.

"But your wife—"

"I want you to be my wife." A woman like Kelli needed that reassurance. He added the final argument that would make her his. "I can't live without you."

She whimpered as he took her lips, hard. That's what she needed. A man who'd overcome her inhibitions.

His ring caught her silk blouse, tearing the delicate fabric. Though she didn't outright resist him, she backed toward his desk. As she leaned away from him, her fingers brushed a command button on his desk. The cameras outside his office activated.

Though her body blocked his view, the partial picture distracted him. Four men were running down the corridor, unescorted by SARC's security team. Immediately, he grew alarmed.

"Voice command," he said. "Lock—"

A blow caught him in his windpipe. Ram reeled away from the desk. Kelli?

She'd lost the frightened look of a timid secretary. Her expression tensed in determination as she faced him, heedless of her torn blouse.

He coughed and attempted again to command the computer. His voice cracked like a twelve-year-old kid's. The men drew closer. He staggered toward the desk to manually key in the sequence.

Crouched in a defensive posture, Kelli blocked his path. He attempted to shove her out of the way. With the expertise that went far beyond a mere assistant, she deflected his blows. With no time to plan, he rushed her. Her slim frame could do little to stop him. He knocked her down, but she grabbed him. Together they fell. Rolling on the floor, she chopped at his arm, then seized his leg from a kneeling position.

Fury fueled him. He rained her with blows. Shielding herself, Kelli released him. Ram shot to his feet, but his triumph was short-lived. A kick to his groin felled him instantly.

He groaned. The doors burst open. Two men grasped his arms. Force-field cuffs hummed into activation, immobilizing his arms and legs. He lay paralyzed.

"You okay, Kel?" One of the men bent over the prostrate woman.

"Yes." She massaged her neck. "What took you so

long?"

"The judge gave us trouble. But we got the warrant."

"Who—?" Ram fought to speak. His body might be shackled, but he wouldn't surrender without a fight.

The men ignored him. The leader helped Kelli to her feet while she salvaged her blouse.

"I thought you took care of everything." Her eyes flashed blue steel. "You gave me the go ahead." With one hand planted on her hip, she looked nothing like the shy woman Ram had courted.

"Sorry." The man shrugged apologetically. "My fault. When we got the call, we thought we had a tight case."

Kelli flung blond hair from her face. "Hold a sec."

From his position on the floor, Ram couldn't see what buttons she pushed. "There. Now the system can't be verbally locked." She walked over to his hidden panel and tapped on the wall. "Behind this, you'll find more than enough evidence to send Ram-boy to the Dzardian penal colony."

"You have no right," he rasped out. Ram coughed, attempting to relieve the inflammation in his esophagus. "I'll have you—"

"Shut up." The man closest booted him.

Ram stared. Wasn't he one of SARC's communications techs?

"Is it safe to escort him out?" Kelli asked.

"Oh, yeah. We've sufficiently intimidated the entire security department. They all know a little cleaning is in order. And not the kind housedroids do."

"What about the head of security?"

The leader shook his head. "Got away."

"I'll have Senator Sherman string you up by your thumbs." Ram coughed again.

"Save your breath," Kelli said in a curt tone. "Once the senator finds out about Empusa III, he'll pretend he never heard of you."

"Empusa III?"

"Yeah." She managed a grim smile. "You know Lieutenant Reese or, I should say, *Senior Agent* Reese? His testimony, plus Aric Lindquist's, will be enough to convict you for all your nasty crimes."

"Aric—?"

"Actually," one of the men interrupted, "I hear it's now Aric *Reese*."

Kelli looked stunned. "Seriously?"

"And without us first giving him a bachelor party. Go figure."

The other men laughed.

She made a face. "That's because he knows you too well."

The reality of the situation began to sink into Ram's mind. Aric? Not dead? Then what about his plans?

"Might as well get the legal aspect over with," Kelli said. "Then let's get out of here. I'm sick of this place."

"I'll bet."

"Oh, another thing." She planted a fist at her waist. "Remove those cameras Ram-boy placed in my apartment a.s.a.p. I want all the discs, too. Your lab boys don't need to preview them."

He grinned, then stepped up to Ram. "You have the right to remain silent…"

Chapter 36

"What is that?" Aric gripped his arm when they reached the outskirts of base camp. Were those voices?

"Nothing to worry about." Sean took her hand.

"But..."

Urging her forward, he ignored her protests.

As soon as she saw the half-dozen uniformed men—USF agents—she cringed. They apparently expected them because a sharp-looking man of Asian descent saluted Sean.

"Afternoon, sir."

"How many times have I asked you not to salute me, Jayd?"

The agent grinned. His dark eyes swept Aric. With his short-cropped hair and spotless uniform, she was suddenly aware of how awful she must look. Her face grew hotter as his nose wrinkled.

"By all that's sacred, what's—?"

"Not another word," Sean cut him off.

"Yes, sir. Wasn't planning to." Jayd snapped to attention again. *"Sir."*

"You can drop the 'sir' as well. Aric's impressed."

His lips twitched. "Glad to see you're both all right." He stuck out his hand. The two men shook.

"This is Aric Lindquist Reese." Sean turned. "Aric, my good friend, Jayden Song."

She could only manage a nod in the man's direction. Aric Reese?

Jayden scrutinized them both. "I heard that marital bliss did things to a person, but you actually seem to be glowing. In a silvery sort of way."

"Long story. Which you'll have to wait to hear." Sean crossed his arms. "Any word from HQ? When nobody intercepted us on our way back, I'd hoped..."

"Everything's A-OK." His friend smiled, glancing between them. "You two are heroes."

Heroes? Aric's jaw went slack, completely out of her league.

Sean blew out a breath of relief. "Not that I ever doubted..."

"Of course not. Your favored status had nothing to do with my eloquence when I argued your case." Jayden smirked.

"Whatever." Sean waved his hand.

"Your status could have something to do with the fact that the director stepped down."

"You're kidding." To Aric, he looked more relieved than shocked.

"Officially retired." Jayden again glanced at Aric. "He saw the handwriting on the wall, so to speak. Especially because of you."

Heat flooded Aric's cheeks. However, she managed a small laugh. "I hope no one wants an interview with us looking like this."

"Which reminds me..." Sean cleared his throat. "Did you get the things I asked for, Jayd?"

"Mostly." His friend cleared his throat. "No women were assigned for this trip, unfortunately. I wasn't able to get some of the more, err, delicate items—"

"Never mind." Sean crossed his arms.

Jayden signaled to someone by the cabin while Aric watched, puzzled. Another man brought a knapsack and exchanged it for theirs. Sean nodded and grasped her elbow, speaking over his shoulder to Jayden. "I'll see you later."

"Yes, sir." Again ignoring Sean's wish, he gave special emphasis to the title. "If you need any help—"

"No."

"How long will you—?"

"That is all, Agent Song," he yelled as he hustled Aric away.

"Where are we going?" When they were well away from camp, she finally got a chance to ask. "And what did he give you?"

"You'll find out."

It didn't take long to discern they were heading toward their pool. "Good idea."

"What is?"

"Bathing before you see your boss."

"Actually, I *am* the boss. And they do what I want, which is allow me some privacy to get rid of this filth."

"Oh." She allowed herself to be pulled along. "How did they know we were coming? And how'd they get here so quickly?"

"I used Geoffreys' radio and told Jayd to meet us there. It was simpler. As far as the timing of their arrival—well, apparently USF took my earlier communication very seriously."

"What communication?"

"When you were ill. Jayd relayed my message to our supervisor who immediately acted upon it. Apparently, an unexplainable amount of Angel Gold—and other minerals—showed up in the market. All indications pointed to Barkley. But when USF started to dig, he backed off. My report confirmed something big was going down and they dispatched Jayd that day."

She shook her head. "You could have told me."

"Truthfully, I only found out a couple days ago. And I wasn't a hundred percent certain of what reception we'd get when we arrived at base camp. When no one intercepted us, I figured we were golden."

"You still could have given me *some* assurance."

He grinned. "It was more fun this way."

"For you, perhaps."

"You need more fun in your life. Lately, you've been too serious."

"Me?" She made a sound of derision. "You're the one who's been as quiet as a dead kawya. And now you dare to..."

She couldn't say anything more because Sean swung her around and gently put his hand over her mouth.

"I intend to show you a more pleasant side of life, Mrs. Reese." His roguish smile made her breath catch. The first sprouts of irritation withered under the scorching rays of promise. When he removed his hand, she had nothing to say.

"Okay?"

She could only nod. Her throat was so tight, she couldn't speak.

When they reached the swimming hole, Sean unpacked some items.

"Liquid soap!" She exclaimed in delight.

"It doubles as shampoo. Here. We have two bottles." Sean tossed her one. "Some of the men donated shirts and pants. I'll leave them here with the towels."

"I don't need..." Embarrassment seized her. And nervousness.

Before Sean said anything more, she slipped off her moccasins and dove into the pool. She paddled to the pool's other side where a small beam of light found its way through the umbrella trees. Aric sat on a flat rock, under the warm beacon. Luxuriating in the wonderful lather, she painstakingly untangled her braided hair before washing it twice.

The sulfuric odor from the tahor continually overpowered the floral scent. She sniffed her hands. Why did they still stink? She scrubbed them, but the silver dye remained. And the smell of rotten eggs.

"Pretty bad, isn't it?" Head bobbing in the water, Sean swam up to her. Though he was clean-shaven, the silver also marred him. She could see it on his neck and part of his chest.

"Your men won't be able to stand being near us." She took another whiff of herself and wrinkled her nose.

"Pity. We'll have the cabin all to ourselves." Sean grinned, then rubbed her ankle. "Don't you want to bathe?"

Her heart did a nervous pitter-patter. "I thought we were here for a swim."

"If this were a swim, I'd still be wearing something."

Aric drew an impossibly long breath. Gold light dancing in his eyes gave him a rascally look.

"Come on." His hand caressed her skin. "I'll even wash your back."

Heat flooded her face. "But your men—"

"Wouldn't dare disobey my orders."

She gulped.

"Come, my love." Sean gently tugged.

"Wait." How best to form her request? "I need to

ask…promise you won't be mad at me?"

"I'm only allowed to get mad at you once a month. And I already used my quota."

She licked her lips. "Do you think the captain— your ship has a captain, right? Do you think he would mind performing a wedding?"

Sean's brows rose. "I'm sure he'd be glad to."

"I'd really—well, I'd like a wedding. One where I'm coherent for the ceremony."

A smile curled at one corner of his mouth. "I can arrange that."

"It's important, Sean. To me."

"Well, then, I'd better leave you alone so you can finish up."

"Thank you." Relief flooded her as he swam off.

In no time, she'd finished bathing. With his back to the pool, Sean waited at the edge while she dressed in the loose shirt and pants. She cinched the belt tightly, studying his broad shoulders. Her heart began to slam against her ribcage as she anticipated their evening together.

When she approached, his raking assessment made her cheeks warm.

"You look…" He stopped and cleared his throat.

"Like a blushing bride?"

"Well you have the blushing part down. I don't think a USF uniform is standard issue bride's wear."

"Or the silver skin?"

"Umm-hmm. This will be a unique wedding for sure."

"You mean I shouldn't expect hugs of congratulations?"

He immediately scowled. "They'd better not hug you. Handshakes will be more than adequate."

Aric couldn't help but laugh. Then she sobered. "You sure you want to do this?"

"Are *you* sure?"

She pressed her lips together to keep her welling emotion from spilling through a gush of words. Instead, she merely nodded.

"Then let's go."

Hand in hand, they headed toward base camp.

"Will USF allow you to take time off for a honeymoon?"

"They'd better. If not, I'll retire."

"What if they won't let you?"

"Then I'm thinking a career at SARC might be more agreeable. Especially since it's going to have a different director."

"But what about—?"

"Aric." He stopped, putting a finger over her lips. "You ask too many questions."

"I just want to know—"

"You'll *always* want to know. That's why you're a scientist."

She giggled.

Face softening, he touched her cheek. "It's good to see you laughing again."

"I'm glad to have a reason."

"Before I forget—or you ask—Ella and your mother

are safe."

Relief washed over her. "Thank you."

"Agents were dispatched to protect them until this mess with Barkley is over."

She placed a hand at her hip. "Speaking of bosses, why didn't you tell me you were in charge of this operation? You would have spared me all the worry about what might happen—"

"Because you'd find something else to worry about. I was merely redirecting your thoughts."

"When we're married—I mean, after we get married again—we need to be honest with each other. You said you'd tell me your secrets if I told you mine, remember?"

"I, indeed, said that." He bowed his head.

"Well, it's your turn."

He crossed his arms, chin sunk on his chest. "I'm done with field work. As soon as I'm debriefed, they'll agree. I've had a change in my belief system. Now I answer to a higher authority. If they won't give me a desk job, then I'll move on."

"Really?" Hope welled up at the thought, eradicating her one nagging fear.

"You've taught me so much, Aric. I couldn't promise 'to have and to hold' if I didn't respect all that you love and cherish."

"But what will happen to Empusa III once word gets out?"

A small grin flitted across his lips. "Well, Ms. Science, I hear Intergalaxia is flexing its muscles. I get the feeling they will back any law you suggest to protect planets like this. And cram it down SARC's throat. So the Edenoi will develop naturally."

"Really?"

"I—and USF—will support you one hundred percent."

Her heart swelled with tenderness. "Yes, I do."

"We're going to make a formidable team, Mrs. Reese."

"Then let's get back to base camp and make the 'Mrs.' part official." She shyly added, "And in more than just name."

His eyes shone. A muscle near his mouth spasmed as he looked away for a moment. Then he gently took her hands and pressed his lips to them. "I've wanted to hear you say that. So badly. You have no idea how long I've waited."

"I've waited too." Her jaw trembled despite herself. "Most of my life, I think."

"I haven't stopped thanking God I took this assignment. And I don't mean that lightly. I've told Him so. Many times."

"We have so much to be grateful for."

He slipped his arm about her shoulder. As they walked toward camp, the late afternoon sky began displaying its marvelous colors, all the more brilliant because of her joy. Aric could look into the future without fear, confident that with Sean by her side, she could face anything.

Don't miss the next book in Anna Zogg's
Intergalaxia series!

The Xerxes Factor

Chapter 1

He was supposed to kill her. Not marry her.

The thought pounded Kelli Layne as she watched
the happy couple at their celebratory reception. She
leaned against a column in the grand ballroom, nurs-
ing a glass of pink synth-ale. With the party in full
swing, everyone appeared in high spirits. But neither
the exotic space station nor the triple moons of Xerxes
IX could banish her melancholy.

Long ago, she'd lost her heart to Sean Reese. How
could she have made that clearer?

Sighing, Kelli scanned the packed room, amazed at
the number of high-ranking guests who attended the
white-tie event. Even delegates from the formidable
Intergalaxia had made an appearance. When Sean and
Aric had saved a primitive planet from being plun-
dered, they had vaulted into celebrity status. Not only
that, but rumors abounded he was up for a big promotion.

Even though technically he failed his last assignment. The woman at his side wasn't supposed to live.

Kelli pressed fingers to her temple, battling the headache that had plagued her all day. Was it because of the artificial gravity or the overly crowded outpost? Seemed like twenty parties were happening on the space station all at once. A security nightmare.

Glad I'm not on duty.

No longer able to ignore the pain, she rummaged in her clutch for the aspirin derivative the concierge had delivered to her hotel room earlier. A passing waiter exchanged her flat drink for champagne, which she used to down the pills. She should leave. No one would miss her. Especially as the revelry escalated.

As she snapped her purse closed, Jayden Song caught her eye. Kelli hiked up her smile as Sean's best friend and fellow USF agent approached.

"Well, well. Aren't you distracting."

Speak for yourself. He cut a dashing figure in his black tuxedo and pants, which contrasted with the white waistcoat, shirt and bowtie. The ensemble emphasized his taupe complexion and dark hair.

"Haven't you been trained not to be distracted?" She spoke coyly.

"No man could resist you in that outfit."

"Really, Jayd, I've heard better pickup lines from a dozen men already."

"Only a dozen?" His gaze roamed her form. "Well, I can't blame 'em. You're drop-dead gorgeous in that red silk gown."

Gorgeous? His words didn't match his cool gaze as

it swept over her again. In the six years they'd known each other, Jayd always treated her like "one of the boys." Of course, their paths usually intersected in USF's gym.

"You're wrong about one detail." She adjusted her long scarf.

He glanced pointedly around. "Unless you hid the bodies, no one's dead, if that's what you mean."

She snickered, then indicated her ankle-length sheath dress. "This is Xerxian textile, not silk. Bought it this afternoon."

"Nice choice." His dark eyes met hers. Funny she'd never noticed before that he was about her same height. Most times, her five feet ten gave her an advantage over shorter colleagues. In her heels she stood an inch taller than Jayd.

Suddenly, he leaned in. "So what's bugging you, Kel?"

She blinked innocently. "Who said anything's bugging me?" The punk always could read her. When she'd once voiced frustration, he told her all Asians had that mystical ability.

One eyebrow rose. "The truth's written all over you."

In spite of herself, her smile faltered. Give her an assignment and she could pull it off without a flaw. But in real life...

She lifted her chin. "I have no idea what you're talking about."

For a few moments he appeared to weigh her

comment, then he shrugged. "I'm curious. What's your assessment of the new Mrs. Reese?"

She shifted from one foot to the other as she glanced at the woman. "Surprised to learn she has a kid. And Sean sticking around when he found out."

Across the room, Aric held her daughter by the hands and twirled to the music.. The girl giggled and then collapsed against her mother.

"She's one special lady." Jayd pressed one finger to his chin as he leaned against the column. "I've never seen a guy so much in love. Although, when I first met her, they both stank of rotten eggs."

"Who said men were logical?"

He grinned without looking at her. "Because of Aric, Sean's a new man."

Guess he would know. They had been friends long before USF.

"What'd you mean he's a *new man?*"

Jayd faced her, a glint of mischief in his almond-shaped eyes. "You're gonna hate it."

"Oh?"

"To use one of your phrases, he 'got religion.'"

"She suckered him into some cult?" Kelli let out a breath of incredulity as she stared at the couple. "I knew his marrying her was a mistake."

As soon as she spoke, she saw the trap.

"So *that's* it." Jayd's eyes narrowed. "You have a thing for Sean. You're disappointed he didn't pick you."

Kelli gritted her teeth. A series of retorts flashed

through her mind — agree with sheepishness, disagree with indignation, punch him.

I so want to deck Jayd.

To her credit, she didn't flinch when he leaned closer and spoke in her ear. "Don't worry, Kel. Your secret's safe with me."

He strode away, the crowd swallowing his lean form.

Blinking rapidly, she willed the burn in her eyes to ease. Jayd had this annoying knack of cutting to the heart of a matter. This wasn't the first time.

Hang him.

A passing waiter took her unfinished drink, but she declined a fresh glass. Her three swallows of alcohol were a mistake, proven by an overwhelming desire to cry. When the persistent waiter hovered, Kelli refused again.

If she didn't get out of there soon, she'd start blubbering. Then her colleagues would name her Big Baby rather than Ice Queen. Everyone would know about her feelings for Sean.

I need to leave. Now. She turned and in three steps ran headlong into her supervisor.

"Ms. Layne." The man spoke with the warmth of granite. "Just the person I wanted."

"Sir?"

"How much alcohol have you had this evening?"

Odd question. "A couple swallows, sir."

"Perfect." He spoke in an overly loud voice, rocking on his feet. "Someone told me you're next in line on the roster."

I'm not, but… She wisely kept her mouth shut. Her boss had a nasty way of punishing any perceived insubordination.

"You need to take over Romero and Black's assignment."

Kelli resisted the urge to cite regulations—she carried no badge or weapon, hadn't been prepped. And she was taking over for two agents?

She carefully crafted her question. "What assignment, sir?"

"Protection of Reese's stepdaughter."

A protest nearly burst from her. Clenching her fist, she pasted her fake smile back on. "There's nothing I'd like better than to take care of that kid."

Her sarcasm was lost on him. He nodded, apparently content with her answer.

"Wait here. Reese is on his way with the girl." Without another word, the man reeled away.

Her jaw jutted. If only she'd gone to her hotel room fifteen minutes ago. Jayd's fault for holding her up with his intrusive questions.

"Kelli?"

Sean's voice jerked her from introspection. She willed her heartbeat to stop its erratic cadence as she turned to the man she still desperately loved. Her throat went dry at how his amazing physique filled his formal attire.

Play the part. Pretend. You've done it before.

"Sorry to spoil your fun." His baritone sent shivers

down her spine.

"No problem." The lie fell glibly from her lips. "I was hoping for a little action."

"Afraid there won't be much with a seven year old." He smiled at the solemn girl beside him, hand in his. The child, a miniature of her mother, was kind of cute in a violet taffeta dress. "Ella, this is Ms. Layne." Sean looked up. "Can she call you Kelli?"

"Sure."

"Kelli's going to watch over you until midnight. That work for you both?"

Midnight? Gah! That was three hours away. "No problem." Kelli managed a frozen smile.

Sean clasped his stepdaughter's hand between both his. "You don't have to stay here the whole time. You can head up to the suite whenever you want."

Kelli's veneer threatened to crack. The honeymoon suite?

He knelt before the girl. "I'm going to go back to your mom now. Okay?"

Ella merely nodded. Sean hesitated a second, then kissed her cheek. "If you need anything, let Kelli know."

He started to rise when the girl threw her arms around his neck. The look he shot Kelli made her heart squeeze. In that second, she saw pure wonder. And something else.

Something she never saw in her father's eyes.

"Have fun, sweetie." His voice grew husky as he hugged her. He rose and touched Kelli's elbow.

"Thanks a lot. I appreciate this more than I can say."

She could only stare after him, skin tingling where his fingers had brushed.

I'd do anything for you, Sean. Anything.

But the words were much too late. And best left unspoken.

She started when a small hand slipped into hers.

"So, um, you hungry?" Kelli struggled to find her voice.

Brown eyes fixed on her as Ella shook her head. Her slim fingers felt frail.

She cleared her throat. "Then how about something to drink?"

Her gaze shot to Kelli, then away as she shrugged with one shoulder.

"Okay." She spoke with more assurance than she felt. *By the stars, I haven't a clue what to do with this girl.* Kelli was an only child with one cousin eighteen years her senior. Never been around kids. "I wouldn't recommend the synth-ale. Stuff tastes terrible."

Ella grinned.

No dummy, this one.

"How about some punch? That sound good?"

"Yes, please."

A server magically appeared and took their drink order—slushies for two.

They waited, hand in hand. Kelli intercepted the smirks of her colleagues, which she doused with a glacial glare. If anyone ribbed her, she'd pummel them the next time they met for physical training. She'd leave a nice bruise to make them regret their teasing. And they knew it.

The waiter brought drinks and had thoughtfully added an umbrella garnish to Ella's. Since the girl liked the punch so much, they got a second. Slightly salty, the icy blue slipped down easily in the growing heat. Kelli marveled that the little girl didn't grow weary of hanging onto her hand. Perhaps the kid was lonelier than she?

A distant memory hit Kelli, one where she'd been to a party as a child. No one had watched over her. A picture of a large dark dining hall buffeted her.

I was eleven. The memory sharpened and came into painful focus. *At Mom's funeral.*

She pushed the thought away, fighting weepiness. What was in that champagne? After grabbing two orange Xerxian berries from a platter, she wolfed them down. Their waiter appeared again, but she waved him away. No more drinks. Not even slushies.

The room dimmed. A spotlight snapped on Sean and his wife as they took the dance floor.

"Can I see?" Ella craned to look.

After leading her to a chair, Kelli helped her balance on it.

Ella's parents made a beautiful couple. Sean's sandy hair contrasted with Aric's brunette. As he escorted her gracefully across the dance floor, he towered over her. Kelli marveled at his ease of movement.

I should be in his arms. Oh, Sean.

But he had eyes only for the woman who smiled up

at him.

Kelli sucked a deep breath, unable to tear her gaze away. Even when Ella leaned against her shoulder, she couldn't stop watching them. Couldn't stop torturing herself. Why not me?

When Sean kissed his wife, the crowd murmured approval. A smattering of applause finally broke her trance.

The girl tugged on her scarf. "I have to use the bathroom, please."

Glad to escape, Kelli snagged their waiter and asked for directions to the nearest facility. Instead of merely telling her, he led them through an exit. "The one down here isn't as crowded."

Before she could ask him which way, the door slammed shut. The ill-lit hallway looked like a storage area with chairs and tables lining the walls. Where was the restroom? She considered going back into the ballroom, but Ella started walking on tiptoes. Time to hurry.

"Let's go...*this* direction." It took forever to pick their way through the narrow maze. When they turned the corner, she found a promising sign.

They rushed inside. While Ella went into a stall, Kelli set her handbag on the counter to rummage for lipstick. She stared at her pasty skin in the mirror. Her blue eyes looked so bloodshot, they appeared fueled by neon lights. The pain reliever she'd taken earlier had done nothing for her headache. "Ugh, I look ghastly."

"I think you're pretty." Ella's voice came from behind a slatted door.

Unlike Jayd's dubious compliment, hers rang true.

"Thanks. I think you are too." When her scarf slipped yet again, she wound it once more about her neck and flung the ends over her shoulders.

The girl washed and dried her hands, the whole time gazing at her with...adoration? Kelli smoothed on lipstick, then tucked a stray tress back into her bun.

The girl continued to stare with large, brown eyes. "I wish I had blond hair."

"Changing brown to blond is easy." She paused, sensing the girl needed assurance. Why the rush of emotion? Like she cared what the kid thought. "What's not so easy to change are your features. Someday everyone will envy your pretty lips and cute chin."

Ella shyly smiled.

"I like you. You're nice." The child's expression added a dimension of seriousness that left no doubt of sincerity.

Kelli released a breath, not even aware she'd been holding it. Heedless of her long gown, she knelt before the girl.

"I like you too, Ella. You're a very special person." She pressed her lips together before adding, "And you have two wonderful parents who love you very much." She blinked rapidly.

"When I grow up, I want to be just like you."

Kelli resisted the urge to say, No, you do not. Instead, she smoothed a strand of hair off the girl's forehead. "That's a sweet thing to say. Thank you."

Ella's skin was soft. Eyes so trusting. She radiated innocence.

Was I ever like that?

Behind Kelli, a whisper of sound alerted her that someone entered the restroom. Ella's eyes widened. Still kneeling, Kelli glanced over her shoulder.

Black shoes. Dress pants. Was it a man?

Feet lunged forward. Kelli struggled to rise. Her heel caught on her gown. She teetered, off balance. *Too late.*

A fist swung. She flinched, deflecting most of the impact. Pain exploded in her head. Something clawed her shoulder. Her scarf tightened. Weight pressed downward. Tile dug into her knees.

Where's Ella?

Kelli slid fingers between the material and her throat. "Ella." She choked out the word. "Run!"

Torturous seconds passed. Then a door banged. Footsteps pattered out of earshot.

Flailing, Kelli reached behind to strike the assailant. Vision blurred. Air became precious. Her fingernails connected. The man grunted, hold loosening. Again she struck, gouging skin. He retaliated by stomping on the back of her ankle. She screamed, the sound gurgling.

The noose constricted. She gagged. The hangman wound the long scarf around the faucet. She tried to push up. One leg flopped. Useless. Her gown imprisoned the other. Flashes of light exploded in her vision.

Her world plunged into dark pain.

Books by Anna Zogg

Letters Across Time

Moon Dancing

"Gypsy Gulch" A *Moon Dancing* Mystery
(an e-only short story)

Books in the Intergalaxia Series

The Paradise Protocol

The Xerxes Factor (releasing Spring 2016)

The Xerxian Problem (releasing late Fall 2016)